NELLIE WILDCHILD

She tensed as his hand crept into hers. 'Will I see you again?' he asked.

'I don't know, Frank. Does it make that much difference?'

'You know it does. Now that I've found you, I don't want to lose you, Nellie.'

And the truth was that she didn't want to lose him either. But a Catholic. She dreaded to think what her da would say should he ever find out—or what he might do.

The taxi drew up at the kerb and they were outside her house in Neptune Street. Withdrawing her hand from his, she opened the door and stepped on to the pavement.

He leaned out towards her before she could turn away. 'Think about it if you have to, but next Friday night I'll be waiting for you outside the Roxy at eight. I'll wait all night if I have to.' And then he leaned forward to speak to the driver and pulled the door shut.

Nellie stood in the dark and dirty street, watching for a second as the cab moved off into the night, then turned and hurried into her close. As she climbed the stairs she felt more lost than she had ever felt in her life before.

Also in Arrow by Emma Blair

Where No Man Cries
Hester Dark
This Side Of Heaven
Jessie Gray

Emma Blair

NELLIE WILDCHILD

ARROW BOOKS

Arrow Books Limited
20 Vauxhall Bridge Road, London SW1V 2SA

An imprint of Random Century Group

London Melbourne Sydney Auckland
Johannesburg and agencies throughout
the world

First published 1983
Reprinted 1983, 1984 (twice), 1985 (twice), 1988,
1989 and 1990

Set in Times by Photobooks (Bristol) Ltd

Printed and bound in Great Britain by
Courier International Ltd, Tiptree, Essex

ISBN 0 09 931540 8

ACKNOWLEDGEMENTS

The author wishes to thank the copyright-holders for permission to reproduce the lyrics of the following songs:

'The Parisien Pierrot' by Noel Coward © 1923 Keith Prowse Music Publishing Co. Ltd, and 'I Belong to Glasgow' by Will Fyffe © 1921 Francis Day and Hunter Ltd, both songs used by kind permission of E.M.I. Publishing Ltd.

'Boy! What Love Has Done for Me!' and 'In the Mandarin's Orchard Garden' by George Gershwin, both © New World Music Corp. (Warner Brothers) Chappell Music Ltd, for territories of the British Commonwealth (excluding Canada). Used by kind permission of Chappell Music Ltd.

I went doon by the sweetie work and my heart began to beat,
seeing all the factory lasses coming doon the street
with their flashy dashy petticoats and their flashy dashy shawls,
five and tanner guttie boots,
oh, we're big gallus molls!

Old Glasgow street song

1

Nellie sang as she combed her long, yellow hair. Her voice was like an angel's, her father often said. An angel come to earth.

'Nellie, it's five past seven! Babs will have been waiting for you down at the close mouth five minutes since!' Betty Thompson, Nellie's mother, shouted from ben the kitchen.

'I'm ready!' Nellie shouted back. And, after a final inspection of her face, shrugged herself into her coat, picked up her handbag and hurried through to the kitchen where she found Betty washing up the tea dishes at the sink and her da sitting slumped in his chair before the fire reading the evening paper. Her wee brother Roddy was sitting in the other fireside chair facing her da with his head buried in a comic. He was a great one for the comics.

'Will I do?' Nellie demanded, her eyes bright with anticipation at the evening lying ahead. For it was Friday night, time for fun and a few laughs.

Davey Thompson glanced up from his paper. 'Come closer so I can get a better look at you,' he commanded.

Nellie took a few steps forward.

Davey shook his head. 'I don't know why you lassies have to wear make-up,' he said. 'You're just spoiling the natural beauty the good God gave you.'

Nellie sighed. Ever since she'd started wearing make-up it had been a bone of contention between her father and herself. Over-gilding the lily was how he usually put it.

'I'm wearing hardly any at all,' she defended. 'Less than half what Babs and the other girls at work wear.'

'I'm not interested in Babs or the girls at work,' Davey said. 'You're my daughter. You're the one I'm interested in.'

'Ma?' Nellie appealed.

'It's the fashion for lassies to be made up,' Betty said from the sink. Drying her workworn hands on a tea cloth, she came to her husband's side. 'She looks all right to me,' she added.

Davey grumbled under his breath, a look of uncertainty still on his face.

Nellie was impatient now, desperate to get on her way. But she curbed her impatience knowing full well that unless her father was placated she'd be ordered back through to the house's one bedroom to wipe her make-up off and start afresh.

'Come on Davey, she's late as it is,' Betty cajoled.

Nellie silently blessed her mother whom she knew she could always rely on. Luckily Ma wasn't an old stick-in-the-mud like her da. Ma understood about things like this.

'I think the eyes are a bit heavy but aye, all right, away you go then,' Davey said reluctantly, adding sharply, as Nellie hurried to the door, 'And mind you're home by eleven. Any later and you're for it my lass. It's bad enough you go out looking like a painted Jezebel. What I'll not stand for is you coming in at God knows what hour when you think we're asleep and don't know.'

Nellie stopped at the door. 'That only happened once, Da, because Babs and I missed the last bus and had to walk.'

'Well see you don't miss it again that's all.'

'I promise.'

'Enjoy yourself lass,' Betty said, an understanding smile hovering round her lips.

'Cheerio', said Nellie. And then she was gone, the

sound of her high heels clattering down the stone close steps.

'And no smoking!' Davey called out. But he was too late. She was well out of hearing.

'She thinks I'm daft but I'm not,' he said to his wife. 'Comes in here smelling like an ashtray and tells me she's not smoking. Well, I know better. I didn't come up the Clyde on a bicycle after all.'

'What did you come up in, Da?' Roddy asked, his eyes twinkling mischievously as he looked up for the first time.

Fast as a striking snake Davey's hand lashed out to clip Roddy's ear.

'And I'll have no cheek from you either,' Davey said, settling himself back into his chair while Roddy howled.

'You asked for that,' Betty said, before turning on her heel and returning to the dishes piled high in the sink.

'Youngsters nowadays think they can get away with murder. Well I've got news for them, they can't in my house,' Davey said, having, as usual, the last word.

'What kept you?' Babs Boyd demanded when Nellie appeared at the close mouth. She and Nellie had been great pals since their schooldays and now worked together side by side at Harrison's sweet factory.

'Och, it was my da wittering on as usual,' Nellie replied.

Babs sighed. 'I know what you mean. Mine's just the same, as you well know. If it isn't one thing he finds to go on about it's another.'

The two girls nodded in sympathy.

'So where's it to be then? Up the town or local?' Babs asked.

Nellie had been swithering about that for the last hour. 'What do you fancy?'

'I'm easy.'

'Me too.'

'There's a new band at the Roxy. Big Jessie at work has heard them before and says they're good.' The Roxy was a dance-hall in the centre of Govan, the area where they both lived, less than a quarter of a mile away.

'Shall we take a chance on that then?' Nellie asked.

'Why not?'

'Then the Roxy it is,' Nellie said, slipping her arm through Babs's, adding as they started down the street, 'I didn't really fancy going too far away in case it buckets which I'm sure it's going to do later.'

Babs glanced up at the heavy, lowering sky which was so close as to seem to be resting on the tenement roofs. 'Aye, I think you're right,' she said, unconsciously touching her brolly to make sure she'd brought it with her.

'Tram or walk?' Nellie demanded.

'May as well walk. It's hardly worth the tram.'

'Right.'

Arm in arm they strode past the tram stop and into the grey, sooty night.

For a while they walked in silence and then, giggling suddenly, Babs said, 'Do you think he'll be there the night?'

'Who?'

'*Him. Mr Right.*'

Nellie smiled. Babs was always going on about her *Fate*. The man, the one and only Babs was convinced destiny had earmarked for her.

'He might well be. You never know do you?' Nellie replied.

Babs's face lit up. This was her favourite subject and one she never tired of talking about or speculating upon. 'What do you think yours will look like?' she asked. It was a question she'd asked Nellie at least a thousand times before.

Nellie's answer always depended upon her mood, or the last man she'd seen whom she'd fancied. 'Tall,' she said.

'Aye, tall,' Babs breathed. A tall man was always the first prerequisite, the vast majority of Glasgow men being under 5ft 6".

10

'Good looking –'

'That goes without saying. A real dreamboat.'

'With a wee tache like William Powell.'

'You don't fancy a wee tache surely?' Babs said in horror. 'They tickle when you kiss.'

'Maybe so but they make a man look more debonair, sophisticated. Don't you fancy William Powell?'

'Oh aye. But without the tache.'

'And he must have broad shoulders,' Nellie went on. 'I can't stand those skinnymalinks you run into. Most of them look like a good puff of wind would knock them over.'

Babs giggled. 'I know what you mean. But I'm not against the skinny ones. Some of them can be awful affectionate, as though they're trying to make up for being so wee and runty.'

Like a lot of Glasgow women, Babs was well-fleshed and rounded, and would have made two of the skinnymalinks they were talking about.

'And he has to be kind,' Nellie said.

'None of your cruel sods for me either,' said Babs. 'Especially those who come home and beat the hell out of you whenever they've had a bucket. And believe me, there's plenty of that kind about.'

Both girls nodded knowingly at one another. Brought up in the tenements, they knew only too well what went on at night, especially on a Friday after the boozers shut and the drunks staggered home with what remained of their pay packets in their pockets. Those were the times when wives, and sometimes children, were likely to be beaten.

Nellie thanked God her da had never been like that. Sure he often took a good drink and came home the worse for wear, but she could never remember him lifting his hand against her ma. It was the same with Babs's da.

Their conversation about Mr Right stopped on reaching the Roxy where they had to stand in a queue.

'It looks like a good turnout the night,' Babs said as they shuffled forward. But then Friday and Saturday

11

nights invariably were at the dancing, Glasgow being the most dancing-mad city in the whole Empire.

Once inside they made straight for the cloakroom where they immediately lit up. 'Jesus, but I was gasping for that,' Babs said, drawing smoke deep into her lungs. She'd been dying for a fag since leaving home but would never have dreamt of smoking in the street. Only a tart would ever do that.

As soon as they had their cigarettes they took themselves out on to the floor where Nellie was asked if she was for up?

She made sure the boy who'd done the asking seemed acceptable before assenting to his roughly made request.

'Do you come here often?' the boy asked as they glided round the floor.

Nellie groaned inwardly. It was the clichéd, standard opening. If only some of them could be at least a little original!

'Now and again,' she replied, resisting his attempts to pull her close.

At the end of the dance he asked if she'd like a lemonade.

'No thanks,' she smiled and excused herself, leaving him standing there looking after her. She'd quickly decided he wasn't her type at all.

She found Babs eyeing the unmatched males lining the opposite wall.

'The talent's not bad,' Babs said. 'One or two right lookers among them.'

Nellie took a quick glance across at the male line-up. Babs was right, there were one or two who weren't half bad.

'Are you dancing?'

Babs flashed what she hoped was a winning smile. 'Are you asking?'

'No, I'm here trying to get a couple of pints.'

'A wit!' Babs exclaimed. Then to Nellie, 'Glasgow's full of them.'

12

'That's not all Glasgow's full of,' the boy retorted.

'What do you mean by that?'

'Come on the floor and I'll tell you.'

Babs laughed. 'You sound like a right patter merchant. Come on then, let's see if your feet are as quick as your tongue.'

Babs and the young man melted into the dancing throng where they were quickly lost to view.

Three times in a row Nellie turned down offers of a partner. She didn't fancy any of them and besides, Babs had been right, the band was good, so for the moment she was content just to stand and listen.

A little later Babs reappeared by her side. 'I thought you'd got a click there,' Nellie said.

'Maybe. Maybe not,' Babs shrugged. 'I think he's gone away to consider the idea. I get the impression he's not exactly the impulsive type.'

Both girls laughed.

'How about a drink?' Nellie asked a few minutes later. Babs agreed and they trooped off to the refreshment bar, but as she drank her lemonade Nellie became aware of a young man watching her covertly from a spot a dozen or so feet away. Glancing boldly in his direction she laughed inwardly when he coloured and hurriedly looked elsewhere. But Babs began to chat again, and the young man was instantly forgotten.

The night passed and they both danced a number of times, Nellie more than Babs as was almost always the case when they went out together. But the fact that Nellie was far prettier than she was never bothered Babs. It was something she accepted and, in fact, secretly enjoyed, basking in a sort of reflected glory.

It had just gone twenty past ten and Nellie was thinking of saying she thought it was time they were for off, when out of the crowd materialized a smallish, dark-haired young man who, stammering, asked her to dance.

She was about to refuse, thinking he wasn't her type at all, when it suddenly came to her that this was the same

13

chap whom she'd caught watching her earlier on at the refreshment bar. Not quite knowing why she changed her mind, she accepted his invitation.

He was clumsy, tripping over his own feet and hers. 'I'm awful sorry,' he mumbled after he'd nipped her toe for the second time. They'd been dancing less than a minute.

His hair was dark brown and curly; his eyebrows thick as ropes; the eyes beneath them brown and liquid.

'My name's Frank,' he said.

'I'm Nellie.'

'I know.'

'Oh, do you now?'

He blushed again, the way he had earlier on. 'I heard somebody mention it,' he said.

'Are you sure you didn't ask?'

He laughed, a deep, warm sound, which was the last thing she'd been expecting. 'Well, maybe I did,' he confessed.

The hand in hers tightened fractionally and his feet became more sure of themselves as though, somehow, that small confession had given him confidence.

'You were watching me earlier on,' she said boldly. 'Why?'

'You'll think I'm soft.'

'Try me.'

'I saw you come into the hall and I just . . . well I just fancied you. Something rotten.' he added hurriedly and looked away.

Nellie found this amusing. And not just a little touching. 'Why didn't you ask me up earlier?' she smiled.

'Now you really will think me soft.'

'Go on?'

He licked his lips and cleared his throat. He was about to reply when the music stopped and they had to applaud along with everybody else.

'Will you stay up?' he asked, a hint of pleading in his voice.

14

'All right,' she said softly, and coming into his arms they moved off again as the music began.

'You were about to say?' she prodded.

'I was too feart,' he replied after a pause of a few seconds.

She'd known that was the answer, of course, but it impressed her that he'd admitted to it. It was rare for a Glasgow man to admit fear in any form – especially to or about a woman.

'Are you usually shy?' she asked.

He shook his head.

'Only with me?'

'A dozen times I was about to come over and ask you up but every time I tried my legs started to shake. I felt a proper fool I can tell you.'

Nellie was warming rapidly to this dark-haired lad called Frank. There was a different quality about him, something which made him stand out from the others. He'd caught her interest.

'You're the best-looking bird here. Do you know that?' he said.

'You're only saying that,' she replied coyly.

'No, no. It's true!'

She allowed herself to be drawn a little closer to him. The extreme heat in the hall had caused him to sweat. A not unpleasant smell, she thought – surprised at herself.

As they birled round she suddenly caught sight of the clock above the main entrance, it was twenty to the hour and if she didn't leave right that instant she risked being late home. She couldn't bear to think of the scene that would follow should that happen. It just wasn't worth it.

Pulling away from him she said, 'Look, I'm awful sorry Frank but I really must fly.'

He looked bewildered. 'But I thought –'

'It's not you. It's my da. He'll kill me if I'm not in by eleven.' Then she added mischievously, 'See, you should have asked me up earlier,' and, turning, she hurried across to where Babs was waiting for her.

15

They were just coming out of the cloakroom when Nellie found her arm being grasped. Anger flared in her but that vanished instantly when she saw it was Frank who had accosted her.

'Can I take you home?' he asked.

She shook her head. 'Thanks for asking but it really isn't worth it. I'll have to run as it is.'

He looked crestfallen. 'Will you be here tomorrow night?' he asked.

'I've already arranged to go to the pictures with some of my pals. Sorry.' Thinking she was giving him the brush off, he started to move away only to be stopped by her hand reaching out to touch him. 'I could come next Friday night,' she said.

'I'll be here waiting,' he replied, a smile lighting up his face.

Long after she was gone he was still staring at the door through which she'd vanished.

Nellie hated the alarm clock whose strident jangling announced it was time for her to get up. Monday morning again. The start of another working week. God, what a life!

Opening her eyes she stared across at the kitchen window, through which she could see that it was a grey, dreich morning. Although still warm in bed, she shivered.

In the bedroom her parents' alarm went off. Her mother would make an appearance in a minute to light the fire and put the kettle on, but her da would wait until she'd washed herself at the sink and got dressed before he got up.

Yawning, she swung herself out of the cavity bed she shared with her brother Roddy. The yawn turned to a sharp intake of breath as her feet made contact with the cold linoleum floor.

Hastily she pulled her dressing gown around her and slid her feet into her slippers. Crossing to the sink she

16

began to wash herself, a lick really more than a proper wash, in the icy water from the tap.

Betty bustled in and set about bringing the house to life. Soon a cheery fire was crackling in the grate and the smell of porridge filled the room. Nellie dressed hurriedly, calling to her father when she was finished.

Sitting at the table drinking her first cup of tea, she thought of the dream she'd had the night before. A knight in shining armour, just like the one in the story book she'd had as a child, had come on a white horse to save her from a horrible dragon, and when the dragon was dead the knight had lifted his visor to reveal himself as Frank, the lad she'd met at the Roxy on Friday night. The dream amused Nellie. Her dreams weren't usually that fanciful.

Perhaps she should have gone back to the Roxy on the Saturday night instead of saying she was going to the pictures, which had been a lie. But no, that would have made it too easy for him. Let him wait a week. Her feminine instincts told her that was the right tack to take.

'Time you weren't here,' Betty said glancing across at the alarm clock standing on a chair by the cavity bed.

'Aye, right,' replied Nellie.

'And hap up warm. It may be April, but it's like the middle of winter out there.'

At the door Betty kissed Nellie on the cheek and then handed her her lunchtime piece. 'See you the night,' Betty said.

Down at the front close Nellie found Babs waiting for her as she did every working morning. 'Another blinking Monday,' Babs sniffed.

'Aye. It would sicken your kidneys so it would,' Nellie agreed.

'You can say that again.'

Arm in arm and with heads bent against the biting wind, the two girls hurried on their way. Thanks to the wind the air was clean and fresh, not filled with its usual stench of cat urine and human waste.

How she hated this place, Nellie thought. The street, as

17

were all its neighbours, was like a tipped midden. Soot, dust, grime and just general filth were everywhere. The tenements lining either side were weighed down with countless years of neglect. Once tall, proud edifices, they were now raddled, diseased shells. Someday, somehow, I'll escape all this, Nellie thought to herself, knowing at the same time that very few of her kind ever did. Except to the graveyard, that is.

Harrison's sweet factory, where both girls worked, was a squat building with nearly a century of starling droppings covering its roof. Like a great, grey cake with icing on its top, as it had once been described. To those who worked there it was known as the Bastille.

Nellie and Babs clocked on, then took themselves through to the long, soulless room where coats were exchanged for overalls. From there the 150 women who worked for Harrison's made their way to their various positions. Promptly on the hour the hooter sounded and the machinery ground into motion.

Every Monday morning was the same for Nellie. Coming back afresh to the heavy, sickly, sugar smell that pervaded everything made her stomach turn over.

On starting at the factory two years previously, having left school at fifteen, she'd vomited every morning for a month. If work hadn't been so desperately hard to come by she'd have chucked the job and gone elsewhere. Trouble was, there wasn't really an elsewhere to go to.

She was damn lucky to be grafting and appreciated the fact. But that didn't make the job any easier to live with.

At half past ten, the hooter sounded again announcing a ten minute tea break. Ladies with trolleys were already in position, the workers helping themselves to the poured out cups of tea.

The girls in Nellie's section assembled as they always did, but although all of them smoked not one lit up; to have done so and been caught would have meant instant dismissal.

'You should have seen the one I got off with on

Saturday night,' Big Jessie, the section's self-appointed leader bragged. 'What a maddie, but nice looking with it.'

'What happened then?' Daisy demanded. 'Did he lumber you?'

'Oh aye, he took me home all right. But when he asked me, he said he'd run me there so I thought that he had a car.'

'And didn't he?'

'Don't tell me he produced a pair of sandshoes?' Agnes said, and everyone laughed. It was an old Glasgow joke.

'No, a motorbike. An old rattly affair that I thought was going to fall apart right there under me. Up and down Sauchiehall Street we went, giving me a wee hurl as he put it, and then back to my house with all the neighbours coming to their windows and gawping because of the noise the damn thing made.'

'Are you seeing him again?' Daisy demanded eagerly.

Big Jessie shook her head. 'No fear. He was a university student. What would I want with the likes of that? Oil and water, we just wouldn't mix.' Looking a trifle wistful she added, 'But he was good-looking. No denying that.'

'What about you Babs?' Agnes asked.

'Aye, what about you?' Big Jessie chimed in. 'Weren't you and Nellie going to the jigging? Did you go into town?'

'We went to the Roxy,' Babs said.

'Bloody dump that place,' Big Jessie said. 'I much prefer the town dances myself.'

'We like it,' Nellie said. She wasn't going to let Jessie turn up her nose at her. The Roxy wasn't *that* bad after all.

'Did you get a lumber then Babs?' Daisy asked.

'I nearly did. I met this chap who I thought had taken a notion, but he went away to think about it and that was the last I saw of him.'

Big Jessie shook her head. 'If you'd fancied him you shouldn't have let him go. Never give them time to think, that's always a mistake.'

'Some of us prefer it that way, having enough confidence in ourselves,' Nellie said sweetly.

Jessie glared at Nellie. There was a rivalry between them that nothing ever changed.

'What was I supposed to do, twist his arm or something?' Babs demanded.

'There are ways and means,' Big Jessie replied knowingly.

'Such as? Throw him to the floor and sit on him?'

The group erupted with laughter at the image of Babs sitting on top of a struggling lad in the middle of a dance-hall.

'What about you Nellie? Did you meet anyone nice?' Agnes asked when the hilarity had subsided.

'Possibly. I'm not quite sure yet,' Nellie replied mysteriously.

'You either did or you didn't,' said Big Jessie.

'Was he tall and handsome?' demanded Daisy.

'Not too tall. But he was certainly handsome. That right Babs?'

Babs nodded to the company that that was so.

'Are you seeing him again? Agnes went on.

'Maybe.'

'What does that mean exactly?' Jessie demanded.

'It means maybe. I haven't made up my mind yet. We left things sort of open.'

'In other words you're meeting him in the hall,' Big Jessie said. 'Too mean is he to pay your way in?'

Nellie stared at her coldly. 'I made that particular arrangement because that's the way I want it. Some of us like to pick and choose you know, and not just be swept along by whoever will have us.'

'You're a right cheeky bitch!' hissed Jessie.

'If I am then that makes two of us,' retorted Nellie.

'I wish I could pick and choose,' said Daisy, trying to change the subject. 'But no such luck.'

'You and me both,' added Babs.

Big Jessie was about to make another barbed remark to

Nellie when the hooter indicated that the tea break was over.

'What about you Agnes?' asked Nellie as they made their way back to their stations.

Agnes was exceptionally short and fat with legs that would have done credit to a rugby fullback.

'I went dancing on Friday and stood there all night. I didn't have one offer for the floor,' Agnes said.

'Still, maybe next week,' said Nellie.

'Aye, maybe then,' replied Agnes.

The machinery, that had been stopped for the tea break, clanked into action putting paid to any further conversation.

The week dragged by for Nellie who found excitement mounting within her at the thought of her forthcoming rendezvous. It was rare for her to be so taken with a chap.

When Friday night finally arrived she left work to hurry to the public baths where she treated herself to a good long, piping-hot soak. They had a zinc tub at home which was used in front of the fire sometimes but it wasn't nearly as good as the luxury of the public baths.

Bath over she went swiftly home for her tea, then took herself into her parents' bedroom to get dressed.

The Thompsons lived in what was known as a room and kitchen, the room being the small flat's one bedroom. The toilet was a communal one on the stairs' half-landing and was shared by the three flats on the level above.

Nellie hated having to share the kitchen bed with her brother, desperately wanting a bedroom of her own and the privacy that it would give her. But there was no chance that they would ever be able to move to a larger, more comfortable flat.

Standing in her slip in front of the wardrobe mirror Nellie scraped her hair back behind her ears. With her face freshly scrubbed and free of make-up, she looked incredibly young and childlike. For the space of a few moments she stared critically at herself. Her figure was trim, her breasts neither large nor small. Her bottom stuck out rather pertly; enough to be noticed but not too much to make it look either peculiar or plump. Her legs were good and there was a nice, attractive curve to her belly.

But it was her face that was by far and away her best feature, the corn-yellow hair that was so unusual in Glasgow where the norm was brunette with the occasional redhead thrown in as a colourful relief. Then there were her eyes, which were a deep sea-green with a golden fleck in them.

Frank had been right when he'd said she was the prettiest lassie in the dance-hall that night. She had been, as she was well aware. In fact, she rarely came across anyone who could top her when it came to beauty.

Humming she got to work on her make-up. When that was finished, and she started dressing, she began to sing in a golden voice that never failed to capture the ears and hearts of anyone who listened to it.

Through in the kitchen, Davey Thompson closed his eyes in appreciation. An angel come to earth, he thought to himself. In a life that had been filled with poverty and hard graft, that description of his daughter's voice – which he'd first thought of years before – was the only poetic expression he would have in his entire life.

Nellie and Babs arrived at the Roxy at the same time as they had the previous Friday night. Trying to appear nonchalant, Nellie glanced around her, expecting Frank to materialize out of the throng and come rushing to her side. Ten minutes later she was still looking, more or less certain he wasn't in the hall yet.

'Are you for up?'

The lad doing the asking was rough and not at all to her fancy. 'Sorry, I'm waiting for someone,' Nellie smiled.

Shrugging his shoulders the lad moved on.

Three-quarters of an hour later, Nellie was still alone

and fuming. Loose as the arrangement had been, it was the first time in her life she'd ever been stood up and she didn't like it one little bit.

'No sign?' asked Babs sympathetically, joining her on the sidelines.

Nellie shook her head.

'Maybe he took ill or something?'

'Aye, maybe,' Nellie said, not believing a word of it.

And then, suddenly, he was there as though he had come out of thin air. He was hot, flushed and his tie was slightly askew.

'I'm helluva sorry,' he said, afraid to look her in the eyes and afraid not to.

He looked like a wee boy who'd done wrong, Nellie thought, and despite herself her anger melted instantly.

'Have you been here long?' he asked.

'No,' Nellie lied.

Babs had opened her mouth to answer but hearing Nellie's reply she quickly shut it again.

'I got caught up,' Frank said.

'Oh?'

'I went into the pub for a pint, you see, and the next thing I knew I was involved with some mates. Well you know what it's like? You daren't leave before you've stood your round and, try as I might, I just couldn't seem to be able to stand mine. I had to practically fight those blokes to get away in the end.' Then, both contrite and pleading, he added, 'I came as soon as I could. Honest!'

Nellie knew only too well what Glasgow pubs were like. It was unthinkable to leave without standing your round. It was certainly an excuse she could understand and accept.

'You're looking great,' Frank said, his eyes shining as he stared at her.

'And you look like you've come through a hedge backwards,' she replied, gesturing to his tie.

Muttering more apologies he straightened the offending article.

'Well, are you two going to stand there all night or are

23

you going to show me how it's done?' said Babs gesturing with a smile toward the dance floor.

'Do you want to cool off first?' Nellie asked.

'No,' Frank replied, and taking her hand in his led her on to the floor.

They moved easily together, two people naturally tuned to each other's rhythm. The first dance was completed in silence, each content merely to be in the other's company. During this time Frank glanced occasionally at Nellie's face, as though reassuring himself that she was actually there in his arms.

'Do you live round about?' he asked halfway through the second dance. The spell had been broken and they began to talk freely with one another.

'Neptune Street,' Nellie replied. 'And you?'

'I come from Drumoyne.'

'And what do you work at?'

'I'm an apprentice at the Langbank Yard.'

Nellie exclaimed, 'That's where my da works! He's a welder there. His name's Davey Thompson.'

Frank thought for a moment before shaking his head. 'It's an awful big place you understand,' he said, 'I'm afraid I don't know him.'

'Apprentice what?' she asked.

'Boilermaker.'

'And how long have you got to go before you're a journeyman?'

'Eighteen months,' he said. 'Then I'll be in the money.'

She grinned in sympathy. All apprentices were traditionally very poorly paid; one step above slave labour she'd once heard her father describe it as.

'And what about you, Nellie?'

She told him then about the sweetie factory, what she did there, and the lassies she worked beside.

'This Big Jessie sounds quite a character,' he said when she'd finished.

'She's that all right. And the bane of my life to boot. A proper madam and no mistake.'

24

Frank looked at Nellie in wonder, still not able to believe his luck that he'd managed to pull this gorgeous creature and that she seemed to like him as much as he liked her.

As they danced he became almost intoxicated by the smell and touch of her. He wanted to wrap her up and take her home with him and never ever let her out of his sight again.

Nellie, for her part, was thinking how funny Frank could be. He made her laugh and she liked that. She'd never before met a boy with whom she felt so empathetic. That realization made her insides tingle. It also scared her a little although she couldn't think why.

Later Frank asked if he could walk her home and Nellie agreed. He insisted they take Babs home first as that was only fair, and so, at the appropriate time, the three of them left the Roxy. Frank walked in the middle with Nellie on his arm and Babs a little apart on his other side. When they reached Babs's close they made their good-byes and Babs ran giggling up the gas-lit stairs.

Nellie's heart was beating quickly now that she and Frank were alone, and they fell silent again as they walked to her close where they stopped in the entranceway.

'Can I see you tomorrow night?' Frank asked in a rush.

Nellie stared at her feet as though she were thinking, but answered quickly, 'Yes.'

'Anywhere particular you fancy going?'

'There's a picture on I wouldn't mind seeing.'

'Then that's what we'll do.'

They fell silent again and in that silence she knew he desperately wanted to kiss her – and that she wanted to kiss him.

'Come down here a bit,' she said in a voice suddenly husky. Taking his arm she led him along the length of the close and round into the back stair where it was dark.

He took her in his arms and held her tightly as their mouths met in a kiss.

When the kiss was over Frank shuddered as though something had gone out of him.

'I like you,' he said.

'And I like you.'

'I mean I *really* like you.'

'And I *really* like you.'

They kissed again. This time he put his tongue into her mouth which she greedily accepted.

Later, after the final good-bye and the final kiss, she made her way upstairs. Arriving at her door she paused for a minute to allow herself to calm down a bit. Standing there in the flickering gaslight she thought about the fact that he hadn't once tried to touch her in any of her private places. She liked that. And how different from many of the boys who'd walked her home and who'd no sooner got her into the back close than they'd started pawing and mauling her.

Smiling to herself she opened the door and slipped inside.

She found her father, mother and a stranger sitting around the kitchen table. Her brother Roddy was fast asleep and snoring in the cavity bed.

Da was wearing his best suit with his tie undone. She remembered then that he'd been to a Masonic 'do' that night. He was a dedicated Mason.

'Come away in lass,' called Davey, his words slurred by drink. 'I'd like you to meet a pal of mine. Jim Biles, this is my daughter, Nellie.'

Jim Biles rose. He was tall and fair with a good broad pair of shoulders on him, twinkling blue eyes and an easy smile and manner.

'Pleased to meet you, Nellie,' he said, eyeing her coolly.

Davey waved at the bottle of whisky and bottles of beer standing on the table. 'Jim had a wee win on the dogs today and pal that he is, he decided to share some of it with me.'

26

'It was a good win,' said Biles. 'And not the first I've had this week either.'

Betty pulled out a chair beside her and Nellie sat down.

'Do you gamble a great deal?' she asked politely.

'A fair amount.'

'And do you win a lot?'

'More often than not. I'm lucky.'

'Lucky my foot!' exclaimed Davey. 'It's skill the way he does it. Isn't it Jim lad?'

Jim smiled modestly. 'Well let's just say I don't rely entirely on luck.'

'A glass of beer, hen?' Davey asked.

'I don't think –' Nellie started to reply but Jim Biles interjected.

'Och, you *must*, Nellie. I'm superstitious, you see, and if you don't have some of my winnings' drink I'll worry in case it breaks my winning streak.'

'A *wee* glass then,' Nellie said.

'Jim's a butcher,' Davey said as he poured out the beer and then retopped everyone else's glass. The whiskies he poured after that were very large ones.

'A butcher?'

'Aye, down the Gallowgate. I work for a man called Sanderson. So any time you're short of a few pounds of sausages, you know where to come.'

Davey laughed loudly at that.

Nellie stared at Jim's hands which she'd noticed for the first time. Unlike the rest of him, which was almost elegant, these were large, extremely thick-fingered and very red as though he had them in hot water all day. There was something about those hands she didn't like at all.

'You mentioned you had a lassie but not that she was so good-looking,' Biles said smoothly.

'And you should hear her sing. The voice of an angel,' Davey said.

'Is that so?'

'The voice of an angel,' Davey repeated.

A bit too smooth, Nellie thought. The compliment was no more than what Frank had said to her earlier but in his case it had come out as though he really meant it. Whereas with Biles it was as though it were something he'd said a thousand times or more.

'I love a good song,' said Jim. 'What about singing for us?'

Nellie glanced across at the sleeping Roddy. 'It's awful late and –'

'Don't you worry about any of that,' Davey cut in. 'I'd love a song, too, so what about it? For your old da's sake if nothing else?'

Put like that Nellie didn't see how she could refuse. 'If you're sure it's all right?'

Betty nodded which was the final seal of approval.

Nellie took a sip of her beer and then, rising, stepped back a few paces. It didn't bother or embarrass her to sing like this as her father often requested her to do so. If there had been any embarrassment at performing, it had long since died.

'Give us "The Skye Boat Song",' said Davey. Aside to Jim he added, 'Just wait till you hear this.'

'Speed bonny boat like a bird on the wing, over the sea to Skye,' Nellie sang.

Jim Biles didn't have much of an ear for music but he knew the voice he was listening to was a good one. And what a cracker it belonged to, he thought. A real jewel amongst the dross.

When Nellie had finished Davey led the clapping. 'What did I tell you, eh?' he said to Jim. 'Sheer magic!'

'I thought that was absolutely grand,' he said. 'A real treat.'

'How was the dancing?' Betty asked, as Nellie sat down. 'Fine.'

'And the lad you thought you might meet?'

Nellie noted that Jim Biles's eyes had suddenly become veiled as he watched her closely. It was as though her answer was important to him.

28

'I met the chap, his name's Frank, and we had a good time together,' Nellie said slowly.

'Seeing him again?'

'Tomorrow night.'

'Back to the dancing?'

'No. The pictures.'

'You like the pictures do you?' Jim asked casually. Nellie nodded.

'So do I. Particularly Westerns. They're my favourite.'

'I prefer the love stories myself. But I suppose that's natural, being a woman.'

And what a one, Jim thought to himself.

'Have you been a Mason long?' Nellie asked. 'Or aren't you allowed to tell me?' She laughed softly. 'I swear I've never come across anyone or anything as secret as you lot!'

'I'm in the process of becoming fully fledged, so to speak,' replied Jim. 'Your father's very kindly been helping me with some of the things I have to learn.'

'And then you'll wear a wee pinny like the rest of them when you do the mumbo jumbo,' Nellie said, and despite herself a combination giggle and snigger burst from between her lips.

Davey frowned. 'That's enough,' he said warningly. He took the Masons very seriously.

'I was only –'

'I won't have the Masons mocked. Not by you or anyone. Is that clear?'

Nellie nodded and looked away, not wishing to continue meeting her father's threatening gaze.

'I think it's time I went,' said Jim Biles.

'Aye, it is getting on and you three have work in the morning,' Betty said.

'One last dram?' suggested Davey. 'It's your bottle after all.'

'Another time,' replied Jim. Turning his attention to the two women he said, 'It's been a great pleasure meeting you, Mrs Thompson –'

'Och, call me Betty.'

'All right. It's been a great pleasure meeting you, Betty. And you, Nellie.'

'Likewise,' Nellie replied.

Davey saw Jim Biles to the door, then took himself off to bed, leaving the women to themselves.

'A nice lad I thought,' Betty said, rinsing the glasses out at the sink.

'A bit of a smoothie.'

'Well mannered I'd say. I've always liked a man to be well mannered.'

Nellie thought of Frank as she started to undress. Now there was someone who was really well mannered, and without being smooth about it either. 'I know what you mean,' she said.

'Goodnight lass,' Betty said at the kitchen door.

'Goodnight Ma.'

Nellie wound the alarm clock before putting the lights out and crawling into bed aside Roddy who was still snoring. Smiling in the darkness she thought back over the evening and her time spent with Frank. '*Mr Right*,' she breathed aloud. And, using another of Babs's expressions, '*My Fate*!'

Was he that? It was far too early to tell. Goodness, she'd only had the one date with him so far. What could you tell from that? An awful lot she decided. An awful lot indeed.

Eventually, feeling warm, contented and at peace with the world, she fell asleep to dream of her knight in shining armour – who, when he wasn't killing dragons, made her laugh.

'There's three-quarters of an hour yet before the picture starts, so how about nipping in for a fly one?' Frank asked.

Nellie was undecided. Although, like most working-class Glasgow girls, she knew a great deal about pubs, the truth of the matter was she'd only actually been in one twice before.

Taking Frank's arm she whispered, 'I'm only seventeen. I'm under age.'

Seventeen? He'd been wondering what age she was. The childlike quality in her face had made him think that she might be younger.

'Och, just have a soft drink then and I'm sure they'll say nothing,' he replied.

'You sound like you're dying for a pint.'

'I could murder one.'

She laughed. 'All right, I'll chance it if you will.'

'Follow me,' he said, leading the way.

The pub was a huge, barnlike affair, smelling strongly of alcohol and cigarette smoke. Although still reasonably early, there were a number of drunks clustered round the bar. Nellie noticed that one of them was so bad he kept slipping to the floor, only to be hauled back on to his feet by the chap he was drinking with.

The pub was pretty busy and soon would become jam-packed, Friday and Saturday nights being the busiest of the week.

'Slainte!' said Frank when he'd rejoined her with the drinks, and, lifting his pint, he saw off nearly half of it.

'You *were* dry!' Nellie exclaimed.

'I told you I was. How's the orange juice?'

She sipped, and as she did so her eyes widened fractionally. 'You've put something in this.'

'You didn't think I was really going to give you a soft drink do you? Help ma bob, what sort of Saturday night out would that be?'

'What is it then?'

'Gin. Haven't you had it before?'

She shook her head.

Leaning close to her he whispered, 'They call it mother's ruin.' And waggling his eyebrows up and down added, 'If you get my meaning.'

She laughed, really enjoying herself. 'My da gives me

the odd whisky and beer at home. But that's all I've ever had.'

'I can see I'm going to have to educate you,' he teased. 'There's more to drinking life than just whisky and beer. For example, have you ever heard of vodka?'

'No.'

'Grand stuff from Russia. Clear like gin but tasteless.'

'If it's tasteless then why bother to drink it?' she asked.

'Only a lassie would ask that question,' he grinned. 'Why bother to drink it indeed!'

'Are you an awful boozer?'

'I like a drink, let's put it that way. Who in Glasgow doesn't? But I know when to stop if that's what you're getting at.'

'As long as you do,' she said primly, causing him to grin again.

They talked for a few minutes more and then Frank went back to the bar to get another round. While he was trying to attract one of the barmen's attention, a rowdy gang of football supporters invaded the pub, wearing the blue and white scarves of Rangers' fans.

'You on your own, hen?'

Nellie stared up at the supporter whom she hadn't notice approach.

'No, my fellow's at the bar,' she replied.

'Is that so? But you wouldn't mind another wee bit of company would you?'

Fear fluttered through Nellie. She didn't like this sort of situation at all. 'Please leave me alone,' she said firmly.

The man swayed on the spot, his eyes glassy and his breath reeking of alcohol. His teeth, when he grinned, were discoloured with decay.

'Now you don't really mean that do you?' he leered.

'Yes she does,' said Frank, who'd come up quietly beside the man. He laid his pint and Nellie's fresh drink on the table in front of her without taking his eyes off the head above the blue and white scarf. 'On your bike,' he ordered now that his hands were free.

For a moment Nellie thought there was going to be a punch-up – but then the moment passed.

'Just a wee misunderstanding,' the supporter slurred.

'Sure pal,' said Frank.

'No hard feelings?'

Frank shook his head.

'All right then,' said the other man, and, turning, lurched across to where his friends were standing.

When Frank sat down Nellie saw that his hands were trembling. 'Bloody animal,' he muttered.

Nellie didn't care that they were in public, after what had happened she wanted a cigarette. She lit two and passed one across to Frank.

'Never a dull moment,' Frank joked, grinning.

Nellie grinned back. 'He frightened the living daylights out of me.'

'Me too,' Frank confessed, sounding so relieved that they both laughed.

'He must have been on the booze all day from the state of him.' She shuddered. 'Those teeth! I could have nightmares about them.'

Frank stared across at the group of supporters who were swallowing whisky as though it was about to be banned come morning. They were all hard-faced working men who had the air of troublemakers about them.

'When you get that down you we'll go,' he said. 'I'll just have a quick trip to the toilet before,' Frank said apologetically. 'Sorry, but it's the beer, it's gone straight through me.'

'Be as quick as you can will you?'

'Not a second longer than I have to,' and rising he hurried across to the door marked Gents.

Through the hustle and bustle Nellie saw that the drunken footballers had gone and presumed they'd moved on to another pub. She watched in fascination as the drunk who'd kept slipping to the floor earlier was dragged to the swing doors by one of the barmen and ejected into the street beyond. Nervously, she kept looking towards the door through which Frank had disappeared, but when it finally did open it was not Frank but the rowdy football supporters who emerged. Nellie's heart sank, and her whole body became cold with dread. When the one who'd tried to pick her up leered across at her she knew for certain what had happened.

Noisily the supporters pushed their way through the drinkers and out of the pub, the last one through the doors shouting as though in defiance, 'Rangers are the boys!'

Numb inside, she rose and made her way to the bar where she finally managed to attract the attention of one of the barmen.

'I'll have a look,' the barman said after she'd made her request.

She stood outside the door of the Gents, staring blankly, not even noticing the stink of stale urine that hung there like a pall. When the barman re-emerged he was supporting Frank under the arm.

Nellie caught her breath when she saw Frank. His face had been badly punched and one cheek was seeping blood from a gash down the side of his nose. His suit was filthy and stained and it was obvious they'd been kicking him.

'Come through the back and sit down for a wee while,' the barman said kindly.

Customers stopped to watch as the barman and Nellie helped Frank round behind the bar and into the room beyond. When Frank was sitting the barman said, 'I'll get you a towel and a dram.'

'Thank you,' said Nellie. After the barman had gone she sat beside Frank and took his hand.

'I walked right into the sods,' he said. 'I didn't have a chance. There were just too many of them.'

'I feel it's my fault.'

'Don't be silly, there was more to it than just you.'

'What do you mean?' she asked, puzzled.

'They were Rangers' supporters,' he said through lips that had already started to swell.

An uneasy feeling – as though she already knew the answer to her own question – suddenly overpowered her.

'So?'

'They recognized me for a Catholic,' Frank said softly, looking right at her.

Catholic. The word was a bombshell.

'Surely you realized?' His hand reached towards her.

How could she have been so dense as not to see it! Everything about him screamed Catholic. The curly black hair. The thick black eyebrows. Why he practically had the map of Ireland written all over his face.

'Nellie?'

But before she could reply the barman was back with a hot towel and a large glass of whisky. Frank's eyes never left hers as she wiped the blood from his face and then applied the sticking plaster the barman had also thoughtfully provided. When she made him as presentable as she could, he knocked back the whisky in one grateful swallow.

'Can you stand?' the barman asked.

Unsteadily, Frank came to his feet. His thighs were shaking from the kicking they'd taken and come morning, he knew, his body would be black and blue. 'I think I'll live. Just about,' he said, grimacing with the pain.

Once outside the pub he suggested they still go on to the pictures, but Nellie replied that he wasn't to be so daft. The only thing for him to do was go home.

'I'll get a taxi and drop you off first,' he said.

Being Saturday night the town was chock-a-block and they had to wait nearly half an hour before being successful in flagging down a cab. During that time they barely spoke.

When they were settled in the back seat of the taxi and headed for Govan Frank said quietly, 'Well? What about us?'

'It's my fault for being so stupid. It was staring me right in the face and for some reason it just didn't dawn.'

Frank glanced out at the passing scenery. A grey

landscape of stone and concrete. Damn this town for its bigotry he thought. The orange and the green, and never the twain shall meet.

'How do you feel?' she asked, changing the subject.

'A bit shaky. I'll be stiff as a board tomorrow but it could've been a lot worse. At least none of them was carrying a razor or any other kind of weapon.'

Nellie nodded. He had been lucky. Only the other week a boy in her street had got into a fight and ended up in hospital with a hatchet embedded in the back of his neck.

She tensed as his hand crept into hers. 'Will I see you again?' he asked.

'I don't know, Frank. Does it make that much difference?'

'You know it does. Now that I've found you, I don't want to lose you, Nellie.'

And the truth was she didn't want to lose him either. But a Catholic of all things! She dreaded to think what her da would say should he ever find out, he being the staunch Protestant and Mason that he was.

The taxi drew up at the kerb and they were outside her house in Neptune Street. Withdrawing her hand from his she opened the door and stepped out on to the pavement.

'Think about it if you have to. But next Friday night I'll be waiting for you outside the Roxy at eight o'clock. I'll wait all night if necessary,' he said.

His eyes were vulnerable and appealing. She felt as though she could fall in them and drown.

'Drumoyne,' he said to the taxi driver, and closed the door. She watched for a second as the cab moved off and then turned and hurried into her close. As she climbed the stairs she felt more lost than she'd ever done in her life before.

The house was asleep. Beside her in the cavity bed Roddy was snoring like a good one. His leg was thrown over hers

36

which he did often and which usually annoyed her. Tonight she found it strangely comforting.

A Catholic! Why hadn't she noticed! She should have seen it the first time he'd asked her up to dance.

What a mess she'd landed herself in, she thought. For she'd meant it when she'd said she really liked him. In one short week he'd come to mean an awful lot to her.

But a Catholic! In any other Scottish city it might not have been quite so bad but in Glasgow the gulf between the two religions was both wide and bitter.

From birth the hatred was instilled into you. You might have to work with a Catholic but you never went to school with one – and as for intermarriage, that was the most heinous crime you could commit.

Let him go, she told herself. See him again and it could only lead to tears and trouble and God knows what. To continue their relationship was a sure path to disaster. And yet . . . and yet . . .

The week was interminable, each day seeming longer than the last.

Hour after hour she toiled at the machine she was in charge of which turned out sherbet boilings. But it wasn't boilings she saw when the machine spewed them forth. It was Frank's battered and torn features staring appealingly back at her.

During the tea breaks she was quiet and morose, which at last prompted Big Jessie to ask what the hell was wrong with her. She replied that she wasn't feeling all that clever, which satisfied Jessie's curiosity and put a stop to any further probing questions.

Earlier in the week she'd taken Babs into her confidence. Babs had been surprised she hadn't realized right away that Frank was a left-footer. 'Obvious as a bloody doorpost,' Babs had said. Then added, in a romantic tone of voice, 'I suppose it was the true love that blinded you. They say it often does.'

She'd scoffed at that. But there was more in what Babs said than she cared to admit.

Babs was sworn to secrecy, of course. This was something she didn't want getting around. Not until she finally decided what was what anyway.

For, even as the week wore on, Nellie still hadn't made up her mind about Friday night. One moment she'd decided not to go, the next she was wondering what to wear.

At home, Betty noticed the change in her and asked what was wrong. To which Nellie replied she was just in a bit of a mood that's all and to ignore her as it was nothing important.

Her sleep was also affected. Night after night she lay staring at the ceiling thinking things through, trying to come to the right decision.

Viewed logically there was only one right decision, as well she knew. And yet . . . and yet . . .

She wasn't going to go. Her mind was made up. Slowly she buttered a slice of bread and listened to her father rattle on about some problem they'd been having down at the Yard.

Betty was also listening to Davey, and although she didn't reply, she nodded her head from time to time to show him she was paying attention.

Roddy was eating his second French cake, a box of which Davey often brought home on a Friday night as a special treat for Betty who had a sweet tooth.

Glancing up at the kitchen window Nellie saw that it had started to smir. Even as she watched, the smir became rain proper which within minutes was bucketing down.

They cleared the tea things away and she helped Betty wash and dry while Davey and Roddy ensconced themselves by the fire. Davey puffed contentedly at his pipe while Roddy buried himself in a new comic he'd bought that day with his pocket money.

'Is it the jigging the night?' Betty asked.

Nellie shook her head. 'I thought I'd stay in for a change.'

'Well, in that case, you can help me patch some of the sheets that need mending,' Betty said. Then, loudly over her shoulder so Davey would hear, added, 'It would be a grand thing to have a sewing machine like Mrs McAllister two closes down. Would fair save on time and effort.'

'McAllister's a gaffer and earns more than me,' Davey retorted. 'That's why they can afford such luxuries while we can't.'

'You might not think it such a luxury if you had to do the sewing yourself,' Betty said tartly.

'No matter how much you give them they're never bloody satisfied,' Davey mumbled into his pipe.

While this exchange was going on Nellie stared out of the window watching a flash of lightning rend the sky. A few seconds later the thunder came.

'Looks like it's going to be quite a night,' said Betty peering over Nellie's shoulder. 'Just as well you're staying in.'

More lightning ripped its way across the heavens. 'Just as well,' Nellie echoed softly.

She thought the storm couldn't get worse but it did. As she sewed her eyes kept coming back again and again to the window.

After a while Davey fell asleep and Roddy took himself off into a corner of the room to play with some lead soldiers and a papier mâché fort that had been his present the previous Christmas.

Seven o'clock came and went, as did the half hour. Slowly the hands on the clock crept towards eight.

When the clock struck eight it was as though an electric current had been shot through her. In her mind's eye she could see Frank standing outside the Roxy. He'd promised to wait all night if necessary, even an hour in this appalling weather and he'd be a candidate for pneumonia.

Suddenly, as though a tap had been opened, her resolve drained from her. She had to go to him. She just couldn't leave him standing about on a night like this.

'I'm going out after all Ma,' she said, laying her mending down and rising.

Betty looked up in surprise. 'But it's coming down cats and dogs!' she exclaimed.

Nellie decided she didn't have time to make up or change. She would just have to go the way she was. 'I'll be in by eleven,' she assured her, and without further ado hurried through to the hallway where she shrugged herself into her raincoat.

When the outside door had banged shut Betty sat open-mouthed in amazement. Now what on earth was all that about, she wondered. Young lassies, she thought, they were all the same. Daft as a brush. And hadn't she been the same way at Nellie's age? She smiled to herself at the memory.

Shrewdly she guessed it had something to do with this new boy Nellie had been seeing. Must be serious she thought. And mulled over that while she got on with her sewing.

Nellie ran all the way through the streets, awash with rain. The gutters she passed were miniature rivers in spate.

At first she didn't see him. Then she caught sight of his face reflected in the street gaslight. One of his eyes was black and his mouth and cheek were puffed out. That same damaged cheek was yellow and brown in patches. When she heard him coughing she was almost overcome with emotion.

'Nellie! You came after all!' he exclaimed, his expression one of absolute joy.

'You're soaked through.'

'A wee bit of rain water never hurt anyone,' he replied with a laugh.

She wanted to take him in her arms and hug him tightly.

For almost a full minute they stood staring at one another. And then, not giving a damn – the street was almost deserted anyway because of the weather – he drew her to him and kissed her on the mouth.

Normally she would have been scandalized. But as it was she didn't give a damn either.

'Shall we go inside?' he asked.

'I'm not dressed nor am I made-up.'

'What did you do? Change your mind at the last moment?'

Taking his hand in hers she said, 'I'm here now and that's all that matters.'

'Yes. That's all that matters,' he echoed softly. For a few moments they simply looked at one another. 'There's the fleapit down the road,' he suggested at last. 'I've already seen the picture that's on but who cares about that?'

She laughed. 'So have I but, as you say, who cares?'

Arm in arm and laughing together they walked into the night.

'Nellie?'

She'd just come out of the wee newsagent's on the corner having run down for some pipe tobacco for her da. At first she couldn't place the man smiling at her, but then the penny dropped.

'My da's masonic pal,' she said.

'Right first time,' he replied, and fell into step beside her as she began walking back to the house. 'How are you doing?' he asked.

'All right I suppose. Getting by like everybody else.'

She really was a cracker he thought. As good-looking a piece as he'd seen in a long time. He could imagine her naked, the shape and colour of her, and the thought excited him. Women, what marvellous creatures they were. With some men it was drink, with others tobacco.

41

But with him it was female flesh. Soft, yielding female flesh. He could never get enough of it.

'There's a good picture on in town this week,' he said. 'I was wondering if you'd like to come and see it with me?'

She could tell by the tone in his voice that this was no spur of the moment notion on his part. He'd been thinking about asking her out. 'It's kind of you to ask, Jim, but I'm afraid I'm already winching.'

'The boy at the dance?'

'That's right.'

'I see,' he replied and continued smiling. The smile hadn't wavered since he'd called out her name.

'I'm awful sorry,' she said.

'My loss.'

There was a hurt look in his eyes and suddenly she didn't think him such a smoothie after all. Maybe he's just shy and the smoothie thing is his way of getting over it, she thought.

At her front close they stopped. 'Are you coming up to see da?' she asked.

'I was on my way to your house but it wasn't Davey I wanted to see,' he said. Behind the smile his eyes probed into her, making her feel guilty and uneasy – as though she was being unreasonable in some way. She shuffled her feet, not quite sure what to say next or how to terminate the conversation.

He was drinking her in. Itching to lay hands on her. Her long yellow hair fascinated him, and he wondered if it was the same colour in other places. Just thinking about it excited him even more. God, he could've done it to her right there against the front close wall.

'I'll have to go. Da's waiting for his baccy,' she said. She was about to turn away when he reached out and caught her by the arm. 'Sure you won't change your mind?' he asked, his voice thicker with the lust raging through him.

'I don't two-time Jim,' she answered softly.

He nodded. 'If sometime in the future you broke up with this lad and I was to ask you out, then would you go?'

42

'I might do.'

She was young he thought. At her age boyfriends must come and go with great rapidity. With a bit of luck his wait wouldn't be a long one.

'We'll leave it at that then,' he said releasing her.

Nellie shivered, and didn't know why she'd done so. 'Someone walking over my grave,' she said.

He waited till the yellow hair had vanished round the gloomy turning on the first-floor landing before turning and walking swiftly away.

There was a bird over in Luath Street whose husband was at sea with the Royal Navy. He'd pick up a half bottle and go chapping her door as he'd done a number of times in the past. His need for a woman was great at the moment and she would happily oblige.

Starting to whistle he increased his pace.

2

Months passed and Nellie and Frank continued seeing each other as often as they could, which meant every Friday and Saturday night. And, as time went by, so did their friendship deepen and strengthen. When September arrived they were hopelessly in love with one another.

It was the Friday afternoon tea break before the long Bank Holiday weekend when Big Jessie said, 'So how are you getting on with this new click of yours, Nellie? You keep helluva quiet about him.'

'It must be love right enough,' added Daisy, causing all the girls present, with the exception of Nellie and Babs, to laugh.

'I'm getting on with him fine enough,' replied Nellie, glancing sideways at Babs. All the girls present were staunch Protestants; to say they would be upset had they known she was going out with a Catholic would be putting it mildly.

Big Jessie had a suspicion there was something fishy about Nellie's boyfriend, or why else was Nellie so close-mouthed about him? That just wasn't like Nellie at all. Especially as she herself hadn't had a boyfriend for some time now and Nellie hadn't even bothered to crow once. No rubbing of salt into the wound. No long accounts of how clever or good-looking or whatever that this Frank was; his name being about the only thing they'd found out about him. No, something was queer all right.

'What are you doing at the weekend then?' Big Jessie asked.

'We thought of going away for the day. Down the coast maybe or perhaps a trip to Loch Lomond. We haven't made up our minds yet,' Nellie replied.

'Just the day and not the weekend?' Jessie asked innocently.

'The *day*,' Nellie replied firmly.

'I suppose you'll be giving him his rights now you've been together this long?' Jessie said.

Daisy, Agnes and a new girl, called Lena, who'd joined their group stared expectantly at Nellie. Was she or wasn't she? That was what they were all dying to know.

'I wouldn't judge everyone by your own standards,' replied Nellie tartly.

Babs grinned and buried her face in her teacup. Good for you, Nellie, she thought. That was telling the big one.

Jessie glowered, then stuck her nose in the air. 'I'll have you know I'm a virgin,' she sniffed.

'You're also a comedienne,' Nellie replied.

Anger flared across Big Jessie's face and for a moment it seemed she was going to fly at Nellie. The only thing that stopped her was the thought of getting the sack, which was automatic for fighting.

'I'm just not that sort of girl,' Nellie said lightly. 'When I get married I'll be in white. And what's more, the white won't be a lie.'

Big Jessie glared and chewed her lip. She would have given almost anything, except of course her precious job, to be able to go across and sock Nellie.

'I'd love to go down the coast myself,' said Daisy. 'Or should I say I'd love to go with a man.' She sighed. 'That must be nice.'

'Especially if the man's your *Fate*,' added Babs.

'Is your Frank that?' asked Lena.

Nellie shrugged her shoulders, 'Too soon to tell.' It was a lie. She knew Frank was the only man for her.

'It'll probably rain all day Monday,' said Jessie viciously.

'When you're with a man who cares?' said Daisy.

'Amen to that,' added Agnes.

'What did you say his last name was?' asked Lena.

Babs glanced up at her friend. That was a loaded question if ever there was one. A Catholic could be identified just as easily by his surname as by his features.

'I didn't,' smiled Nellie. 'If you think I'm going to tell you his full name so you can look him up and try to steal him away, then you're daft.'

'You think I'd have a chance then?' asked Lena.

'No. But why should I take the risk?' Next to Nellie Lena was the best looking girl in the group.

'Maybe he's got a brother?' suggested Lena.

'And maybe you should away and raffle your head,' retorted Nellie, which raised a laugh, Lena joining in against herself.

The hooter sounded.

'Back to bloody work,' said Big Jessie sourly. 'Still, only a few hours to go and that's it till Tuesday morning.'

Nellie returned to her boiling making machine, having successfully fended off the probing questions one more time. But that was something she wouldn't be able to go on doing for ever. The longer she went out with Frank, the more curious people became. At home as well as work.

The Bank Holiday dawned a scorcher. Nellie met Frank down at the red bus station where they queued for the Balmaha bus, Balmaha being on the shores of Loch Lomond.

Frank's mother had made up some sandwiches which he'd brought along with some bottles of beer. Their plan was to find a nice spot and have a picnic.

At Balmaha they started walking north, wanting to get well away from the other day-trippers. After a mile over

46

undulating countryside they came to a beautiful little inlet where the waters of the loch were lapping gently.

Nellie stretched out on the grass and stared up at the duck-blue sky. There was a soft wind stirring which took the edge off the intense heat blazing down. September is nearly always a good month in Scotland, far better than July or August, which are often cold and wet.

'Like the South of France,' said Frank lying down beside Nellie.

'Oh, you know it do you?' she teased.

'Och, aye. I'm always going there on my holidays. Makes a change from down the Clyde.'

Nellie laughed. 'Daftie!'

She closed her eyes and let the heat sink through her. What a change from the grey, griminess of Glasgow. It was amazing to think the city was so close, just over an hour's bus-drive away. The contrast between the city and Loch Lomondside was so startling that she might have been on another planet.

'Fancy a paddle?' asked Frank.

'No, but you away in.'

He grinned at her as he stripped off his shoes and socks, rolling up his trouser legs before striding down to the water's edge.

Nellie sat up to watch him. She felt so at peace, so together with him. There was no doubt at all in her mind that he was the right man for her. In a lifetime she'd never meet another more right for her, or her for him.

'It's blinking freezing,' he said pulling a face.

'It looks warm enough.'

'You come in and you'll find out differently,' he retorted. A few seconds later he yelped, saying, 'There's a bloody fish down here having a chew at my toes.'

Nellie laughed at the comical, outraged expression on his face. 'You'd better come out before you poison it,' she said.

'Very funny!'

'Is it still there?'

47

'Aye, and it's got a wee pal with it now as well. I think you're right. It's time I came out before there's a whole shoal of them here having a go at me.' And having said that he beat a hasty retreat for the bank.

Nellie set out the sandwiches while he opened the beer. 'This was kind of your ma,' she said.

'She's not a bad old stick.'

'Does she know I'm a Protestant?'

He glanced sideways at her. 'Ma assumes you're one of the green, just like us. For the moment I thought it best not to shatter her illusions.'

'And what'll she say when she finds out?'

'She'll have a knipshit, as will my da. They'll probably disown me. Ordered out of the house never to return and all that bunk.'

Nellie shook her head. So much energy and emotion wasted on what was such a little thing after all. Only the green and the orange didn't see the differences between them as being little. And as time went by, rather than trying to bring their two sides closer together, the factions built on the existing hatred and bigotry so that the gulf separating them became wider and wider.

After the sandwiches and beer they lit cigarettes and lay side by side smoking. Nellie was so happy she felt she could have stayed there till the end of time. Or till hell froze over as her da would have put it.

He came into her arms and they kissed. A languorous, indulged-in kiss, very different from the frantic, passionate ones of the back close. The kiss went on and on and it seemed to Nellie it would never stop. Nor did she want it to.

His hand crept up to her breast, cupping and squeezing it. She made no resistance when the same hand undid the top buttons of her dress and slipped inside. He didn't undo her bra, but rather pulled it out and over so that her breasts fell free. Having exposed them he buried his face in their softness.

Nellie stroked the back of his head while he kissed and

48

nibbled her nipples. They'd gone this far before in the back close but it was so much nicer here in the open air with the sun beating down.

'Oh, Frank,' she murmured.

He was like a little boy, she thought. But then weren't all men when like this? They certainly were in her experience. A little boy sucking greedily at her breast. She liked the idea.

His breath was coming in short, laboured gasps. He brought his hand up the bottom of her dress to tug at the cotton knickers she wore. He jerked when his hand came into contact with downy pubic hair. Then it was her turn to jerk as his finger went inside her.

Nellie groaned and writhed. It was such a marvellous, marvellous sensation. His finger was like a column of fire. Probing, touching, exploring what, for the moment, was the very centre of her universe.

She was suddenly aware that he was using his free hand to undo his trousers. 'No Frank!' She grabbed hold of the hand to stop it.

'But Nellie –'

'It's my fault for letting you go this far,' she broke in, pulling herself free.

'Please?' he pleaded, desperation in his voice.

'Do you think I don't want to?' she said, tugging her knickers into place.

'Then why not, for God's sake?'

She sat up readjusting her bra and buttoning her dress.

'Nellie?'

'Not until I'm married,' she said firmly. 'What if I was to get pregnant?'

'There are things you can use, you know.'

'I'm well aware of that. Just as I'm well aware they're never a hundred per cent certain. Anyway, being a Catholic you're not supposed to use those.'

'You sound like the priest now,' he said, and laughed.

'Have you got some with you?'

'Some what?' he asked, feigning innocence.

49

'What we've just been talking about.'

'I might have,' he replied coyly.

Her eyes narrowed fractionally. 'Were they bought especially for the occasion?'

'Could be. Then again they might be something I carry around in my wallet all the time.'

'Have you . . .' She was embarrassed to ask the question and it showed by the blush that crept across her face. 'Have you . . .?'

'Oh lots,' he said, guessing her question.

Mixed emotions sparked in her eyes. 'How many are lots?'

He put his hand to his mouth and pretended to think. 'Twenty, maybe twenty-five. You lose count after a while.'

'What!'

'Then again it could be more. I have that effect on women, you see. They just can't keep their hands off me.'

Nellie was scandalized and shocked. Twenty-five. She'd thought maybe one or two. But twenty-five!

Then she noticed the amused glint that escaped his otherwise fixed expression and knew he was having her on.

'You bugger!' she exclaimed and launched herself at him.

He laughed as they rolled on the ground, she pummelling his chest with clenched fists.

To stop her he encircled her with his arms and hugged her tight. With her breasts pressing into him he kissed her.

'You're rotten, you know that?' she said breaking away.

'Will I tell you how many there have really been, Nellie?' he asked softly.

She stared at him, waiting.

'None. Not one.'

'Maybe I shouldn't have let the cat out the bag,' he went on, suddenly unsure of himself. 'Women like to think their man has been around a wee bit. That he's got some experience.'

Her man, it was an expression she liked. Her man. Yes, that was exactly what he was.

'Well this is one woman who doesn't,' she replied. 'I like you just as you are. I wouldn't want to change anything at all about you.'

'Nor I you.'

He felt awkward, clumsy; wishing he could find the words to express what was in his mind and the emotions he felt for her.

'You sure you won't do it till you get married?' he asked, looking at the ground.

'No, Frank. And nothing you can say will make me change my mind. That's the way it's going to be with me.'

'You're scared of getting in the club?'

'That's got a lot to do with it. But it's more than that. Can't you understand?'

'Aye. Although I don't really want to.'

She grinned. He was now looking even more like a little boy.

The words came out in a rush. 'Well, I suppose that's what we'll just have to do then,' he said.

She wasn't quite sure if she'd understood him properly. 'What exactly do you mean?'

'We'll just have to get married. What do you think I meant?'

For a moment or two she forgot to breathe as the enormity of what he'd just said sunk in. 'Are you proposing?' she asked huskily.

'Well, I'm sure as hell not asking you to pass what's left of the bloody sandwiches!'

Although she was already hot from the sun, a different kind of heat enveloped her. She wanted to leap to her feet and sing and dance but she restrained herself.

'We can't. Not yet anyway,' she said quietly.

He blushed. 'Are you turning me down?'

Immediately she was in his arms, resting her head on his

shoulder. 'Of course I'm not. I love you, Frank Connelly. And I have done since the night we first met.'

He wanted to say he loved her too but it just wasn't in him to utter the word. He would've felt a prize idiot had he done so. A man just didn't say that word. Not in the daylight, anyway.

'Is it the religious thing that's bothering you?' he asked.

'That, and other things. To marry you now I'd need my da's permission and there's certainly no way he's going to give me that when he finds out you're a left-footer. And then there's the fact you're still an apprentice. We'll have to wait till you're time served before we get married. We're going to have to move away from Glasgow, there's just no two ways about that. And besides these other problems we just couldn't live on what we earn now. Together we don't earn a full man's wage.'

What she said was true. Even skimping and scraping in the extreme, their combined wages wouldn't cover the cost of a house and the other necessities. He had no choice but to accept the facts.

'How long till you finish your apprenticeship?'

'Fifteen months,' he replied.

'By which time I'll be well eighteen and not have to ask anyone's permission to get wed.'

'Near the time I could start writing away, Newcastle maybe. And when I line myself up with a job then we could elope.'

Elope! It was so romantic.

But he went on, 'That way there'll be no problem from anyone here in Glasgow. No priest screaming in my ear, or da in yours. We'll leave them all to stew in their own bloody juice.'

It was a marvellous idea. An inspiration. She kissed him deeply and considered giving in. But no, she would do what she'd always said she would do – wait until her wedding night.

'Does that mean we're engaged?' she teased.

'I suppose it does. But we'll have to keep it secret, mind.

You know as well as I do, if it gets out there'll be hell to pay.'

'Will you buy me a ring?'

'Do you think that's wise? In the circumstances, I mean.'

'I wouldn't feel properly engaged without a ring, Frank. And I don't have to wear it as such. I could just keep it for times like this when we're alone.'

He thought about the wee bit of money he had put by. It wasn't much, but it was enough to buy her a ring of some sort.

'It'll be an awful wee diamond. You'll probably need a microscope to see it,' he joked.

She snuggled close. 'The fact that it'll be from you will be the important thing. The size of the stone won't matter at all,' she whispered.

'We'll go into town and get it Saturday afternoon,' he replied. He brought his hands down to encircle her bottom. 'Now that we're engaged and almost married, how about it then?'

'Frank!'

He sighed. He was going to have to wait – but at the moment fifteen months seemed like two eternities. 'Is there any of that beer left?' he asked at last, resigned.

Nellie broke away. 'I'll get it for you,' she said.

After the beer he went back for another paddle. As he explained, he needed cooling down.

So did Nellie, but she didn't tell him that.

Arm in arm they strolled along Sauchiehall Street, gazing in jewellers' windows until at last they came to one that Nellie decided she fancied.

Frank had already been to the bank to withdraw every penny he possessed. Although little enough he'd never had so much money on him before and the thought of it bulging out his wallet made him feel ten feet tall.

There were only two trays of rings within their budget,

but even so Nellie spent over an hour poring over them, each ring being tried on and considered at least half a dozen times. Finally the choice was made, and as no adjustment had to be made to the band, Nellie was able to wear it away with her.

Outside the shop again a beaming Nellie said she had a spot at the back of her drawer at home where she would plank it. But in the meantime was it all right to wear it till they got on the tram?

'Och, aye, there'll be no harm in that,' smiled Frank.

Before slipping her arm into his, Nellie held the ring up to have yet another look at it. 'It's a right smasher,' she said.

'Just like you.' Laughing, they continued down the street.

If Nellie hadn't been so caught up in her ring she might have seen Big Jessie standing across the road, staring open-mouthed at her and Frank. There was nothing wrong with Big Jessie's eyesight, nor her powers of deduction. Nellie and her bloke had obviously been buying a ring, and the fact that it was the left hand Nellie was wearing it on could only mean it was an engagement one.

But the real turn-up for the book, as far as Jessie was concerned, was Frank himself. He just had to be a Fenian, everything about him screamed it.

Suddenly it all clicked into place. No wonder Nellie had been so reticent to talk about her man. He was a bloody Catholic. That was why they'd never got his surname, or any other facts out of her.

'A Fenian,' Jessie breathed aloud. That really was something. She stared after the departing couple till they'd been swallowed up in the Saturday throng. Then, turning, she hurried in the opposite direction. She was meeting up with Daisy and Agnes for coffee. Did she have something to tell them!

She couldn't wait to see their faces.

*

Monday morning Nellie teamed up with Babs at the close mouth, and, as they did every working morning, they trudged off to the Bastille together.

For a change Nellie had been down before Babs arrived. She was dying to show Babs the ring which Babs had known she and Frank were off to buy the previous Saturday.

With the ring duly admired, Nellie recounted every detail about the jeweller's shop and the other rings she'd had to choose from, and why she'd preferred this particular one over the others. Babs hung on every syllable. In her mind she saw herself choosing a ring with the man who was *her Fate* – and whom she'd still to meet.

When they reached the factory Nellie put the ring back in its box, which she then stuffed into her coat pocket. Later she would transfer the box to her overalls, so it would be on her and safe for the working day.

It wasn't till the break that she realized something was up. Agnes, Daisy and Lena were studiously avoiding looking her straight in the eye. Big Jessie on the other hand had a curious exultant glint in hers.

She glanced at the other groups of lassies standing and sitting around. Two, who were usually quite chummy, turned their heads away when she started to smile at them. And Bella Murcheson, who was another out of the Big Jessie mould, positively glowered at her.

She brought her attention back to her own group, where Lena and Agnes were talking about the dancing they'd gone to on the Saturday night. It was an ordinary enough conversation of the sort they were always having, only this time there was something forced about it, as though they were somehow talking for talking's sake. Were they talking to one another so they wouldn't have to talk to her? Then there was that glint in Big Jessie's eye. What did that mean?

Suddenly she knew with absolute certainty what it meant. Big Jessie, as well as the others, had found out about Frank. She didn't know how, but guessed that they must have been seen together.

Well, what did she expect, after all? She and Frank had been going out long enough. It was a miracle they'd gone on this long without being spotted. Glasgow might seem a sizeable place but it wasn't really. There was no way you could get lost in it like she was told you could in London.

Mind you, they'd done their best not to be seen together. After their first few dates in Govan they'd met in town or an area where the odds against them running into someone they knew were greatly diminished.

Their lovemaking in the back close was surreptitiously conducted: she going in first to be followed shortly after by him, having trailed her from the tram.

The hooter sounded, rousing her from her reverie. On the way back to her machine she saw Bella Murcheson was still glowering hate at her, and remembered then that Bella's father was a fanatical Orangeman. She shivered. Bella's look of hate was only a foretaste of what she could expect to come.

Two days later, on the Wednesday night, the Thompson family was sitting round the table having tea. Normally a good eater, eight-year-old Roddy was playing with his food, pushing it with his fork round his plate.

'Will you stop that and get on with it,' Betty said with a frown.

Roddy muttered something unintelligible and stuck some egg into his mouth. He chewed it slowly as though it was something distasteful.

'Are you not feeling well, son?' she asked.

'I'm fine, Ma,' Roddy replied morosely.

'Well, there's something wrong. It's not like you to lose your appetite.'

'Have you had an upset at school?' asked Davey.

Roddy pulled a face.

'Well?' Betty demanded.

'One of my pals said if you're a pageboy you have to dress up in a velvet suit. Is that right, Ma?'

The question caught Betty by surprise. 'Pageboys don't *have* to wear velvet suits but it's often the done thing.'

'You'll not make me wear one then? Please, Nellie.'

Nellie's fork stopped halfway to her mouth. She was acutely aware of her mother's and father's gazes coming to rest on her. For years she'd been telling Roddy that when she got married he'd be a pageboy at her wedding.

'Please Nellie?' Roddy pleaded. 'All my pals would laugh at me if I had to dress up like that.'

'I'm sure you'll be far too old for a velvet suit by the time Nellie gets married,' Davey said with a grin. Then to Nellie, 'Eh, lass?'

Nellie was about to reply when Roddy said, 'And you'll not make me go to the chapel either, will you Nellie? My pals at school would make my life a misery if you did.'

Oh, Jesus! Nellie thought. He'd landed her right in it now.

Very slowly and carefully, Davey put down his knife and fork. 'What are you talking about?' he asked his son.

'Nellie marrying a Catholic.'

'Who told you that?'

'Tam Gray in my class. He heard his sister Fiona talking about it. She works at the sweetie factory same as Nellie.'

Fear and apprehension had tied a knot in Nellie's stomach. The look Davey turned on her caused her to shrink in on herself.

'Well, girl?' Davey demanded.

'Tell us it's not true,' coaxed Betty.

'I eh . . . I . . . Yes it is,' she whispered.

A long hiss of breath escaped from Davey. His daughter marry a Catholic! The very thought made his skin crawl. Catholics were little better than vermin.

Betty had gone quite pale, looking at Nellie as though seeing her for the first time.

57

'*Will* I have to go to the chapel, Nellie?' Roddy asked.

She wanted to reach across the table and slap his face. Don't take it out on him, she chided herself. He was too young to realize what it was he'd just done.

'The boy you've been going out with all these months?' asked Davey.

Nellie nodded.

'A Catholic?'

Nellie nodded again.

'What's his name?'

'Frank Connelly.'

'Frank Connelly,' Davey said, tasting the words as though they were something nasty that had found their way into his mouth. 'I suppose amongst his own kind they call him Francey?'

'I don't know.'

'He's asked you to marry him?'

'You didn't accept did you?' Betty put in quickly.

'He bought me an engagement ring last Saturday,' Nellie said slowly.

Betty caught her breath and put her hand to her mouth.

'Behind our backs, eh?' Davey said. 'Like a couple of thieves in the night.'

'I knew you would be upset and that's why I didn't tell you,' Nellie defended.

'Upset! That's putting it mildly!'

'Are you going to turn?' Betty asked anxiously.

Nellie opened her mouth to reply but before she could do so Davey's clenched fist came crashing down on the table causing everything on it to jump, and a teacup and saucer to fall to the floor and shatter. 'There'll be no bloody turning in my family!' he roared.

'I hadn't planned to,' Nellie said.

'What *had* you planned to do?'

'We were going to wait till I was eighteen and he'd served his apprenticeship – he's at Langbank Yard same as you – and then we were going to elope to somewhere religion didn't matter so much.'

'Oh, were you now?' mocked Davey.

'I love him, Ma,' Nellie pleaded. 'He's the only man for me.'

Tears came into Betty's eyes. 'But he's a Catholic, lass. He's not one of us. He's a different kind altogether.'

'I don't care what he is. I love him and that's all that matters.'

'Love? What do you know about it at your age?' Davey said scornfully. Coming to his feet he started unbuckling his belt.

Originally brown, the belt was now black with age. Nellie stared at it in fascination. It was years since her father had used it on her.

'Ma?' But when she looked at Betty her mother averted her gaze.

The expression on Davey's face was terrifying. At that moment he looked quite capable of murder.

'You're going to tell this Connelly that your so called engagement's off. Understand?'

'No,' Nellie breathed more than said.

Davey came slowly round the table. 'In the other room,' he said.

'No.'

She screamed when he grabbed hold of her hair and yanked her from her chair. She screamed all the way to the bedroom as he dragged her stumbling through. He closed the door behind them before throwing her from him. His nostrils were dilated and his eyes hooded as he wrapped a section of the belt around his fist. 'Now, you're going to break off this engagement,' he commanded.

Nellie stared at her father in terror. Her legs had started to shake so much she thought she was going to lose control of them.

'You haven't answered me, girl.'

She had never seen her father so angry; his anger so intense it seemed to be sparking off him like electricity.

'I won't,' she whispered.

She screamed as the belt curled viciously round her

59

backside raising an ugly red weal under the material of her dress.

'I'll never give him up,' she said defiantly and screamed again as the belt struck her a second time.

Again and again the belt lashed her buttocks and legs till she thought she must surely faint from the pain. But she didn't. Even that release was denied her. She lay on the floor with her father towering above her, her bottom and legs were covered with blood.

Davey paused. 'Will you break it off?' he demanded.

Her face was drenched with sweat and tears, her long yellow hair matted and sticking to her cheeks and neck. From the waist downward she felt as though she'd been skinned alive. She made a fist and screwed it into her mouth, her body convulsed with uncontrollable sobs.

Davey reached down and grabbed her arm, 'Well?'

'No,' the word so faint as to be almost inaudible.

Even in his rage he knew he couldn't leather her any more. 'I'll have my way over this. One way or the other, Nellie, you'll break with that Catholic.'

He strode to the door where he paused to stare back at her. 'You'll stay in here till you come to your senses. Your mother and I will sleep in the cavity bed with Roddy until you do.'

He went out closing the door hard behind him. Nellie listened to the key turning in the lock. She wouldn't give in, she wouldn't, she swore to herself. There was nothing he could do to her that would make her give up Frank.

Groaning in pain, she crawled across the linoleum floor to the bed. It took her long, agonizing minutes to heave herself up on to it, and she collapsed, face down, burying her tears in the cool softness of the feather quilt.

She'd had some beltings in her life but nothing to compare with this. Da had behaved like a man possessed. But then he was possessed, she told herself. Possessed with hatred and bigotry.

'Oh, Frank,' she cried into the quilt, her eyes filling again with hot, salty tears. 'Oh, Frank, what can we do?'

*

Sun was flooding the room when she came to, her position on the bed exactly as it had been when she'd fallen asleep.

She whimpered when she tried to move. It was well after going to work time, though it would have been impossible for her to go anyway.

Gritting her teeth, she forced herself up on to her arms and legs. Then, with a monumental effort, she got off the bed and on to her feet. She removed her dress, having to pull it away in places where it was stuck to her with her own dried blood. Then she took off her petticoat, stockings and pants. Clad only in her bra, she forced herself over to the wardrobe to look at herself in the mirror.

Her bottom was puffed up and swollen, and beneath the blood were large areas of flesh already turning black and blue.

The key twisted in the lock and the door opened. Betty came in carrying a jug of water and a plate on which were several slices of unbuttered bread. 'God Almighty!' she exclaimed. Setting the jug and plate down she hurried over to Nellie's side.

'Pretty isn't it?' Nellie said bitterly.

'You've no one to blame but yourself,' Betty snapped back, adding, with a shake of her head, 'but he shouldn't have gone that far.'

'I hate him! I hate him! I hate him!' Nellie suddenly burst out, her cheeks flaming with anger. Then with a strangled sob she threw herself into Betty's arms where she rested her head on her mother's bosom.

Betty stroked her hair and made soothing noises while Nellie wept. When the crying fit was finally over she said, 'I'll away through and get some hot water and antiseptic. I'll soon have you washed and cleaned.'

'Wouldn't it be easier if I came through to the kitchen with you?'

Betty's face hardened. 'Your da said you're to stay in

here, and that's what you'll have to do. He also says you're on bread and water till you see sense.'

'Then I'll be on it for the rest of my life.'

'You really love him, eh?' said Betty, softening.

'He's the only one for me, Ma. And please don't say that because I'm only seventeen I don't know my own mind, for I do.'

She'd always had her father's stubborn streak, Betty thought. Nellie and Davey were more alike than they knew. As much as Nellie swore she wouldn't break off this engagement, Davey was equally determined that she would.

'Lie on the bed and I'll get the hot water,' Betty sighed, and left the room.

Nellie hobbled to the door which her mother had left unlocked. Silently, she went out into the hallway to where her coat was hanging. It took only a moment to slip the box containing her engagement ring from her coat pocket.

She had told Frank that she was going to hide the ring in a secret place of hers in the kitchen, but she'd changed her mind about that. Instead, she'd taken it with her to work so that she could have it with her during the day. She might not have been able to wear it, but she'd found great comfort and pleasure in being able to reach down and touch its box from time to time.

Back in the bedroom, she took the ring from its box and slipped it on to her finger. The time for secrecy was over. From now on she'd wear it for all the world to see.

Nellie was lying on the bed reading a book when she heard the front door slam, followed by the sound of her father's footsteps in the hall. She cringed involuntarily, wondering if he was going to come in and belt her again. Surely Betty wouldn't allow it?

Still, she winced when the key turned in the lock and her father entered the room. It was something of a relief to see his belt was round his waist and not in his hand.

His face was rock hard as he came to the bed to stand beside her. 'Have you anything to say to me?' he asked.

'No.'

'You won't change your mind?'

'Never.'

His lips thinned and his eyes flashed fire. 'Well I've got something to say to you,' he said. 'I looked up this Frank Connelly with the intention of having it out with him. But then I had a better idea, and one which will solve this nonsense once and for all.'

Having said that he seemed to relax a little. Crossing to the fireplace he placed his baccy tin on top of it and proceeded to fill his pipe. When his pipe had been puffed into life he went on. 'Shipbuilding yards are dangerous places as you well know. Despite safety precautions and regulations, accidents happen all the time. Bad accidents that maim and cripple people.' He paused before adding ominously, 'Kill them even.'

Nellie was rigid, her eyes never leaving her father's.

'You say you love this boy?'

She nodded.

'Then you wouldn't want anything to happen to him, would you?'

'You're not capable of that,' she challenged. Or so she'd thought until last night.

'Oh, but I am lass. I'll do anything to stop a daughter of mine marrying a Fenian. And you'd better believe me.'

Despair welled in her and her resolve began to crumble.

'It would be a fall, probably. Or a heavy weight dropped on him. Something substantial like a girder.'

'I'd go to the police.'

He gave a terrible smile. 'That wouldn't do you any good. When it happens I'll be somewhere else and with plenty of company to vouch for me. No, I wouldn't be doing it personally, not when you could put the finger on me. I've been at Langbank an awful long time and have many pals there. Pals who'd do anything for me. And do it happily when they knew a Catholic was involved.'

This wasn't the father she knew. It was a monster she'd never seen before. She couldn't match this man making such dreadful threats with the kind, but strict, dad she'd known all her life.

It came to her that she'd finally stepped through the door into adulthood. No more was there to be the protection afforded children. She was now in the harsh world of reality where she had to stand on her own two feet without support.

'What do you say now?' he asked.

She had to capitulate. There was nothing else for it. The alternative was simply too horrible to contemplate. 'I'll give him his ring back when I see him on Friday.'

Davey nodded. 'You'll not only give him his ring back, but you'll tell him you never want to see him again. You'll say you made a mistake, that you thought you cared for him but you don't. You'll tell him he's never to contact you again.'

Like hell, she thought. She'd tell Frank the truth and then they'd just have not to see one another till his time was out when they could elope as planned. 'All right,' she lied.

But Davey wasn't stupid. 'Furthermore, when you do tell him, I'll be within earshot,' he said. 'I want to make sure you get your story just right.' He held her chin so that her eyes met his. 'And I want you to be quite clear about this. If you do see him again, or contact him to try and arrange something between you, then he'll still be for the high jump. The accident will take place and that *will* be the end of it. Understand?'

She wanted to be sick. He'd thought of everything. But she'd find a way. Somehow or another she'd let Frank know the truth.

'You say you're seeing him Friday night?'

Nellie nodded.

'Then you can stay locked up in here till then. Where does he live?'

'Drumoyne.'

'Which street?'

'I don't know, and that's the truth. He was never able to invite me to his house for the same reason I was never able to invite him here.'

'You're sure you don't know?'

'No!'

He was satisfied she wasn't trying to put one over on him. 'That'll rule out letters then.'

A cloud of smoke wafted behind him as he walked to the door.

'Can I get something decent to eat now?' she asked.

'No.'

Nor did she until Friday dinner time.

Frank was waiting for her when she got off the tram. Smiling, he came straight to her and took her arm. 'Hello,' he said.

She'd been crying all morning, and her eyes were rimmed in red. She wanted to take him in her arms, to kiss him, to smother him with love. Instead she nodded towards a shop entranceway. 'We have to talk,' she said.

'What is it Nellie?' he asked once they were in the relative privacy of the entranceway.

Through the glass window she could see her father out in the street, pretending to be studying the window's contents. It was a position from which he'd be able to overhear every word that was about to be said.

'I've changed my mind about the engagement. In fact, I've changed my mind about us. We're finished, Frank.' Taking the box containing her engagement ring from her handbag, she pressed it into his hand.

Frank was dumbfounded. 'What?'

She was close to tears but fought them back. 'It just wouldn't work,' she choked.

He looked at the box then back at her. 'You can't mean it, surely?'

Of course she didn't mean it, she screamed inside

herself! In her mind's eye she saw a falling girder with Frank below it. She shuddered. 'I'm afraid I do.'

'But just last weekend you said –'

'I know what I said, but I was wrong.'

'You don't love me?'

A sideways flick of her eyes told her Davey was watching her intently. The hard face nodded.

'I thought I did, but I don't. I'm sorry. I don't want to see or hear from you ever again.'

His face had gone grey, his shoulders slumped – as though he were suddenly beginning to age.

I do love you! I do! she desperately wanted to shout. And I'll go on loving you till the end of time!

Frank pulled himself together. 'That's it then,' he said. His initial shock was now giving way to anger. Anger against Nellie, against himself, against the world in general.

'Good-bye,' she said, and hurriedly kissed him on the cheek.

Her high heels clattered on the ground as she rushed out of the entranceway.

When she was gone, Frank touched the mark of her kiss with the fingers of one hand. He'd been suckered, taken for a ride. The mark of the kiss was cold on his cheek. Slowly he rubbed the flesh warm again.

Back out on the street, he saw she was gone. 'And good riddance,' he said out loud.

It was later, when he was well in his cups and feeling sorry for himself, that the idea came to him. He knew as soon as he thought of it that it was what he was going to do.

Babs listened wide-eyed as Nellie told her what had happened, on the way to work the following Monday morning.

'So it's all off then?' she said when Nellie had finally come to the end of her tale.

66

'I'll find a way of letting Frank know I was forced into doing what I did. He'll understand once I've explained.'

'It's a right mess and no mistake,' Babs said. They were walking at half the pace they usually did as Nellie was still stiff and sore.

'You should have seen his face when I told him. It was terrible,' Nellie whispered, seeing again that face, that look.

'I can imagine.'

'And in a shop entranceway too. But my da insisted it was done somewhere he could overhear. When I left Frank I got halfway along Sauchiehall Street before my da caught up with me. He said I was running, but I wasn't aware of it. The ride home in the tram is a complete blank as well.'

They arrived at the factory and after clocking on went through to change into their overalls. Nellie found herself beside Big Jessie.

'And how was your weekend? Did you see your boyfriend?' Jessie asked with a smirk.

She didn't reply.

'And when are we going to see the engagement ring he bought you? Or are you ashamed to wear it seeing as how it came from a Mick?'

Nellie glanced at Babs, who shook her head. 'How did you know about that?'

Big Jessie's smirk became even wider. 'There I was, minding my own business, when who do I see coming out the jeweller's shop but you and him. The way you were goggling at your left hand it wasn't hard to put two and two together.'

So it was Jessie who'd seen her. Now she knew. And thanks to Jessie she'd lost Frank.

Fury blazed inside of Nellie. And the centre point of that fury was Big Jessie.

*

The lassies came streaming out the factory gates, all of them eager to get away home. Many of them were laughing and chatting gaily, now that the working day was done.

Nellie stood waiting with Babs by her side. She'd already confided to Babs what she intended to do.

'There she is,' said Babs out the side of her mouth, nodding with her head.

Raucously, Big Jessie's voice rose above those of the others she was with. She swaggered as she walked.

Nellie was icy cold inside. All day she'd been thinking about this and looking forward to it. It didn't matter at all that Jessie was taller and carried considerably more weight than she did. Her strength lay in the fact she didn't care what happened to her as long as she got a good few in on her enemy.

Quietly she stepped forward in front of Jessie. 'I want a word with you,' she said.

That infuriating smirk came back on Jessie's face. 'If it isn't the Fenian lover,' she said spitefully. 'And what can I do for you?'

'Your mouth is as big as your arse, which is saying something,' Nellie said clearly.

The chatter from the girls crowding round stilled instantly.

'What did you say?' Big Jessie demanded. Her smirk was gone.

'You're a born troublemaker of the worst kind. And what's more, you've got a head on you that's as thick as your ankles.'

Jessie coloured. 'You mind your tongue,' she warned.

'No, Jessie, it's you should've minded yours.' Having said that, she suddenly leapt forward.

Jessie screeched as Nellie's nails raked her face. The screech became an anguished howl as Nellie yanked at her hair.

Jessie got Nellie into a bear hug and started to squeeze. Finding her hand close to Jessie's breast Nellie sought out

68

the nipple and pulled it viciously. It was a massacre. Jessie was completely unable to cope with this hissing, spitting ball of venom.

'I give in! I give in!' she screamed.

The two were on the ground, with Nellie sitting astride Jessie, banging her head on the pavement.

'She'll bloody murder her,' yelled a voice from the crowd of onlookers.

Babs knew it was up to her to stop this before it got completely out of hand. Certainly none of the others was going to try. None of them wanted to tackle the hellcat that Nellie had become.

'It's all over. You've beaten her,' Babs said taking hold of Nellie's arms.

At first Nellie didn't hear her friend's voice, so overcome was she with fury. It was as though a red curtain had descended in front of her eyes.

'Nellie! Nellie stop it! Stop it! You've won.'

Big Jessie was crying, the tears streaming down her face.

Slowly, Nellie stood to stare down at Jessie. Her chest was heaving and her bottom was throbbing again from her unhealed cuts.

'Let's go home,' Babs said gently.

The crowd parted for them. With Babs's arm hooked in Nellie's, they continued on their way.

'That showed her,' said Nellie.

Babs thought of the battered, bleeding Jessie they'd left lying back there on the pavement. 'Aye, it certainly did that,' she agreed. 'Just promise me one thing though?'

'What's that?'

'If you ever get upset with me, let me know so I can get well out of town.'

They were still laughing when they reached Nellie's close.

*

A month passed and Nellie still hadn't been able to get in touch with Frank. If only she knew his address or a special friend she could contact. But she knew neither.

Her efforts were further hampered by the fact she was now indefinitely confined to the house after work and at weekends.

Babs had tried to help her by going to the Roxy several times in the hope that Frank would show up there, but so far she had failed to meet him.

Then, one night, the family had finished tea and Davey had settled into his chair with the evening paper, when he discovered his tobacco tin was empty. 'Nellie!' he called, reaching into his trouser pocket. 'Away down to the newsagent's and get me half an ounce.'

Nellie, who had been helping Betty with the dishes, wiped her hands on the tea towel before taking the money from him. 'Are you sure you trust me out for five minutes?' she asked bitterly, the abhorrence she felt for her father burning in her eyes.

'Less of your cheek, girl. And five minutes is all you've got. Any longer and I'll want to know why.'

'It's like being in jail,' she snapped.

She was emerging from the newsagent's when she saw a chap who'd taken her out several times in the past. His name was Colin Cunningham, and at one time he'd been rather keen on her.

'Colin!' she called suddenly. She'd just remembered that she'd pointed him out to Frank one night at the pictures, and Frank had said he knew him from Langbank.

'Hello, Nellie, how are you?' Colin greeted her.

'Listen, I've only got a moment. Will you do me a favour?'

'Aye, sure. What is it?'

'If I was to send you a letter with another letter inside would you pass the inside one on to Frank Connelly at the Yard? I haven't time to explain, but you'd have to promise to keep it secret. Would you do that for me?'

'I would if I could Nellie, but I can't.'

'Why not?'

'Was Frank a friend of yours?'

There was a sharp, constricting pain in her chest. 'What do you mean *was*?'

'He just didn't turn up for work one day and no one has seen him since. The rumour is he upped and left for Canada or New Zealand.'

The world reeled and Nellie staggered where she stood. It wasn't true! It couldn't be!

'Are you all right?' he asked, taking her arm to steady her.

'Are you sure about what you've just told me?' She could barely speak.

'I'm sure that he hasn't been to work in weeks and that his card's been removed from the time clock. As for him going abroad, well that's what's being said.'

'Canada or New Zealand,' she repeated, shaking her head. It was so unexpected.

'A queer business right enough. No one knows what caused him to go charging off like that.'

Colin looked at her expectantly but all she said was, 'Thanks', in a voice that was little above a whisper.

So Davey had got his way after all. She'd had it all planned, too. Fifteen months of lying doggo and then on a prearranged day it would be goodbye to Glasgow and a train south to marriage and a happy life together.

She'd never see him again her father had said. And he had been right. Frank Connelly would never come back to the city or the woman who'd betrayed him.

Damn you father! she raged. I'll never forgive you as long as I live.

Never.

71

3

Nellie sat staring into the fire while her mother ironed and Davey dozed in his chair.

Although allowed out at nights again, it had been months since Nellie had been anywhere, the last time being a trip to the pictures with Babs. Since Frank, she wasn't interested in enjoying herself or meeting anyone new.

'Cheer up, for Pete's sake!' said Betty. 'You look like you lost a pound and found a tanner.'

Nellie glanced up at her mother. 'I'm all right.'

'No you're not. Your face is tripping you.'

'I'm sorry it if bothers you. I'll try to be more cheerful, but I haven't exactly got a lot to be cheerful about have I?'

'Och, lassie that's just not true. You're bonny, you're healthy and you've got your whole life stretching ahead of you. What more could you want?'

Nellie went back to staring into the fire. But it wasn't coal and dancing flames she saw; it was a knight in shining armour whose face was Frank Connelly's.

She never had found out exactly where it was he'd gone. She'd even heard later that it wasn't Canada or New Zealand at all but South Africa. No matter where, really. Wherever it was it was far away from her – and that was what mattered.

She glanced across at her father's sleeping form. She'd

never have believed it possible to hate anyone so much.

'Nellie? Is that a knock at the door?'

With a sigh Nellie stood. It must be Roddy back from his pal's she thought, as the outside door was lightly chapped again.

But it wasn't Roddy.

'Hello. Remember me?' Jim Biles said with a smile.

'Of course I do. Come away in.'

Betty exclaimed with pleasure as Jim entered the kitchen. 'Davey! Davey!' she called out. 'There's someone here to see you!'

Davey woke with a snort, blinking open his eyes and elbowing himself up in the chair. When he saw it was Jim Biles who was calling his face broke into a warm smile.

'I hope I'm not intruding?'

'Och, no, no, it's good to see you,' Davey answered, waving Jim to the other fireside chair.

Jim produced a half bottle and placed it on the table. 'A wee something I bought on the way up,' he said.

Davey's eyes shone. He was a man who enjoyed his drink. 'Is it a special occasion then?'

Jim shook his head. 'I just thought a bevy would go down a treat.'

'You can say that again. Nellie, get some glasses.'

Still smiling, Jim watched Nellie as she moved to the sideboard. She was the reason for his visit. He'd asked after her a few days earlier and, in great confidence, Davey had told him the story of her and Frank Connelly.

So, she was now free again and as desirable as ever as far as he was concerned. He stared hungrily at her slim body and long yellow hair. And those green eyes – they were magic.

Nellie poured drinks for the two men.

'Grand stuff, right enough,' said Davey, sipping appreciatively.

Nellie sat at the table while Betty got on with the ironing. Jim and Davey chatted for a while about this and that, and then Jim turned his attention to her. 'And how are you?' he asked.

'Fine, thanks.'

'You're looking well.'

Davey saw the gleam in Jim's eyes. So that's how the land lies, he mused to himself. Well, he certainly had no objection. He was a good man, Jim Biles. One of the best. And a Protestant.

'Are you still going to the jigging?' Jim asked.

'Not of late. I haven't bothered going out much recently.'

Jim nodded, as if it were news to him.

'And how about yourself?'

He thought of his bird in Luath Street. Thank God for the Royal Navy! And then there was the widow in Penilee he saw from time to time. Now, she was nice. But neither she nor Luath Street were in the same league as Nellie.

'I'm not much for the jigging myself, but I get around,' he replied casually. Then, conversationally, to Betty, 'What are you planning to have for your Christmas dinner?' Christmas was only a fortnight away.

'I'm hoping for a nice chicken but they're awful expensive and difficult to come by besides.'

'Aye, there's a shortage of them right enough. But you leave it to me. I'll see you get one at a price that won't dint the housekeeping too much.'

Betty beamed. 'That's right kind of you, Jim. We fair appreciate it.'

'What else are friends for?' he laughed.

When the bottle was empty and it was almost time to go Jim said, 'I've had an idea, Nellie. I've been asked to a butchers' Christmas do next week and I was wondering . . . Are you still winching?'

'No,' she said slowly, averting her eyes from his.

'Well why don't you come along as my partner? Should be a good night with lots of food and drink. What do you say?'

'I –'

74

'Sounds like a great idea to me,' Davey broke in. 'Why don't you go, lass? It would do you good.'

Jim's eyes flicked across at Davey. He'd found himself an ally.

Nellie was uncertain. Her initial reaction was to refuse. But she had to start going out again sometime. She could hardly stay at home for the rest of her life.

'Aye, all right then,' she sighed. 'I'd like that.'

'I'll look forward to it,' Jim smiled.

Together they made the arrangements.

Nellie was enjoying herself for the first time since Frank. She'd never seen so much food and drink! And the band was a right laugh that did crazy novelty numbers every so often.

'Do you fancy getting up again?' Jim asked. They'd already danced a number of times.

'Lovely,' she replied, really smiling at last.

He took her into his arms and they moved off into a foxtrot. 'Are you enjoying yourself?'

'Isn't it obvious?'

He grinned. 'Just making sure.' He'd already decided how he was going to play the Frank Connelly business. He reckoned the time had come to bring it up.

'You broke with your lad then?'

She looked up at him. 'Has my da not said anything to you?'

He shook his head. 'Should he have done?'

'Frank was a Catholic,' she said simply.

'I see.' He paused for a few seconds. 'I can imagine how upset Davey must've been.'

The hate Nellie felt for her father welled up inside her. 'And what about you? How do you feel about Catholics?' she demanded.

Jim shrugged. 'I may be a Mason, but that doesn't mean I'm against them. There's nothing in the Masonic Order that specifies we hate Catholics. I suppose I take them as I find them. Some are all right, others I wouldn't give the time of day. In other words they're just like any other people as far as I'm concerned.'

'And what would you do if you had a daughter who wanted to marry one?'

Jim pretended to furrow his brow in thought. 'I think, at least I'd like to think, that I'd tend to let them get on with it.'

Nellie's face softened. It was the answer she'd wanted to hear. Which, of course, was why Jim had said it.

'We were going to go to Newcastle or somewhere like that when he'd finished his apprenticeship,' she said. 'Anywhere away from this town and its prejudices.'

He could see how deeply hurt she still was. He was going to have to continue playing this very coolly indeed if he was going to get anywhere. Well, he could be patient when the prize was Nellie Thompson. She was worth waiting for.

As he walked her home, he didn't attempt to take her arm as he'd normally have done. When they stopped at her close he could sense her tensing, worried that he was going to try and take her into the back.

'I really have enjoyed myself. Thank you, Jim,' she said formally.

'I know how you feel about Frank, you've made that quite plain.' Gently, he took her hand. 'But I'd still like to take you out again. What do you say?'

'Could we just be friends?'

'We'll be whatever you want us to be, Nellie. I'm just happy to be in your company.'

She stared at him. He was quite nice really. A bit too smooth, perhaps, but that might just be his manner.

'There's a new picture on at Green's in the town that I wouldn't mind seeing,' she answered hesitantly.

'Right, then. I'll chap your door half past six Friday night.'

And without waiting for a reply he turned and strode off quickly down the street.

*

It was a Sunday afternoon and the thirteenth time he'd taken her out. He knew it was thirteen because he'd counted them. Being a Sunday everything was shut, even the swing parks remained locked. They were sitting in an Italian café sipping coffee, Italian cafés being the only establishments to break the Protestant Sabbath.

He'd kissed her by now and had a few cuddles, but that had only whetted his appetite. What he really wanted was her in bed with him.

Nellie stared into her coffee, her mind a million miles away.

'Nellie?'

She looked up and smiled. 'Sorry, I was dreaming.'

'About Frank?'

She looked back into her cup.

'He's left Glasgow, you know. Gone abroad according to your da.'

'I didn't know,' she lied. This was the first time she'd officially been told, his name never having been mentioned again in the house.

'It's time to try and forget him, Nellie. This way you'll only keep on hurting yourself, and what's the good in that? He's gone and you'll never see him again. Accept the fact.'

'Have you ever been in love, Jim?'

'Yes.'

'Was she pretty?'

'Very.'

'What happened?'

'Oh, I haven't given up hope yet. The trouble is, you see, she's still in love with someone else.'

He was talking about her. 'Let's just not go too fast,' she said.

'At whatever speed you like, Nellie. That'll be all right with me.'

She reached out and held his hand. 'Thank you.'

It was the first time she'd ever voluntarily touched him in a tender way. Progress, he thought. Small, maybe, but progress all the same.

They were on their way to the pictures one Saturday night when their path was suddenly blocked by a man who must have been waiting for them. He had a razor scar running from his ear to the corner of his mouth.

'Hello, Jim,' he said almost politely.

Jim came up short: for a brief moment fear showed on his face. 'Hello.'

Scarface looked from Jim to Nellie and then back again. 'Wee Mo would like to see you,' he said slowly.

'Right,' Jim tried to sound cheerful. 'Tell him I'll be round next week.'

'Now,' the stranger said shortly, steel creeping into his voice.

Jim knew any further protestations were useless. 'It won't take long,' he said to Nellie. 'Do you mind?'

She didn't like the man's look – he sent shivers racing up and down her spine. How had Jim come to be acquainted with a man like this?

Without a further word, Scarface led the way to a car parked nearby. A jerk of his thumb told them they were to get in the back. They then drove up west to a posh part of the city.

'Wee' Mo was well over six feet tall and must have weighed all of twenty stone. 'Glad you could come,' he said politely as they entered the room where he was holding court. There were two more hardmen present, neither of whom was introduced.

'My girlfriend, Nellie Thompson,' Jim said when Mo raised an enquiring eyebrow.

'Pleased to meet you, Miss Thompson,' Mo said, shaking her hand.

It was a curious handshake, she thought. Light and sensitive, almost like shaking hands with another woman.

Except that the hand which enveloped hers was of massive proportions.

'Now how about a dram?' invited Mo.

'We're really in a hurry,' said Jim.

Wee Mo smiled, the effect being more sinister than pleasant. 'I'm having one myself. I'm sure our business together won't take long.'

'Then a dram would be grand,' Jim said quickly. Although he, too, was smiling there was sweat under his armpits and in the small of his back. He had noticed that one of the hardmen was openly carrying razors in his waistcoat pocket.

'And you, Miss Thompson?'

'Please.'

Nellie's eyes glanced round the room while Mo poured the drinks. There were lovely pictures on the walls, and the furniture and furnishings were far nicer than anything she'd ever seen except in magazines.

She sat close beside Jim on a pink, satin-covered sofa. Wee Mo eased his huge bulk into a very large armchair facing them.

'You lost again on the dogs today, I'm told,' said Mo.

Jim licked his lips. 'I'm having a bad run. It happens.'

'Oh, it does that. Which is how people like me make money.'

The penny dropped for Nellie. The man was a bookie, Jim's bookie by the sound of things.

'You've been a good client, Jim. A very good one over the years, which is why you're one of the couple dozen I allow credit.'

Jim shifted uncomfortably.

'What you dropped today brings it up to two hundred pounds. An awful lot of money for a butcher to find.'

'You'll get your money. There's no need to worry about that,' Jim assured him.

'I'm not worried. I always get what's due me – one way or another. Eh, boys?'

The two hardmen stared gravely back at their boss, one of them giving the slightest of nods.

The threat wasn't lost. Jim knew what to expect should he fail to pay up. Sweat beaded on his forehead at the thought of himself razor-scarred for life. And it would be a terrible scarring too, they'd make sure of that.

'Now, about what you owe,' said Mo. 'I'm going to have to ask you to settle that before I accept any more of your bets. That's fair isn't it?'

Jim tried to regain his composure. 'Yes, entirely.'

'And as for the two hundred, when can I expect it?'

Jim's mind was whirling. Damn this losing streak he'd been on recently. Look where it had landed him. His back against the wall and Wee Mo's boys all set to jump on him from a great height. And all he had to his name was his week's wages. 'A month?' he asked hopefully.

'A fortnight,' Mo decided. 'As from today. In fact,' he glanced at his watch, 'as from now.'

Mo rose. Jim was free to go.

'It's been a pleasure meeting you,' Mo said to Nellie.

'Likewise,' she replied.

'I'll be in touch,' said Jim.

Mo's sinister, chilling smile returned. He didn't reply.

At the door to the room the man with the scarred face was waiting to see them out. There was no offer to drive them back.

Jim sat with Nellie's hand in his, staring up at the silver screen. The picture was an exciting swashbuckler but he was taking none of it in. Instead, he was feverishly trying to work out where he could lay his hands on £200.

He could tap his employer for twenty, twenty-five maybe. But that still left £175 to find. An absolute fortune.

Then he thought of the Masons. Surely he could expect some help there. For the first time all night he began to think there might be hope. But he would have to decide the best way to approach them.

'You all right?' whispered Nellie in the darkness.

'Yes,' he whispered back.

'Worried about Wee Mo?'

'I think I know how to sort that problem out now.'

She squeezed his hand.

For the first time since entering the cinema he concentrated on the picture. It was rather a good one after all.

He had her pinned against the wall in the darkness of the back close, his tongue in her mouth and his hand on her breast.

Nellie pulled her mouth from his. 'I'll have to go on up,' she said quietly.

Jim was quite beside himself with passion. He wanted this woman like he'd never wanted any other. His hand travelled down the front of her dress.

'No, Jim,' Nellie said firmly.

She was proving amazingly stubborn. Far, far more than he'd ever imagined. 'Please.'

'It's your own fault for getting yourself all worked up.' She pulled away. 'I've told you, nothing's going to come of it.'

Desperate with wanting her, he took her hand and held it against him.

'No Jim!' she hissed, jerking away.

'Nellie. Please.'

'Not in a back close, Jim. Is that all you think of me?'

'Of course not. I'd much rather we were at my place, but you'll never come.'

She smiled wryly. 'Do you blame me? If you're like this here what would you be like there?'

'Nellie you're driving me crazy. I swear to God, I'm going out of my mind with wanting you.'

'Then you'll just have to control yourself. You know how I feel.'

'Don't you fancy me, Nellie? Is that it?' He stood so close to her she could hear his heartbeat.

'No it isn't, as you well know,' she answered tenderly.

'What can I do?'

'Well, right now you can see me to my door.' Then, seeing the expression on his face, she had to smile.

'I'm glad you think it's funny!' he said bitterly.

'You're too serious about it, Jim, and that's a fact.'

'I only wish you would be,' he grumbled as they went through to the front close, where they stood bathed in the flickering gaslight.

'I have to see someone else tomorrow afternoon,' he said.

'Are you angry with me?'

'No. I've just got some things to see to.'

She touched his arm. 'Those men – that *will* be all right won't it? They frightened me.'

'Don't you worry about me. I'll come up smelling of roses. You wait and see.'

'Till Friday then.'

'Aye. Till Friday.'

He gave her a final kiss, and stood watching as she ran up the stairs.

Outside the tenement he stood under a street lamp and lit up, deciding what to do next. It was a toss up between the widow in Penilee and the bird over in Luath Street.

The bird in Luath Street won for the simple reason that she was the closest. The silly cow thought he was in love with her. She'd murder him if she discovered he was using her to work off his frustrations with Nellie.

Jim hurried off into the night.

The next time they were out together, Nellie invited him up for a cup of tea when he took her back home.

They found Davey at home. Betty and Roddy were out visiting her sister who lived a few streets away.

As always, Davey was delighted to see Jim, immediately

82

ushering him into the other fireside chair while Nellie put the kettle on.

Jim was morose and preoccupied, not wanting to talk in front of Nellie, not sure how to say what he wanted to say. But Davey was full of conversation. Jim listened politely, trying to seem enthusiastic, until Nellie finally gave him his opportunity.

'I'm away downstairs a minute,' she said, meaning she was off to the landing toilet.

The instant she was out the house, Jim changed the conversation by saying, 'I'm in bad trouble, Davey, and was wondering if you could give me your advice?'

Davey frowned. 'If I can son.'

Jim explained the position, ending up by saying, 'So do you know anyone in the lodge who could lend me that sort of money? I know it's an awful lot, but I just have to have it. And there'll be no risk involved. I swear to God I'll pay it back. It may take a while, mind, but they'll get back every ha'penny, I promise you.'

Davey tamped down his pipe and looked thoughtful. 'Aye, it is a lot indeed,' he agreed.

'But do you know anyone?'

An idea had come into Davey's mind. He was fond of this lad, as it seemed Nellie was. He knew how bitter she still was about the Frank Connelly affair. Perhaps this was his chance to make it up to her.

'I could lend you two hundred,' he said at last.

Jim was surprised. He would never have thought Davey would have that much.

Davey interpreted Jim's expression correctly. 'Och, I've been prudent, you understand. Putting a bit by every week. And it's amazing how it soon adds up.' He leaned forward, gesturing that Jim should lean forward also. In confidential, hushed tones he went on, 'I also have a wee fiddle going with a scrap man I know. There's me and another chap at work been pulling the same stroke for years. We split it like.'

'Well, well,' said Jim, nodding his admiration.

'You'll keep this strictly to yourself, of course.'

'You can trust me never to breathe a word of it, Davey. I'm not one for breaking a confidence.'

Davey cleared his throat and sat back in his chair to peer at Jim through a fug of acrid blue smoke. 'What was in my mind was to give it to you rather than lend it,' he said.

Jim was taken aback. 'Give it to me? What do you mean?'

Davey's eyes were sparkling. 'I was thinking two hundred pound would make an awful generous wedding present. And there would be something else forbye, so Nellie need never know about it, unless you want her to.'

Elation welled through Jim. Here was the chance he'd been praying for. This could get him off the hook once and for all. But marriage: that was something he'd never even considered.

Well, why not, he asked himself. At twenty-three he wasn't getting any younger. If he wasn't careful, he could end up with someone who'd make his life a misery.

And he'd told Nellie he loved her, which was true enough, he supposed. He certainly fancied her rotten. That yellow hair and those green eyes were driving him mad! And all along she'd made no bones about it: marriage was the price for having her. And he wanted her. He wanted her more than anything he'd ever wanted in his life before.

He was going to get married someday, wasn't he? That being the case, he'd be daft not to grab this opportunity: two hundred nicker and Nellie. Anyone who turned that down needed his head felt.

'I had intended asking her anyway when this trouble I'm in had sorted itself out,' he lied smoothly.

'I could see that's the way things were going,' said Davey. 'Knowing Nellie, she'd hardly have gone out with you this long if she hadn't thought awful highly of you.'

The door banged shut and Nellie was back. 'What are you two up to? You look like a right couple of conspirators,' she said, going right to the stove where the kettle had been boiling its head off for the last couple of minutes.

'Wouldn't you like to know?' replied Jim mysteriously, and laughed. He wouldn't ask her tonight; he'd set it up specially.

When Nellie's back was turned Davey nodded to Jim and winked. The deal had been made.

'You can sure think up places to take me that I've never been before,' Nellie said. She was staring up at a palm tree from which hung clusters of coconuts.

They were up west, not far from where Wee Mo lived, at the Botanical Gardens.

'Is it the first palm tree you've ever seen?' he asked.

'Course not. There are thousands of them in Govan. You can hardly move for bumping into the damn things,' she retorted.

He chided himself for asking a stupid question and leaving himself wide open, but his mind had been on working himself up to proposing.

It was extremely warm in the greenhouse, a complete contrast to the bitter cold outside.

'Nellie?' he began.

'Yes?'

'I eh . . . I . . . eh –'

'What is it?'

He couldn't remember ever being stuck for words like this before. But then, he'd never asked anyone to marry him before.

Nellie giggled. 'You've got the most amazingly comical expression on your face. What is going on in that head of yours?'

In a sudden rush, he grabbed her hands and blurted out, 'Will you marry me?'

Nellie lowered her gaze to the floor. 'Can we walk a little?' she replied quietly.

They strolled side by side. Outside there was snow on the ground and in the distance they could see some wee boys sledging down a hill. Nellie thought of how strange it was to be amongst tropical lushness while staring out at such a landscape.

Was she going to turn him down, Jim wondered. He knew how deep her feelings still ran for Frank Connelly. Well, whatever her answer, he couldn't lose. Wee Mo was paid off with Davey's money. If her answer was in the negative then all it meant was he had to pay the money back as he would've had to do to Mo anyway. Only with Davey he could take his time without worrying about a razor in the face.

But the other side of the coin was how much he wanted her. If she turned him down he knew he'd have lost and would never have her.

Taking her by the arm he said, 'I'll be a good man to you, Nellie. You have my word on that. I'll see you want for nothing.'

Nellie had known for some time that he was going to propose. After all, he'd said he loved her, and a man didn't say that unless he had something permanent in mind. She should have made a decision before now, but had shied away from doing so. Now she would have to. Only not right here and now.

'Can I have a day to think it over?' she asked.

'If you like.'

'I want to be absolutely sure, Jim.'

'I understand.'

She smiled up at him. 'You've been awful patient with me. I appreciate that.'

He glanced around to make sure no one was watching. Catching her in his arms he said, 'I'll call round tomorrow night and we'll go out for a walk. You can give me your answer then.' Slowly, tenderly, he kissed her fully and deeply. And for the first time she responded with none of her usual initial hesitancy.

*

Out came the boilings in a steady flow. Hundreds a minute in a seemingly never ending stream.

Nellie glanced around. God, how she hated this place. The boredom, the smell, the sheer mindlessness of the job.

Day in, day out, five-and-a-half days a week, fifty weeks of the year. On and on and on till all she wanted to do was throw her head back and scream with frustration.

Up until a fortnight ago she'd thought her life at the factory couldn't get any worse, but she'd been sadly wrong. For a fortnight ago Big Jessie had been appointed supervisor of this section, and after the hammering Nellie had given Jessie, the big one was out to make life for her an absolute hell.

She could see Jessie now, watching her from behind one of the machines further along. What would she find wrong with her work today she wondered? For she'd find something wrong all right. She always did.

Jessie, she knew, was out to get her the sack. It was only a matter of time before she succeeded. They both knew that.

Her mind came back to Jim Biles. She didn't love him, but she was fond of him. She didn't think she'd ever love a man again. All her love, that kind of love anyway, had gone to Frank whom she'd love to her dying day. No other relationship could even begin to approach that one.

But she had to face the fact that Frank was gone – probably never to return. So where did that leave her? Clinging to a memory, that's where. And beautiful as the memory was, she didn't want that to be all she had to sustain her for the rest of her life.

Then there was her father whom she hated for what he'd done to break up her and Frank. At the moment she was forcing herself to be friendly towards him. What else could she do in a house the size of theirs, where they practically lived on top of one another? Besides, she had her mother and brother to consider. Open warfare would have made their lives intolerable.

Marriage was the answer. Once out the house she could

87

cut all ties with her father and have a life of her own.

Whichever way she looked at it, the odds were in favour of her marrying Jim. If she couldn't get Frank, then Jim was as decent a man as was likely to come her way. And once married she wouldn't have to worry about her job because Jim wouldn't expect her to continue working. A married woman's place was in the home looking after her family.

She smiled at the thought of children. She couldn't wait for a babe of her own. In fact, the more the merrier to fill the house with gaiety and laughter.

Yes, she told herself, if she couldn't have Frank – then why not Jim? If she didn't love him, at least he loved her. She could do an awful lot worse than that.

It was the first time Nellie had ever been in his house, which was no more than a one-room apartment.

She was impressed by how neat and tidy it was. She'd been expecting a bachelor tip but that just wasn't the case.

'Do you have someone come in?' she asked.

He grinned. 'You've found me out. There's a wifey upstairs who I pay a dollar to come in twice a week. For another two bob she takes my washing to the steamie when she goes.'

'And your ironing?'

'She does that as well.'

'You get your money's worth don't you?'

'I try,' he replied, taking her in his arms.

'We'll need new curtains and I'm wondering what your bed linen's like?' she continued, ignoring his advances.

'And I'm wondering what you're like.'

She pushed his arms away, and, going to the bed, threw the covers back. The sheets were old and threadbare, the blankets as thin as she'd ever seen. 'We'll need new bedding,' she decided.

It was a lot better than Nellie had thought. The walls had been distempered fairly recently and underfoot the linoleum was almost new. Given a few improvements and a women's hand here and there, she could soon have this a wee palace.

'You like it?' he asked.

'It'll do for the moment.'

'Now don't be too enthusiastic will you?' he said sarcastically.

'All right then, Jim,' she laughed, giving him a hug, 'it's very nice. And in far better condition than I'd dared hope.'

'Aye, well I never could abide living in a pigsty. There's plenty that do around here mind you, but not me. It doesn't take that much of an effort.'

'Expecially when you can afford to get someone else to do the dirty work?'

He grinned. 'That's one of the big secrets in life, Nellie. Never forget it. Delegate when you can.'

He had a good brain on him and she admired that. He would go far in the butchering trade, getting his own shop one day, of that she had no doubt.

His only drawback that she could see was his addiction to gambling, which bothered her. But he'd got himself out of the scrape he was in with Wee Mo the bookie, though she never had found out how he'd pulled that one off, and was now back on a winning streak again.

He certainly seemed to know what he was doing when it came to the dogs and horses. Still, it worried her all the same. A wee flutter was one thing: wholesale addiction quite another. She was going to have to work on the gambling, she thought as she looked around her new home – but there was time for that.

'Nellie?'

She came out of her reverie to find him sitting on the bed staring at her. He had a look in his eye which she'd come to know only too well.

'No Jim,' she said flatly.

'Why the hell not? We're going to be married aren't we?'

'*Going* to be. We're not yet.'

'Does it make such a big difference?'

'To me it does.'

He sighed. She was the most exasperating woman he'd ever come across. And yet maybe she was right. He'd waited this long so why not a little longer? When he finally did have her he wanted her full co-operation and it was obvious that was only going to happen on the wedding night. Some things, he was sure, were worth waiting for.

'You win,' he said resignedly. Later, when he'd dropped her off home, he'd slip up to Luath Street and work off his itch there.

'How do I look, Ma?' Nellie spun slowly around in place.

Betty stood back to admire her daughter. 'A proper treat, lass. As beautiful as any bride I've ever seen and that's a fact.'

Indeed, even in the simple shop dress she looked like a princess, her hair so golden and her beauty so radiant.

'Are you excited?' Betty asked, fussing with the skirt.

'Yes, Ma. Yes, I am,' dismissing the phantom thought of Frank with a smile.

'I can remember our wedding –' Betty started, but trailed off. 'But never mind that. It's ancient history now.' Then, 'You're getting a right good chap, Nellie. I hope you appreciate that?'

'I appreciate it,' she whispered, though that would never mean that she had forgotten.

'Fine. As long as you do.'

Nellie turned around once more. 'Do you think the hem could do with coming up a fraction, Ma? It looked all right in the shop but now I'm not so sure.'

'Let me see,' said Betty, and bent to have a look.

Jim walked down the aisle with his best man, a chap called Phil Drummond who worked alongside him at the shop. He'd been drunk out of his skull the night before at the stag booze-up which had gone the round of all the local pubs, and, thanks to Phil, already had a goodly number of halves and chasers under his belt since getting up that morning. He was feeling no pain at all.

Until he saw Marj Henderson.

He came up short and his jaw fell open. What in the world was she doing here? God Almighty, he thought suddenly, surely she hadn't come to denounce him! What a showing up that would be. What would Nellie say? He daren't even think about that.

'What's up?' Phil whispered.

He watched in horror as Marj raised a hand and waved at him. If he could have wished himself a thousand miles away he would have done so.

'Jim?'

'Aye, it's all right, Phil. Just something that flashed through my mind that's all.'

Side by side, they continued walking toward the front of the church while around them none too expertly executed organ music rent the air.

Thankfully, Nellie didn't keep him waiting long as some might have done. The music changed to 'Here Comes The Bride' as she appeared at the top of the aisle with her father.

'Here you go,' whispered Phil.

Jim put a smile on his face and tried not to look as shocked as he felt.

When the ceremony reached the part where the minister asked the congregation if there was anyone who objected to this marriage he tensed, fully expecting Marj's voice to be raised saying, yes, she objected as he really loved her and had been seeing her secretly and frequently for the past year to prove it.

No voice came. If she wasn't here to object then what?

Phil handed him the ring which he slipped onto Nellie's finger. She was absolutely stunning, the perfect bride. He'd never fancied her more than he did at that moment – which was saying something.

91

'I now pronounce you man and wife,' said the minister. And that was that. They were wed.

'You may kiss the bride.'

It was a moment she'd dreamed of nearly all her life, and yet she didn't feel at all as she'd imagined. She had the ghost of Frank Connelly to thank for that.

She put Frank from her mind as Jim's lips met hers. From now on the less she thought of Frank the better. Having married Jim she now had to give that marriage a chance. She had to forget about her lost love.

People crowded round them, shaking her hand and slapping Jim on the back.

'Congratulations, lass,' said Davey, pecking her on the cheek.

She wilted under the kiss, feeling as though she'd been scalded. God, how I loathe you and how marvellous it is to be rid of you she thought, staring at her father.

Then her attention was diverted to Betty who was having a right good cry. She squeezed Betty's hand and said, 'It's a wedding Ma, not a funeral. You're supposed to be happy for me.'

'But I am!' wailed Betty.

'Women! I'll never understand them,' said Davey pulling a face.

Cars were outside the church waiting to take them on to the reception which was being held directly after the ceremony in the local Co-operative Hall.

'What a day!' said Jim when they were in the car and driving away. Behind them a swarm of small boys were fighting for the scramble, the money the bridegroom traditionally throws from the car window.

'I could murder a drink,' he added.

'From the smell of your breath you've murdered quite a few already,' she said.

'Now you're not going to start our marriage off by nagging are you?'

He was right. 'I'm sorry,' she apologized, leaning against him.

'If a man can't have a few bevvies on his wedding day, then when can he have them? After all, it only happens once.'

'You hope,' she said. And they both laughed.

They took a long detour round Govan so that when they arrived at the hall, most of the guests were already there waiting for them. They entered to applause and some ribald shouts from the back.

Phil Drummond immediately came forward to hand them each a glass of champagne. 'To the bride and groom!' he toasted.

While the guests toasted them they toasted one another.

A band had been hired which consisted of accordion, piano and saxophone. At a signal from Davey they started to play.

Those who wanted to dance danced; those to eat ate; and those to drink drank. It was an informal, neighbourly affair, the main criterion being to enjoy yourself.

Later speeches would be made, but not until most people would be too drunk to remember them.

Jim took the floor with Nellie to a round of applause and more ribald shouts from the back. They danced two dances and then decided to take a breather. Jim was at the makeshift bar, collecting some whisky, when a voice beside him said, 'Hello? And wasn't I surprised to find out you were the bridegroom.'

He nearly jumped out of his skin at the sound of that so familiar voice. He turned to find Marj Henderson smiling at him.

'What the hell are you doing here?' he hissed, drawing her to one side.

'I might ask you the same?'

'I'm getting married. What in the name of the Wee Man does it look like?'

'I didn't mean that. What I meant was, what are you doing here after all the things you've been telling me for the past year? "I *love* you Marj." "I'd do *anything* for you." Why only the other night –'

'Sssh! For God's sake!' he whispered, having just seen Nellie closing on them.

'Hello Marj. It's good to see you,' Nellie said on joining them.

'You look marvellous, Nellie. May you have all the happiness in the world.'

Nellie turned to Jim. 'I didn't know you two knew one another?'

'We don't,' he replied hastily. 'We just got chatting.'

'Then let me introduce you. Marj, this is my husband Jim.'

'Hello.'

'And Jim, this is my cousin, Marj Henderson. She lives over in Luath Street with her husband who's in the Royal Navy.'

'How do you do,' said Jim thickly.

He swallowed half his drink. Cousins! What a turn up for the book. They didn't look at all alike. Not even the hint of a family resemblance.

'Jack's at sea, I take it, otherwise he'd have been here the day?' Nellie said.

'Aye. But he'll be back soon. He's been out to the Indian Ocean and back. Last word I had they were steaming through the Med.'

Nellie shook her head. 'Wouldn't suit me being married to a sailor. Being left alone so much.'

'Och, you get used to it,' Marj replied, smiling as she caught Jim's look.

They talked for a few minutes more and then Jim took Nellie back on the floor. As they were excusing themselves from Marj he saw a mischievous glint in Marj's eyes. She'd enjoyed watching his discomfiture, knowing she could drop him right in it at any second. She was a cool one that, and no mistake. He was going to miss his visits to Luath Street.

An hour-and-half later Jim had nearly drunk his fill

and was feeling decidedly unsteady. He'd danced with Betty and just about every other female he could lay his hands on. He was having a whale of a time. The air was rent with wheechs and cries as a reel got under way.

Blearily, he gazed round the floor to see that Nellie was up with Phil Drummond. He decided to go to the toilet.

Lurching down the dingy corridor that led him to the turn off where the toilets stood side by side, he was just about to enter the Gents when the door to the Ladies opened and Marj emerged.

'Well, if it isn't Romeo himself,' she said wickedly.

'Oh, come on, none of that now,' he coaxed. But secretly he was pleased. He liked the idea of being thought of as a notorious lover.

Marj had also had a fair amount of drink. Her cheeks were flushed and her eyes slightly watery. 'I've been watching you give everyone else a dance, but not me. What's wrong? Have I suddenly got the plague or something?'

He leant against the wall to steady himself. 'I thought it best to leave you alone, in the circumstances.'

'Did you now?'

He suddenly laughed. 'It is helluva funny when you think about it. You and Nellie being cousins I mean.'

'Very funny indeed.'

'Ah, well,' he sighed. 'Maybe you don't think so.'

'I really thought you cared, Jim,' she said in an accusatory tone.

'You're married, Marj.'

'Marriages have been broken before.'

He shook his head. 'I really am sorry the way things have turned out. I never meant to hurt you. I promise.'

'You should've seen your face in the church,' she said, her lips twitching upward.

'I thought you'd come to make a scene. I nearly died when the minister asked if there was anyone in the congregation who objected to our marriage. I was sure you were going to leap to your feet and give me a right sherricking.'

'I was tempted, I can tell you. But no, I wouldn't do that, if for no other reason than I've got my own marriage to consider. Divorcing Jack's one thing. But standing up and making a spectacle of myself is quite another.'

'Aye, I understand,' he replied.

'I'm going to miss you, Jim.'

'And I'll miss you.'

'No you won't. You'll have Nellie to keep you warm.'

'I'll still miss you, Marj. I swear it.'

They were alone in the turn off and there was no one in the corridor. Putting his arm round her neck, he drew her face to his and kissed her. The kiss was full and luscious. As always happened when he kissed her, he was instantly aroused.

'Oh, Marj,' he whispered, all thoughts of Nellie momentarily forgotten.

'You should have told me what the situation really was,' she whispered back.

'You would have told me to take a running jump.'

'Maybe. Maybe not.' Through an alcoholic haze she thought of the awful, long lonely nights when Jack was away at sea. A body needed some comfort and you took it where you could. She'd lied to Nellie; you never got used to the long separations. Especially when you were a passionate, loving woman like herself.

Jim could smell her; the warm body he knew so well.

'Marj,' he sighed, and kissed her again.

It was time to be changed and be off, Nellie decided. Crossing to where Babs and Phil Drummond were deep in conversation she told them she thought it was time.

'Right. I'll away out to the car and get the things. Where are you going to change?' asked Phil.

'Nowhere else but the toilet.'

'All right, you and Babs away along there now and I'll be by with your things in a minute.'

Nellie glanced around. 'Have you seen Jim? I seem to have lost him.'

'He'll be around somewhere. Don't you worry about him, I'll root him out.'

Nellie smiled and squeezed his arm. 'Thanks Phil.'

'Just doing my duty as best man.'

He was a really nice chap, Nellie thought. And from the way Babs was looking at him she wouldn't disagree with her. She'd keep her fingers crossed that something developed out of this meeting. They'd make a good couple together.

'Come on then,' said Babs as Phil left them for the hired car that had been patiently waiting outside all this while. In its boot were their suitcases for the honeymoon.

'Another hour and most of this lot will be flat on their backs,' said Babs as they made their way through the boisterous crowd.

'As long as they've enjoyed themselves, that's the main thing,' Nellie laughed.

'There's been some booze drunk I can tell you.' She stumbled and would have fallen if Nellie hadn't caught her round the shoulders. 'And I've had my fair share,' Babs added.

They were almost at the toilet when Nellie heard the noise which brought her to a halt.

Babs frowned; she'd heard it too.

A sort of moan, Nellie thought, as though someone was in pain.

But Babs knew differently. A grin spread across her face as it dawned on her what they were hearing. Gesturing Nellie close she whispered in her ear, 'There's more than one person in there.'

'No!' protested Nellie, understanding dawning.

Babs nodded. As if in confirmation, a female voice said clearly, 'Oh, that's lovely, lovely.'

The sound was coming from behind a door facing the

toilets. Nellie placed her finger over her lips and nodded that they should move on into the toilet. They were about to do so when suddenly an unmistakeable voice said, 'Christ, the feeling!'

Nellie froze, completely shocked. A glance at Babs's face told her she hadn't misheard.

Babs took Nellie by the arm. 'Come on, leave it,' she whispered.

Nellie jerked her arm away.

'Leave it, Nellie!' Babs said urgently.

Taking a deep breath, Nellie turned again to face the door from behind which the voices had come. She had to be absolutely certain. She had to see with her own two eyes. There must be no mistake.

She swallowed hard as she put her hand on the doorknob. Then, feeling so light inside that a decent puff of wind would blow her away, she opened the door.

It was a bucket and broom closet. But she didn't take that in right away. The scene that etched itself forever in her memory was that of Jim with his trousers down round his ankles and her cousin Marj with her knickers off and kicked to one side.

'Oh my God!' exclaimed Marj when through the light which had suddenly invaded the privacy of the closet she saw Nellie staring at her.

For a moment or two Jim wasn't aware of anything. He swore as Marj pulled herself off him to fumble with her skirt. And then, for the first time, he noticed the light and realized they weren't alone. Still dazed, he turned to find his wife of a few hours staring at him in horror.

Marj picked up her knickers and slipped into them, turning her back on the others as she did so. Her face and shoulders were beet coloured. Although not exactly sober, she was considerably more so than she'd been the moment before the door opened to reveal Nellie.

Anger and disgust raged through Nellie. She was both hot and cold in the same instant. She wanted to be sick.

'Nellie –' he began.

'Cover yourself,' she snapped, her voice like steel.

He did as he was told without a murmur.

'Nellie, don't do anything daft. It's not what you think,' Marj said.

'What do you mean, it's not what I think?'

Marj bit her tongue. She was genuinely fond of Nellie, although Nellie would hardly believe that after what she'd just witnessed.

'We'd both had too much to drink. It was one of these stupid things. Nothing more. I swear it,' Marj said.

'You lied when you said you'd never met her before didn't you?' she accused.

For once words deserted him. He couldn't begin to think of a reply, and in failing to do so confirmed Nellie's accusation.

'It's time for us to go. Phil will be here any second with your change,' Nellie said. Then to Marj, 'Get back to the reception.'

'You won't tell Jack will you? Please Nellie?'

Nellie felt nothing but contempt for her cousin. 'Jack will never know from me. Nor Babs here. You have my word on that.'

'You're still going on the honeymoon?'

'Of course. It's all been paid for. I'm not going to waste that.'

'Forget it if you can Nellie. It was the drink, nothing else.'

'Good-bye.'

Marj hurried out of the turn off and along the corridor in the direction of the reception.

'Someone's coming. Sounds like Phil,' said Babs who'd been spellbound ever since the door had been opened.

'Knock on the toilet door when you're ready,' Nellie said to Jim.

Phil arrived with the suitcase containing their change. 'There you are. I've been looking all over for you,' he said when he saw Jim.

Babs took the suitcase. 'I'll take Nellie's stuff out and then I'll pass it through.'

'Aye, fine,' replied Phil, wondering what had been going on. Half cut as he was, he still couldn't fail to be aware of the atmosphere he'd walked into.

Once in the toilet Nellie leaned on the washbasin, shaking with shame and revulsion. She still wanted to be sick but it wouldn't come.

Babs lit two cigarettes and passed her one. 'What are you going to do?' she asked quietly.

Nellie drew heavily on the cigarette. She felt dirty and unclean somehow. She also felt years older than when she'd got up that morning. 'I don't know. I'll have to think about it.'

'Don't go off half-cocked. I'm sure Marj was right and it was only the drink. We all do bloody stupid things when we've had too much. I'm positive it was no more than that.' Then, when Nellie didn't reply, 'It's your wedding day, Nellie. You can't end things before they've even begun.'

'I'll have to think about it. Long and hard,' Nellie said, wondering how their relationship could ever be the same again. It wouldn't, of course. Not after what she'd just witnessed. With her own cousin too!

'Let's get on with it then,' said Babs. And started to help Nellie to strip.

When Nellie was changed and combing her hair she said to Babs, 'You'll never breathe a word of this will you?'

'You know better than that.'

There was a knock on the door and Phil's voice called out, 'Ready when you are, ladies.'

'Won't be a jiffy!' Babs called back.

Nellie lit another cigarette feeling, her hands still shaking. 'Jim can wait,' she said.

All the folk from the reception came out to wave good-bye to them when they left for the station. Despite the fact that her world had just come crashing down around her, Nellie somehow managed to put on a brave and beautiful smile, waving back to the well-wishers until they were left far behind.

Settling back into her seat she gazed out at the passing scene. Beside her, Jim fidgeted.

The journey to the station was made in silence; he was desperate to speak, his emotions a combination of anger and guilt, but couldn't, because there was no partition between them and the driver. She did not even respond when she was offered a cigarette or acknowledge the offer in any way.

At the station Jim tipped the driver then lifted their suitcases. 'Platform 3,' he said.

Nellie strode off, leading the way.

He'd wanted an empty compartment but there were none to be had. They had to settle for one containing a blowsy, middle-aged woman and a wee girl who throughout the journey chattered non-stop about 'goin' doon ra watter', as going down to the Clyde Coast was often called by Glaswegians.

Troon was a sleepy little city on the Firth of Clyde. There they got off the train and hailed a taxi which took them to the hotel. The room was a nice double with a good view of the Clyde. Nellie took off her gloves and hat. Sitting on the bed she stared straight ahead.

'Please forgive me, Nellie,' he said.

She looked up at him. 'What I can't understand is why you'd even want to? And on our wedding day of all days?'

'We told you, it was the drink. Phil had been feeding me the stuff long before we even got to church. By the time the reception came round it only took a few halves to send me away with the fairies. And she was the same way.'

'Why didn't you admit to knowing her before?'

He sat in a wicker chair and twiddled his thumbs. He couldn't very well tell her the truth. 'I don't really know,' he hedged.

101

'I take it then you'd . . . well, made love to her before that incident in the closet?'

'I knew her before you,' he said, which in itself was true. 'We were gey close for a while. You understand?'

'Was she married to Jack at the time?'

He nodded.

'I see.'

'I packed in seeing her ages ago,' he lied. 'She never crossed my mind after we met.'

'And the wedding was the first time you've seen her since going out with me?'

'Yes.'

That seemed to mollify her a little.

'I suppose I denied knowing her because her turning up had caught me so much by surprise. And on top of that I felt guilty. I had no idea she was your cousin.'

Somewhere in the depths of the building a gong sounded to announce the evening meal. The last thing she wanted was food.

'Nothing like it will ever happen again, Nellie. You have my solemn word on that,' he pleaded.

She regarded him thoughtfully. Babs was right. She couldn't allow this to be finished before it had even begun. Everyone was allowed one big mistake, after all. The pity was he'd made his so soon.

She'd forgive him. But not yet. He was going to have to suffer a little while longer. A couple of days at least.

'Let's away down,' she said rising.

'Nellie?'

'We'll talk about it over the meal,' she said.

He smiled inwardly, thinking he'd won the round.

It had been an excellent meal. At least they'd thought so. They'd even had a bottle of wine, which they'd considered very posh.

At the door to their room Jim excused himself saying he

102

had to go to the toilet. Humming he went off down the corridor.

Nellie undressed and put on the special nightie she'd bought for the occasion. She wouldn't have worn it now except it was the only one she'd brought with her.

She took off her make-up and then tied her hair back. When that was done she took several blankets from the bed and arranged them on the floor. At their head she put one of the bed's two pillows.

Having crawled between the blankets she tucked herself in. The floor was hard and unyielding but she'd endure it.

Coming into the room, Jim gaped when he saw her. 'What the hell are you doing down there?' he demanded.

She regarded him coldly. 'This is where I'm sleeping.'

'But why?'

'You have the affrontery to ask me that after what you did the day?'

He walked over to stand glaring down at her. 'I thought we'd sorted that out?' he said.

'Surely you don't expect me to let you sleep with me only hours after you've been with my cousin? Oh no, you've another think coming if that's what you had in mind.'

'Be reasonable, Nellie,' he pleaded. 'It's our honeymoon, after all.'

'You should have thought of that before you went into the broom closet with Marj.'

Squatting, he placed his hand on her shoulder. 'Please?'

'No!' she said, finality ringing in her voice. And closing her eyes willed herself to sleep.

Nostrils dilated and breathing heavily, he came to his feet. Turning abruptly on his heel he strode from the room, banging the door behind him.

The bar was still open for residents so he ordered up a large whisky. He drank it off in a single gulp and immediately ordered another. Four large whiskies and quarter of an hour later found him sitting at a table overlooking the sea. Okay, he thought, so he'd been bloody stupid, but to do this to him! It was inhuman after all these months of waiting. To be denied like this on the first night of his honeymoon was just too much to bear.

He thought of her lying upstairs. That body he'd so desperately craved for so long. The hair, the eyes, the form he'd never seen unclothed.

By the time midnight struck he was the only one left in the bar. He was lolling at the table, having consumed a little over three-quarters of a bottle of whisky since coming down. From behind the bar the barman watched him anxiously.

By now he'd convinced himself Nellie was being completely unfair in denying him his rights. Her behaviour was totally out of order. Just not bloody fair at all.

'Are you all right, sir?'

Jim stared drunkenly up at the barman. 'Why, what's it to you?'

The barman took a step backward, only too familiar with Glasgow drunks. He knew how mean and nasty, not to mention violent, they could be.

'It's just that you look a working man yourself, sir, and you'll appreciate I have to be back on duty at six in the morning.'

Jim grunted. That seemed reasonable enough. Not like some bloody people he could think of.

'Do you know I got married the day?' he mumbled. The barman was now a friend rather than a foe.

'Congratulations.'

'One for the road, eh?'

The barman relented. It was the chap's wedding day after all. And at this late hour what was another five minutes?

'Coming up, sir.'

'And one for yourself, John. A large one, same as me.'

'Thank you very much.'

The large one became four before Jim finally staggered

out of the bar and up the stairs to his room. He stumbled twice on the stairs and nearly fell but managed to save himself both times. Entering the room, he stood with his back against the door. He could see her lying there, yellow hair gleaming in the moonlight. Staring at her all the while, he slowly stripped in the darkness. When he was finally naked he crossed to stand staring down at her, swaying like a young tree in the wind.

All those months of waiting, wanting her. And here she was, his legal wife – and still denying him.

Nellie awoke with a start, only just managing to stifle a scream when she saw the swaying figure looming over her. 'Jim?' she breathed tremulously.

Suddenly he was on her, ripping the blankets away. Taking hold of her nightie he tore it straight down the middle so that her body was exposed and vulnerable. The body that had driven him nearly crazy all these months and for which he'd had to find a substitute in Marj Henderson.

Nellie couldn't cry out. That might have brought someone – the last thing she wanted. No! she screamed inside herself. Please God not like this!

Drink had never interfered with Jim's ability to get aroused, and it certainly didn't now. Forcing her thighs apart he rammed himself viciously into her.

She gasped, then whimpered with the shock and acute pain of his entry. Grabbing his hair she pulled; he slapped her viciously across the mouth.

He was far too strong for her. To continue struggling would only result in her getting hurt further. Oh, God, she silently prayed, just let him get it over with.

She lay with her head to one side so that she couldn't see the white shape pounding relentlessly into her. Tears trickled from her eyes to run hot and scalding down the length of her cheeks. Would it never finish? He was going on and on, oblivious to her, almost unaware that he was not alone.

With a grunt and final heave he came. 'That'll teach

you, you bitch!' he snarled. Stumbling to the bed he fell face down across it. Within seconds he was snoring.

She lay in the darkness feeling completely violated. It was as though her very essence, the core of her being, had been beaten and betrayed.

To think she'd saved herself all these years for this to happen. She'd dreamed of it being gentle, loving, a thing of beauty. Instead, it had been a crime. A joyless and violent nightmare.

Come morning she'd be covered in bruises, but they would heal in time. Her heart never would. The experience would never fade. That would be with her, like some festering canker, for the rest of her life.

'Oh Frank!' she whispered into the cold, still dark. If only she'd known. If only . . . if only . . .

4

Nellie started drying her hands on the tea towel the moment she heard the front door snick shut. It was Jim's second day back at work after their honeymoon. She made up, combed her hair, and put on one of her best dresses. Once outside she headed for Harrison's, the sweetie factory.

She was going to leave him. She'd made up her mind about that the night of the rape.

Nor had she any intentions of returning to her ma and da. Davey, as the saying went, could go and bile his can as far as she was concerned. If she never saw him again it would be too soon.

She wasn't sure how she was going to solve her living problem yet, but she would, somehow. Perhaps Babs's parents would take her in as a lodger. That was one of several possibilities running through her mind. But first she had to find a job.

Although she'd left the factory partly because of Jessie, she wasn't particularly worried about the big one now. It was highly unlikely she'd be put back in the section she'd been in before, which would mean Jessie would have nothing to do with her. She would have a new supervisor.

As she walked she thought of the nightmare that had been her honeymoon. There had been no apologies the next morning, not that she would've forgiven him anyway. Instead, on waking, he'd dragged her up on to the bed and taken her again.

She'd felt totally cold towards him then as she'd felt every time he'd had her since. When he approached her her body would go tense and rigid. She'd lie inert, giving no response and feeling none.

She'd come to hate his hands. During their courtship she'd forgotten how horrible they were, but now the very sight of them was enough to make her grue. Large, thick fingered and very red – as though they'd been skinned – she wanted to shriek every time he laid them on her flesh. She thought of them as the hands of a beast and not a man.

It might not have been so bad if he'd shown even a little tenderness. But he didn't. He was on her like an animal, whenever he wanted, and when he'd finished turn and walk away, though, the act completed, she no longer interested him.

In those moments she felt like a whore. Degraded, defiled, humiliated in the extreme.

She put these thoughts from her mind as she entered the factory, amazed to find that it was as though she'd never been away.

The room she was ushered into was sparse and utilitarian. She sat there for nearly an hour before being seen.

'Why do you want to come back to us, Miss Thompson?' Mr Geddes asked. He had a hard face, like a slab of granite from his native Aberdeen.

'Mrs Biles,' she corrected. 'I'm married now. And that's why I left, to get married.'

He waited, his expression one of irritation. She hadn't answered his question.

'We need the money,' she said finally. It was none of his business she intended leaving Jim.

'I see. Didn't you realize that before you left?'

'Things have changed at home during the last few

weeks. Family responsibilities you understand.' She hoped he wouldn't ask her to elaborate on the lie.

Geddes pursed his mouth. 'You're lucky, there is a vacancy. Wait here a minute.'

The minute became twenty. Then he was back and this time he didn't sit down.

'I'm sorry, Mrs Biles, we've nothing to offer you.'

'But you just said –'

'I was mistaken.'

She was bewildered. What had she done? If he'd said there was a job available there must be. No one else could've been taken on without his knowledge as he was solely responsible for all hiring and firing.

'Good-day, Mrs Biles,' he said, indicating the open door.

Suddenly she knew what had happened. He'd left her to go and have a word with her ex-supervisor. That had to be the case.

She could just imagine what Big Jessie would have said about her. Slack, lazy, a bad timekeeper. Oh, she would have had a field day! None of it true of course, but Geddes wouldn't know that. He'd have swallowed every lie Jessie fed him as gospel.

Geddes left her in the corridor, hurrying the opposite way on other business. She found her own way out.

It was raining, a drizzle that fell relentlessly out of an iron grey sky. For a moment or two she stood, undecided about what to do. That her guess about why Harrison's had turned her down was correct, she had no doubt. Her lips thinned in anger. She'd made a bad enemy in Big Jessie.

Well, Harrison's wasn't the only place of employment in Glasgow. She'd just keep on chapping doors till she found work somewhere.

She thought of Coates, the thread people. Now that was a possibility.

Hunching her shoulders against the rain she hurried down the street to the tram stop.

*

Nellie sat staring into the fire, while across from her Jim dozed in his chair. He'd gone out after his tea, coming in again only half an hour since. He'd said he had a wee bit business to attend to. She presumed it had something to do with horses, dogs or bookies. His business always had.

She lit a Willy Woodbine, the last from the packet of five she bought herself every day. Their budget didn't stretch to more. Then she went back to staring into the dying coals of the fire. Her front was nice and toasty hot, but she wore a shawl to keep her back warm against the chill of the rest of the room.

She was filled with despair. Four months they'd been married now and she was no nearer to finding herself a job than she'd been that first day she'd gone to Harrison's.

She'd known things were bad but had been sure she'd have come up with something in this time. How wrong she'd been. God alone knew how many endless miles she'd trudged, how many doors she'd chapped, how many hard-faced men she'd asked for work, all to no avail.

The only offers she'd come up with were two part-time jobs, both working the same hours or she might have been able to dovetail them, paying so little money it would have been impossible for her to exist on her own.

Full of despair she might be, but she was still a long way from giving up hope. Somewhere there was a job for her. She just knew it. If she persevered she was bound to knock the right door one of these days.

With a snort Jim came awake. 'Bed,' he growled.

She sighed inwardly. *That* time had come round again. Morning and night without fail.

She'd hoped that, as time went by, she might come to find it less repugnant. But every time he touched her she found it as loathsome as the first.

She undressed quickly, with her back to him, slipping

110

into a warm flannelette nightie that could never have been accused of being arousing.

Lying back, she waited for the hands to touch her. Those hands she'd come to have nightmares about. All day long they handled meat. At night and in the morning they handled her the same way.

'G'night,' he mumbled.

She couldn't believe her ears. 'Good night,' she replied in a whisper.

It was a game, she thought. He was teasing her. Making her think she'd got off before pouncing the way he always did.

She lay staring at the ceiling, rosily tinged with fire glow. Hurry up and get it over with so I can get my sleep, she thought. He started to snore.

Relief surged through Nellie. It was the first night since their marriage that he'd failed to want her, failed to take her.

She finally fell asleep praying that the cycle had been broken and that from now on he would leave her alone.

She laid the mince and potatoes on the table while he washed his hands at the sink. It was Friday night and he was just home from work. They ate in silence, as they usually did. A year they'd been married now. To Nellie it seemed like ten.

After they'd finished she cleared the dishes into the sink. As she put on her pinny she said, 'Well? Where is it then?' It was pay night.

Jim took a small, buff-coloured envelope from his pocket and threw it down on the table.

Nellie opened the envelope to count its contents, frowning as she did so. It was only a quarter of what she was usually given for the housekeeping.

'What's going on?' she demanded.

'I lost a few bob on the horses last week. I had to settle up the night before coming home.'

111

She spread the money on the table and stood staring at it. 'How in God's name am I supposed to manage on this?'

He shrugged. 'You'll manage somehow.'

His gambling had always been a bone of contention between them. There had been a time when she'd thought she could wean him away from it but she'd soon learned her mistake. He was addicted to gambling the way an alcoholic is to drink, and, since paying Wee Mo the £200 he'd owed, he'd been on a winning streak.

Not that she saw any of his winnings. She was given the housekeeping and that was that. They never went out together, they rarely spoke.

Her only pleasure in life was her cigarettes and the odd night, usually about once a month, when he allowed her to go off to the pictures either on her own or with Babs, who now was engaged and shortly to be married herself.

'Have you nothing put by? A wee fly something?' he asked.

She laughed. 'From what you give me? You must be joking!'

'Well you don't have to worry about meat. I'll see we're all right there.' He normally brought home the meat which he paid for at cost price. But that wasn't what he was talking about now.

'You mean you're going to steal it?' she demanded.

'I'll think of some story to cover the fact I'm not buying it as usual. I could say you've developed a sudden mania for fish and chips.'

She stared at him in contempt. 'Wouldn't it just be a lot easier if you didn't lose what you can't afford?'

'Shut up!' he ordered.

Anger flared in her. 'Don't you speak like that to me. I won't have you coming in here taking out on me the fact you've lost nearly all your wage packet on some bloody horse!'

He glared at her, his hands automatically knotting into fists. 'Don't nag. I could never abide a nag!'

'Then don't give me anything to nag about.'

'I said we wouldn't go hungry next week!'

'And what about the rent? How am I going to pay that?'

'There's almost enough there. Tell them you'll pay the rest the following week.'

'Oh, aye. And if I give the factor what you say, how will I get coal in? Or bread, or potatoes?'

He had no answer to that.

'I can just imagine you getting up in the morning to a freezing cold room with no fire. You're going to love that.'

'Dry your eyes,' he said angrily. He ran his fingers through his hair. He knew damn well he was wrong. There was no need to go on and on about it.

'And another thing –'

But she got no further. 'Oh for God's sake!' he exploded, leaping to his feet to send his chair crashing to the floor behind him.

She tried to duck the fist that came punching toward her but wasn't quick enough. She cried out as it took her in the eye knocking her head backward and sideways.

'I said shut up!' he screamed.

Sobbing she held her hand over her eye. Already she could feel the flesh there puffing and closing.

He pulled his jacket from the peg behind the door and savagely thrust his arms into it, one after the other. 'I'm going out,' he said.

She didn't reply. What she was thinking was if only she'd have been born a man she could have stood up physically to Jim Biles. Just ten minutes of a man's strength and she would have thrashed him the way he'd so often thrashed her. Oh the glorious satisfaction there would be in that!

'And I don't know when I'll be back,' he added. He hesitated for a moment or two, turning something over in his mind. Then, coming to the table, he scooped two half-crowns into his hand before banging his way out of the house.

He's taken drinking money she thought bitterly. Now there was even less to get by on than there had been before.

Crossing to the sink she wet a flannel under the tap and held it to her eye. There was enough coal in the bin to see them through to the next day. And after that?

There was Barrie's coalyard not that far away where they bagged the coal and loaded the carts which brought it round the streets. The coal was kept in buildings under lock and key. But at night the yard was deserted and easy to get into.

She knew from playing around there as a child that if you were prepared to go along and pick it up there were always lumps to be found. That's what she would do tomorrow, after the men had gone off for the weekend.

The factor would just have to be put off with a story, for she needed what was left of Jim's pay for essentials. The factor fancied her, she knew that from the way he stared at her every week when she went to pay the rent. She'd play on that. Flirt with him a wee bit. Win him around.

Jim had been right. She'd manage. That was a woman's lot.

The other wives in the steamie were chattering nineteen to the dozen. 'Have you heard about her down in Beresford Street?' 'You mean her with the ginger hair?' The chattering became a medley of whispers, punctuated every second or two by giggles and the odd raucous laugh.

Nellie waited patiently for the copper to come to the boil. She enjoyed steamie days. They were an escape from the incredible boredom of the house. There were days when she was sure she'd end up screaming because of it! All day long on her own, and then at night *him*.

And he was certainly no company. When he was at home, which wasn't all that often nowadays, he would doze and read the paper exactly the same way her father had done. But most evenings he was out, on business as he called it.

And she knew all about that, didn't she just! This new losing streak of his seemed to be going on forever. She rarely got her full housekeeping money each week. She could hardly show her face down at the factor's, so behind were they with the rent.

Nor had she given up hope of finding a job and getting the hell away from him. But there were just no jobs to be had.

She would have been able to get something up the town if she could type or take dictation, but she had no skills at all. It would have to be a factory, boilings or thread or something of the like. She didn't care what. Anything would do.

The copper was bubbling now so she picked up the pile of clothes and the water received them, glugging them into its depths.

One of his shirts was the last item in. She was about to poke it under the surface with the large wooden tongs when a red smear on the shirt's tail caught her eye. Frowning, she pulled the shirt out again, draping it over the rim of the copper in such a way that she could examine the smear.

Lipstick. No doubt about it.

It could have been hers, of course. Even in such a queer place. Except for one thing. Her last lipstick had given out months ago and she hadn't had the money to replace it since.

She prodded the shirt back into the copper and pushed it down amongst the rest of the clothes. Putting the top on the copper she moved away to a work surface for folding clothes and sat. Sweat was running down her face and back. Her hair clung damply to her head and neck. She felt a hundred years old.

So, he had another woman. That explained why his sexual demands hadn't been nearly so great of late. She should have been able to put two and two together before now. A man like Jim demanded his full quota. If he wasn't bothering her for it then someone else just had to be involved.

But did she care? That was the question she asked herself. Shouldn't she be grateful to this other woman who'd taken the pressure off her?

As she sat thinking she again became aware of the hum of conversation from the other women present. A laugh rose stridently to saw the air.

'And her none the wiser!' a voice said.

Mocking laughter filled the steamie like a roll from a timpany.

'Poor bitch!' another voice said.

'And him the sort you wouldn't think to look at twice. Just goes to show you, you can never judge a book by its cover.'

'It's what's under the cover that counts,' the first voice said.

Again the laughter swelled, to die into whispers interspersed by chortles and giggles.

A thought had struck Nellie making her chill despite the heat. Were her neighbours talking about her and Jim like that? Laughing and sniggering behind her back? Had they realized before she herself had? Have you heard about Nellie Biles's man? Did you know that . . . ?

She could hear it all now. A short while married and already lost her man. Of course, maybe it's not his fault, they'd say. Could be he's got to look elsewhere for what he should be getting at home. The tongues clacking. The fingers pointing. The eyes watching behind curtains and blinds.

Gossip. There was nothing the women of the tenements liked more. And when sex or morality, or both, were involved they were in their element. She couldn't bear the thought of the neighbours talking about her like that. Scorn, derision and even pretended pity.

She couldn't mind that he had someone else, but he

should be discreet about it. He owed her that. She'd make him promise. Make him swear.

'Are you going out the night?' she asked.

He was just finishing his tea. Without looking up he grunted a yes.

'With her?'

He threw his knife and fork clattering onto the plate, then regarded her biliously. 'Who?'

'Your fancy woman.'

His eyes hardened and shrunk to slits. Fear turned her stomach over. She'd learned to be scared of him when he looked like that.

'What are you talking about?' he demanded harshly.

'I know you're seeing someone else, so don't bother to lie about it.'

'How do you know?'

'Lipstick on your shirt. You should tell her to be more careful. And what the hell was she doing anyway to get it on your shirt-tail? Isn't that sort of thing a bit difficult up a back close?'

He let the jibe pass. She was only fishing for information.

'Who is she?'

'None of your bloody business.'

'I think it is.'

He stood, scraping the chair away from him. 'I haven't got time for a fight. I'm late as it is.'

'It's not Marj is it?'

'No. You finding us in the broom closet scared the living daylights out of her. I haven't spoken to her since. I have seen her once or twice in the street, but seeing me coming she's ducked down a close or round a corner.'

Well that was something Nellie thought. At least it wasn't her cousin he was two-timing her with.

'Why? Are you jealous?'

'Not me. Whoever she is, she's welcome to you.'

He decided to stick the knife in. Christ, to think how he'd once panted after this woman! He could hardly credit it now. For now she meant nothing to him. Nothing at all.

'At least she doesn't lie there like a stookie. She gives me a bit of come on, shows that she's enjoying it.'

'If I'm like that you've only yourself to blame,' she answered hotly.

'How so?'

She was flabbergasted he had to ask. 'What you did to me on our wedding night was enough to put anyone off for life.'

'I'd have thought you would have forgotten about that by now.'

'Forgotten about it? Forgotten?'

'I think you're just making that an excuse anyway. You'd have been the same whether that night happened or not. And it was your own bloody fault it did. Trying to refuse me my rights after keeping me at arm's length like you had all those months.'

'If I'd known what you were really like I'd never have married you. Not in a million years. I thought you cared.'

'Cared!' he spat contemptuously. 'Sure I cared. To get you into bed.'

'Was that all I meant to you? Bed?'

'No. You meant more than that. You meant two hundred quid which got me out of trouble with Wee Mo.'

'What?' she said, appalled.

'You heard me.'

'I don't understand. What two hundred quid?'

'The two hundred your father gave me for taking you off his hands.'

'This is the first I've heard of it.'

'It was between him and me. Nothing to do with you.'

'Nothing to do with me!' she laughed. 'It had everything to do with me I'd say.'

'Well now you know,' he said.

'God you are an evil bastard!'

He laughed cruelly. She was devastated and that pleased him. If he'd had the time he'd have taken her there and then. Perhaps in her present state he'd get some response out of her.

She thought of her da, hating him, detesting him. He'd not only lost her Frank but he'd saddled her with Jim. Surely that man had a lot to answer for.

'Two hundred quid,' said Jim cruelly. 'And I've suffered for every penny of it. You're useless, you know that? Bloody useless. Pretty packaging with nothing underneath. Why, I'd be better off with a tailor's dummy than with you.'

He was close to her now, leering down at her. How she hated that face. She reached out to grasp hold of the bread knife.

'You would, would you!' he cried as the knife swept up in an arc aimed at his belly. He dodged to one side and then, using a chopping, motion hit her wrist to send the knife clattering to the floor.

Grabbing hold of the front of her dress, he half hauled her to her feet. His open hand smashed again and again into the face that once had mesmerised him.

When he let her go she slumped to the floor where she lay, sobbing. He picked up the knife and placed it on the table.

'No use bitch!' he said, and left the house slamming the door behind him.

If only she could run away! But she couldn't. Until she found a job she was trapped with this animal who was her husband.

Still sobbing, she brought herself into a sitting position. She knew Babs's parents would take her in for nothing until a job came up, but she couldn't ask that of them. Like everyone else their resources were stretched to the limit. Another mouth to feed would mean them getting less themselves.

No, she would just have to endure it for the time being. Somehow.

'I'm sorry Mrs Biles, but I can't put anything else on the slate for you. You owe me,' And here Mr Simpson consulted the book he kept account of the tick in. 'Three pounds, nine and six as it is. That's a lot more than I allow most of my customers.'

Mr Simpson smiled kindly at her, but behind the smile he was resolute. He'd learned to be to stay in business.

'My husband will soon have –'

'Sorry, Mrs Biles,' he interjected firmly. 'Not another item out this shop until this bill's paid off.'

She sagged where she stood. How in God's name was she going to feed them for the rest of the week? It was only Tuesday and she hadn't a penny left to her name. It had been months since she'd had a full week's housekeeping money.

'I understand,' she said dully.

'I'm sorry lass,' Mr Simpson replied.

Outside she stood for a few moments to gather herself. She felt like running screaming down the street. Instead, she set off home at her normal pace, even managing a smile on passing folk she knew.

Once in she sat in front of the lifeless fire. The scuttle was empty which meant she would have to go scrounging round Barrie's coal yard again that night. She hoped she could at least find a few lumps in the dark to bring home.

Her head rested in her hands. Jim was earning good money but she was seeing little of it. Wee Mo's runners were getting the lion's share and most of what was left he was holding on to to pay for his nights out.

Her stomach rumbled, reminding her of just how hungry she was. Her last bite had been yesterday dinnertime. Some fish she'd got cheap because it wasn't as fresh as it might be.

She thought of the meat he used to bring home from the shop: the chops, the sausages, the joints. Those had stopped now, too. For a while he'd helped himself without paying, but that had come to an end when he'd got the idea his boss was getting fly to him.

She was still sitting in the chair a little while later when there was a knock on the front door.

'Can I have a word with you, Mrs Biles?'

Her heart sank on seeing it was the factor. There was only one thing he could have come about. She ushered him through.

In the kitchen he took off his bowler to reveal his balding head. He was a tall man, beaky and gaunt.

'I'm sorry, Mr Butter, but I'm still not in a position to give you anything,' she said.

'You're six months behind now.'

'That much?' She was genuinely surprised. She hadn't realized it had been so long.

'Aye, I'm afraid it is.'

She ran a hand over her face. 'What are you going to do?'

'Give you a week's notice of eviction I'm afraid,' he said, apologetically.

'But you can't do that!'

'Oh, I can Mrs Biles, I assure you. The Corporation's not a charity, you know. We can't afford to let you live in our house for free.'

She bit her lip, thoroughly ashamed and thoroughly lost.

'Your man's working isn't he?'

'Yes.'

'So,' he said, nodding his head. He'd seen it all before. 'Drink is it?'

'Gambling.'

'I see.'

Tears filled her eyes. If the bailiffs came they'd be thrown out on to the street, lock, stock and barrel. The shame and humiliation would be bad enough – but where would they go? What would they do? For he had no relatives that would put them up. None that would offer, anyway. Which left Betty and Davey. But no, she wouldn't go back there, she couldn't go back home. She'd sworn that much to herself.

'Please?' she pleaded.

Mr Butter's heart went out to Nellie. He pretended to be a hard man, but he wasn't really, and he'd always had a soft spot for Nellie.

'I can't extend any longer. It would be more than my job's worth.'

Those eyes, he thought. He'd never seen anything like them. What a contrast to the wife he had at home, who was fat and homely. Chalk to Nellie Biles's cheese. He'd fantasized a number of times about Nellie after she'd been to see him. He could imagine himself, twenty years younger and handsome, stepping out with her up to the town. And then he'd imagined making love to her.

Nellie took hold of his arm. 'I'll do anything,' she said.

Suddenly he was nervous, the insides of his legs trembling.

Nellie was well aware of what she was saying. But she meant it. She'd do anything rather than be thrown out in the street or have to go home to her da. Mr Butter had a kind face. What was one slice off a cut loaf, anyway?

She could see the indecision on his face and guessed that he was wanting to be absolutely certain about the offer and that he hadn't misinterpreted her meaning.

'*Anything*,' she repeated.

He licked his lips, unable suddenly to meet her gaze. 'Perhaps . . . I could put on your file that there were extenuating circumstances and because of this I was allowing you extra time to pay.'

'How long?'

'A month.'

'Two?'

'Six weeks.'

Crossing to the bed, she removed her dress, which she folded neatly before laying it to one side and then took off her bra and knickers to stand totally naked before him.

'Well, Mr Butter?' she asked.

She felt nothing while he was doing it to her, but, unlike with Jim, she pretended otherwise. He told her that she'd been absolutely marvellous.

When he was gone it surprised her that she didn't feel tainted in any way.

She just felt hungry.

Nellie huddled in her thin coat against the wind cutting through her like a knife. The wind was off the sea and you could still smell the salt in it despite its corruption by city smoke and other odours.

She was on her way to see about yet another job. How many was this now she'd gone after? If it wasn't a thousand it certainly felt like it.

She was in the Gallowgate, not all that far from where Jim worked, when, looking up, she saw his boss, Mr Sanderson, coming towards her. She was preparing to nod and pass by when, in desperation, it occurred to her that he might be able to help her.

'Mister Sanderson?'

He stopped and smiled. From the expression in his eyes she knew he hadn't placed her.

'Nellie Biles. Jim's wife.'

'Oh, aye, of course,' he replied, his smile widening.

'You're probably in a hurry, but could you spare me a minute?'

'Certainly. What can I do for you?'

In a voice cracking with emotion she told him about Jim's gambling and how, with this losing streak he was going through which seemed to be going on forever, nearly all his wages were ending up in the pocket of Wee Mo the bookie.

'I'm desperate,' she ended, close to tears.

Sanderson was frowning. An elder of the kirk, he strongly disapproved of gambling and strong drink.

'Jim thinks an awful lot of you. I know, he's mentioned it a number of times,' she went on. 'And what I was wondering was, if you could have a word with him? Try to convince him that gambling's a mug's game and that the only person who wins in the long run is the bookie. He might just listen to you, Mister Sanderson. At least I think it's worth a try.'

Sanderson thought of the money he'd lent Jim in the past. Jim had always said it was for domestic matters, but he could see now that was a lie. 'I had no idea Jim was a gambler,' he said.

'Will you speak to him?'

Sanderson nodded. 'I consider it my duty.'

She took his hand and shook it. 'Thank you,' she said.

'I just hope it does some good.'

'It certainly won't do any harm.'

She looked drawn and haggard, he thought, but even so she was still beautiful. Jim Biles was a lucky man, in more ways than one. On an impulse he took two pound notes from his wallet and slipped them into Nellie's coat pocket.

She protested and tried to hand them back but he wouldn't accept them. 'Give yourself a treat,' he said. 'And don't worry, I can afford it.'

As she hurried on her way she thought of the meal she'd make when she got home. And to hell with Jim, he could go without. What she bought she'd eat herself.

'Does that mean I've got the job?' Nellie asked eagerly.

The manager nodded. 'Provided you're here at eight sharp in the morning. We set a lot of store by good timekeeping at Goldman's. You're either on the dot or not at all.'

'I'll be early,' she said.

'That's the idea,' the manager replied, his lips smug with approval.

She could scarcely believe her luck. After all this time she'd done it. She'd landed a job! She'd leave Jim, find a room somewhere. Life was going to be marvellous at last.

The Gallowgate was abustle with people hurrying

hither and yon. She passed among them; seeing nothing, hearing nothing.

What a day it was turning out to be! First of all there was the two pounds Mr Sanderson had given her, which meant she would be able to eat her fill, and now a job!

Nor was it a bad job either. Goldman's was a big china importers. She was to be employed downstairs in the packing room at a wage which was eight shillings more than she'd been getting at the sweet factory.

Her luck had changed. No doubt about it.

Tea was bread and scrape, and he was lucky to get that considering the amount of money he'd given her to get through the week on.

She was feeling gloriously happy. It was amazing what a full stomach and a job to start in the morning could do. Another ten days till she got her first full week's wages and then she was off. Jim Biles could hang as he grew for all she cared. Let his fancy woman look after him. She'd had enough.

She put the kettle on the moment she heard the key in the lock. When he entered the room he had a face like a thundercloud. He stood by the door, glowering at her.

'What is it?' she asked, already tensed.

He was so angry he had trouble speaking. 'Sanderson kept me back after work. He told me you'd been complaining to him about me.'

Fear exploded inside her. What a stupid thing Sanderson had done, putting it like that.

'Well?'

'You can't go on the way you are,' she pleaded. 'It's madness. We're months behind with the rent and when was the last time we had a decent meal? I can't manage on what you're giving me, Jim. I've told you that till I'm sick of telling you. You've got to give up gambling.'

'Got to, have I?'

'For your own good. It's become an illness with you.'

Slowly he stalked forward, his eyes, dark and evil, stabbing right through her.

She backed away. 'No Jim,' she pleaded.

His hands knotted into fists. 'You'll not do the likes of that to me again,' he said.

He'd beaten her badly before but nothing like he did now. Finally, reluctantly, he forced himself to stop. Breathing heavily he stood staring down at the woman lying curled at his feet.

'You can't do this to me,' she gasped at last, painfully crawling away from him towards the bed.

'Who bloody can't?' he asked. 'I've just done it, haven't I?'

She stared at him, her body burning with pain, hating him.

'I'm going out,' he said. 'On business.'

She let the tears come after he'd gone. She ached all over. Every muscle, every joint, every inch of flesh. The crawl to the bed had been indescribable agony.

She felt so lost and alone. She thought of Frank and what life with him might have been like. Frank whom she loved and had never stopped loving. Frank who she had never let make love to her.

Frank, who . . .

She fell asleep, to dream.

The alarm clock burst into a strident jangle to bring her awake. Without thinking she reached to turn it off causing a wave of pain and nausea to sweep through her.

She had to make it to Goldman's, she told herself, and as early as she'd said she'd be. To lose a job after spending so long looking for one didn't bear thinking about.

Jim came out of bed, hardly bothering to glance in her direction as he got dressed. He drank his tea and ate his bread in silence. When he was finished he left the house without having spoken a word.

Every step was a torment. Every movement of her body

the same. She couldn't walk a yard without having to stop for a breather.

She cleared up and then got herself into her coat. Taking tiny steps which seemed to minimise the pain she made her way out on to the landing and down half a flight of stairs. By the time she got to the end of the first flight she knew she wasn't going to be able to make it. And even if she had, how would she get through a day's work in this state? She could hardly move, far less cope with what would be expected of her.

Leaning against the wall she bent over. She had no control over her legs when they slowly gave way under her. She ended up sitting on the cold stone stair with her back against the wall.

Her chance had come and gone. She would have to stay on, and at that thought her heart filled with terrible despair. Was there to be no end?

There *will* be another job, she told herself as, gritting her teeth, she forced herself back up the stairs. There just has to be!

Please, God.

She sat staring into the empty grate. It was a week since Jim had beaten her and even now she still wasn't fully recovered. Not even enough to go down to Barrie's coal yard to scrounge some lumps for the fire. Because there was nothing else to do she started to sing, a soft crooning melody that warmed her heart and made her feel better. She often sang when she was alone. It was a pleasure and comfort that didn't cost anything.

She broke off when there was a chap on the door. Now who can that be she wondered, coming stiffly to her feet.

Betty smiled nervously when the door was opened. 'Hello, hen, it's me,' she said.

'Come in,' said Nellie, gesturing into the hallway.

Betty entered, looking round as she did so. It was the first time she'd been in Nellie's house.

Betty sat by the empty fireplace while Nellie made tea. 'How are you?'

'Stiff,' Nellie replied, not having intended to tell the truth.

'Why's that?' asked her mother, politely.

'Because I've a man who's forever beating the living daylights out of me,' Nellie sobbed, her voice breaking.

Betty stared at her daughter, shocked, unable to think or speak.

Nellie pulled herself together, sweeping the hair back from her face. It was dull and lifeless of late. Like I am, she thought.

'What does he beat you for?' Betty asked gently.

'For the sheer pleasure of it, mainly. Other times it's because I've done something dreadful, like complain about not having any housekeeping money.'

'But he earns a good wage –'

'Oh, aye,' Nellie interjected. 'Only he's got a wee weakness that takes care of most of it. His gambling. Remember?'

'But he always won, I thought.'

'Used to, Ma. For a long time now he's been losing.' And, then, with her mother's arms around her, she spoke for the first time of what life was like with Jim Biles.

'Och, you're exaggerating a bit, surely?' Betty tried to soothe.

'I've not exaggerated anything, not one thing.'

Betty stared into her tea. 'Your da will go daft when he hears,' she said at last.

Nellie's laugh was sharp and mirthless. 'Will he, now? Will it annoy him because he'll think he hasn't got his money's worth?'

'What are you talking about?'

'Hasn't he told you either, then? He paid Jim Biles to take me off his hands.'

'I don't believe that!'

'It's true. Two hundred pounds that Jim needed to pay off a gambling debt. He and da arranged it between them.'

There was an enormous pause and then Betty said her voice half-dead, 'Is that why you haven't been to see us?'

'I never want to see him again. And that's why I got married. I couldn't stand being in the same house with him.'

'But he's your da, Nellie, no matter what he's done.'

'He lost me Frank Connelly. He lost me Frank, and, not content with that, he landed me with Jim. I wouldn't spit on him if he was on fire. As far as I'm concerned he doesn't exist.'

Betty's eyes were wet with tears. 'And me? What about me?'

'I've nothing against you, Ma,' holding her mother's trembling hand. 'You've always tried your best.'

Betty stared at her daughter in silence, noting how thin she'd become. And how pale. She looked like a half-starved animal. 'What are you going to do?' she finally asked.

'Leave him when I get the chance. It's getting the job to support myself that's the problem. Something always goes wrong.'

'You won't consider coming home, then?'

Nellie shook her head, averting her mother's eyes.

'Your da will want to come round when I tell him.'

'You tell him from me to go to hell first.'

'What he did he thought he was doing for your own good.'

'Then Heaven preserve me from my enemies,' Nellie sighed.

'I never knew about the money. I wouldn't have let him do that,' Betty said. 'It wasn't right.'

They talked for a little while longer and then Betty rose to go. 'Now that I know I'm welcome can I come back?'

'Anytime you like, Ma.'

She opened her purse and took out four single pound notes and a ten shilling one, it was all the money she had.

'No Ma,' said Nellie.

'Ach, away with you,' Betty replied, placing the money on the mantelpiece above the fire.

The two women stared at one another. Joined for the moment by more than the bond of flesh and blood. Each, in her own way, had experienced the hardness of life and it was the understanding of this which now flowed between them.

'I'd better be off,' said Betty at last.

At the door, with a hint of tears still in her eyes, she kissed Nellie on the cheek.

'Look after yourself, Ma.'

'And you, Nellie. And you.'

Nellie went back through to the kitchen, put on her coat, and took the money from where it was lying beside a china dog. Folding it carefully, she put it into her pocket.

A glance at the clock told her it was just gone 8 p.m. None of the shops would be open at this time, but the chippie would. That was where she'd go to treat herself.

It was foggy out, not too bad, but thick enough that you had to be careful how you went. As she walked, yellow-eyed cars passed her, and the fog caught in her throat making her cough. A line of Corporation buses, like arthritic dinosaurs, lumbered by. Somewhere in the distance a foghorn sounded.

There was a queue at the chippie, but the wait was worth it. Standing outside the blazing window, she ravenously dug into her fish supper. She was halfway through her feed when she saw them.

Disbelief stamped itself across her face. She was imagining things, she thought. She had to be!

But she wasn't. There was Jim coming towards her, holding hands with a woman. And the woman was Big Jessie.

Even as she watched Jim paused to kiss Jessie on the mouth. Then, laughing like a couple of schoolchildren or newlyweds, they continued towards her.

He'd promised her. Given her his word he'd be discreet. And here he was, holding hands and canoodling for all the world to see. And not more than a few hundred yards from his own front door. And with *her*.

How long it had been going on she didn't know, but how Jessie must have laughed at her behind her back. How she must have enjoyed Nellie's shame.

In her mind's eye she saw Jim and Jessie, together, in a back close, behind a midgie, wherever, laughing at her, making a fool of her.

And Jessie wouldn't have wasted any time putting it round the sweetie factory. Hey, guess who I'm going out with? Jim Biles. That's right, Nellie's man. That's one in the eye for her, eh?

Why the hell hadn't Babs told her? For Babs must know. Babs must think she was protecting her in some way.

Big Jessie! Of all the women in the world, he had to pick her!

She wasn't aware when the remains of her supper slipped from her hand to fall messily on to the pavement. The red mist of rage had descended on her, an anger transcending anything she'd ever experienced before.

Her hands formed themselves into claws. She'd rip the witch's face to shreds. She'd gouge out her eyes.

Big Jessie saw her first. It was a moment she'd been anticipating for a long time, but the look of triumph, that flashed across her face disappeared almost instantly, to be replaced by one of fear when she saw Nellie advancing on her like an avenging angel.

'Oh, my God!' Jessie whispered.

Eyes popping, hair flying, Nellie ran at Jessie who, with a screech, turned and fled.

Jim grabbed hold of Nellie as she tried to go past him, and taking her by the shoulders shook her vigorously. When he saw her hands coming at his face he hit her hard on the side of the head. Nellie fell, rolling into the gutter, lying there momentarily stunned among the refuse and dirt.

Whirling, Jim shouted, 'Jessie! Jessie!' and ran out into the street after her.

There was a split second when he might have saved himself. But the sight of the motorcycle – bursting out of the fog straight at him – made him freeze as if he'd taken root.

Nellie saw none of it. By the time she registered the sound and turned to look, it was all over.

A horrible wailing noise tore through the night. Jessie had come running back to find herself staring down at Jim's inert body.

Within seconds a crowd had gathered, one man galloping away for the police while others hauled the bike off Jim and the motorcyclist.

Jim was lying in a pool of blood, his face the colour of milk. He looked asleep.

Jessie, with several women trying to console her, continued wailing.

'This one's dead,' one of the men said, looking up from the body of the motorcyclist. Then he put his head to Jim's chest and listened. He screwed up his face as though not sure if he was hearing something or not. 'This one's still alive. Just,' he said finally.

Jessie had totally given herself over to hysterics. Breaking away from the women who'd been trying to console her, she threw herself down on her knees by Jim's side. Curiously detached, Nellie watched Jessie's wailing grief. Her gaze went from Jessie to Jim. She was unmoved to see him lying there, more so than if he had been a complete stranger.

'Are you his wife, missus?' a policeman asked quietly, hunching down beside Jessie.

Nellie stepped forward. 'No, I am,' she said, in a voice she didn't recognize. 'I'm his wife.'

It was a glorious feeling, having the bed to herself for the first time since she'd been married. The only glorious feeling she was likely to have. She yawned and stretched. It was past midnight and she wasn't long back from the hospital. Jim was going to make it after all, but he'd lost his right leg below the knee.

She felt no pity toward him. Try as she would, she felt he'd brought it on himself. She had no tears left for him.

Was she being too hard? No, he'd been nothing but cruel toward her, treating her the way she wouldn't treat a dog. How could she feel pity for a man like that?

Part of her wished he'd died out there on the street. For now she could never leave him. Now she was going to have to live with a cripple for the rest of her life, and God alone knew how they were going to manage. God alone knew how they would ever survive.

'It's bad news I'm afraid, Mrs Biles,' the doctor said. He'd taken her into the Sister's room at the head of the ward.

She looked at the doctor, waiting for him to continue. It was only the morning after the accident, but already it seemed so long ago.

'Your husband's paralysed down his entire left side,' the doctor said, in what he thought was his most consoling manner.

She was almost afraid to ask the only important question. 'Will he ever get better?'

The doctor shrugged. 'It has been known. But in the majority of cases like this, the chances are very small. However, you mustn't give up hope,' he said, patting her on the shoulder.

She stared out of the window at the sandstone wall opposite. 'What happens to him?' she asked at last, from very far away.

'How do you mean?'

It was funny how all hospitals smelled the same she thought. Sharp and antiseptic, and something else. Fear perhaps.

'Will he be in hospital for the rest of his life?'

'He'll certainly be a few months with us. But then, we hope, he'll be able to go home."

133

The old trapped feeling descended on her like a shroud. Home, and her having to look after him, for there was no one else. None of his family would take him on. In the eyes of the law, after all, *she* was his family.

'Aren't there special places? Institutions?'

She could see the doctor was looking at her strangely, wondering what sort of woman she was.

'Yes, there are,' he said slowly. 'But there's usually a long waiting list.'

'How do I get him on it?' she asked.

She didn't fail to notice the coldness in his voice during the remainder of their conversation. I wonder how you would have reacted in my place, she thought. But then men didn't know what it was like to be a woman. Or to have their bodies violated and their pride destroyed.

They just didn't know.

Later that day she opened the door to a man she'd never seen before.

'Mrs Biles?'

'Yes.'

'I was supposed to meet your husband last night but he never showed up. My name's Hendry, I work for Wee Mo.'

'If it's money you're wanting I haven't any,' she said harshly.

'No, no, you've got it all wrong. I've come to give you some.' And he pulled out a wad of notes from which he peeled off eight fivers.

Nellie took the money, hardly believing her eyes.

'I'm away through to Edinburgh this evening for a couple of weeks and I thought I'd better let Jim have his money before I went. He might think I'd done a moonlight with it otherwise,' said Hendry grinning.

'Aye, he might,' Nellie replied.

Hendry cocked his head. 'Give him my best and tell him I think his luck's changed at long last.'

With a wave of his hand Hendry went clattering down the stairs.

Nellie closed the door and leant her back against it. She clutched the fivers to her bosom.

A grin split her face. 'Tell him his luck's changed at long last,' she repeated.

Oh that was rich! That was bloody marvellous! His luck's *changed*. She started to laugh hysterically, holding herself tightly from the ache of it. She had a husband who'd beaten and abused her, and now she would have to look after him, waiting on him hand and foot. His luck had changed all right, but for the worse. As had hers. *Hers*.

She wasn't laughing anymore. Tears streamed down her face as she sobbed. What had she done to deserve all this? Why had she been given such a cross as Jim Biles to bear?

Filled with despair and self-pity she sank down to the floor and buried her head between her knees. She cursed the day she'd first met Jim Biles. And she cursed the day she'd become his wife.

She cried so hard, and so long, that, exhausted, she eventually fell asleep where she sat. But there was no peace in that sleep. For in it she was being pursued by a pair of large, red, raw hands.

Hands she knew so well.

Three months and one week later they brought Jim home.

The ambulancemen brought Jim up the stairs on a stretcher to which he had to be strapped. Because it was impossible to get the stretcher through the door they unstrapped him and brought him into the kitchen carrying him between them in a chair position.

The cavity bed he was laid on had been transformed from what it had been formerly. Workmen from the hospital had been to turn it into a sort of cocoon.

When Jim was tucked up, she bid the ambulancemen good-bye, then she put the kettle on.

When the tea was made she gave Jim his. He could still eat and drink by himself.

As she drank her tea, she studied him while he, in turn, studied her. He'd lost a considerable amount of weight, his face now almost emaciated. The once broad shoulders had shrunk and become bony.

'I take it they told you I've put you down for an institution? But a bed won't become available for some time as the waiting list is a lengthy one,' she said at last into the empty silence.

'They told me,' His speech was thick and slurred. He'd been fortunate not to have completely lost the power of speech. When he spoke it was out of the right side of his mouth only, the words he produced having a curious elliptical sound. But at least they were understandable.

'I've paid off the back rent and we're now up to date. I've enough money for a few weeks more and then that's it,' she said.

'What are you going to do?'

'Go on the parish till I can find work,' she replied.

'Aye, I suppose so,' he sighed. 'I take it Harrison's won't give you your old job back then?'

'Your friend Jessie put the mockers on that for me some time ago. Didn't she tell you?'

'No,' he replied, looking at her with his old loathing. 'I blame all this on you you know,' he said carefully. 'You've been nothing but a Jonah ever since I married you.'

'And how I wish *that* had never happened.'

'That makes two of us, I can assure you.'

They glared at one another, only the hatred between them real. 'I'll give you your rub and then I'm going out for a wee while,' she said. She wanted some fresh air. She wanted to be away from him. She was finding his presence hard to bear after thirteen weeks on her own.

*

136

'And your husband will never work again?' one of the men asked. There were six of them on the Parish Board interviewing Nellie.

'There's a doctor's statement there confirming it,' she replied.

God, how she was hating this. Her neck was burning with embarrassment and shame. She felt totally humiliated.

All six men were looking at her as though she were a prisoner in the dock. From their stern gazes you would've thought she was trying to lie to them. Make the facts worse than they were. Well that she certainly didn't have to do. They were bad enough as they were.

'Can't you get a job and support him?' another man asked. This one was the army-type with a monocle and clipped moustache.

'If you know of a job going, *any* job, I'll happily take it,' Nellie replied.

'Hmmh!' said the army-type, nodding. Her reply pleased him.

And so it went on. Question after question until it seemed her entire life had been laid bare before these inquisitors.

Later, when she'd left the room, they told her that she'd have their decision in a few days. It took every ounce of willpower she had to keep her head held high and stare those she met in the eye.

It was hours before her mortification began to fade.

Several months passed and she got into a routine for looking after Jim. They were scraping by, just, on the money the parish had awarded them.

The funny thing was, Nellie thought, they were actually marginally better off than when Jim had been on his losing streak and most of his wages had been going straight into Wee Mo's pocket.

Then, early one evening, just as she was thinking about making the tea, there came a rapping on the front door.

'Hello!' said Babs, kissing Nellie on the cheek. Then, indicating Phil Drummond who was standing behind her, 'We thought we'd pay you a visit.'

Nellie ushered them through, consciously grateful for the company. Most of the time she spent alone with Jim, her only alternative being to go out for a walk.

'We brought fish suppers. Thought you'd like a change,' said Phil.

'His idea,' said Babs, staring with unashamed love at him. They were now engaged, the wedding scheduled for later on in the year.

Nellie stuck on the kettle and put out plates. While she was doing this Babs said, 'After we've had this I thought you and I might go up the town and see a flick. Phil's only too happy to stay with Jim.'

Nellie's eyes shone with excitement. She couldn't remember the last time she'd been to the pictures.

'I'm paying, of course,' said Babs. 'And Phil will give us money for chocolates to take in with us.'

'Thanks for telling me,' exclaimed Phil, pretending to be put out.

Babs had been lucky with Phil, Nellie thought. A real nice, easy-going fellow who worshipped the ground Babs walked on. In many ways he reminded her of Frank Connelly. And, as usual when she thought of Frank, a small, black creature passed through her; despair and regret nibbling her insides.

They went into town on a tram, going upstairs so that they could have a smoke.

'We could've gone locally but I thought you'd enjoy the town more,' said Babs.

Nellie smiled and nodded.

'Any news of Jim going into an institution yet?'

'No.'

'Is it bad having to look after him?'

'Bad enough. I can think of a lot of other things I'd rather do.'

'Aye,' said Babs, her voice sympathetic.

'I'm still looking for a job, mind you, but it seems I'm fated never to find one.' And then, thinking of Goldman's, added, 'Or lose it again when I do.'

'Big Jessie's getting married. Have you heard?'

'No. Who to?'

'Some chap she met at the jigging. A sheet-metal worker from over Shieldhall way.'

'God help him for taking her on.'

'Exactly what we all said.'

They rode for a little while in silence, the tram rattling and swaying. Schoogling they would've called it.

'You should've told me about those two,' Nellie said, a little further on.

Babs pulled a face. 'How could I, Nellie? She was aye like a red rag to a bull where you were concerned.' Then, giving a sudden grin, 'Let's be nasty and hope she's marrying a right sod who beats hell out of her every week.'

Just like I married, thought Nellie bitterly. Well, at least one thing was certain. Jim Biles would never beat her again.

He'd been a bastard in his day. But by God he'd paid for it. And would continue to pay.

But even the grim satisfaction gave her no real comfort.

'A real smashing film,' said Babs as the lights came up for the interval. 'Now how about an ice cream?'

'If you can afford it.'

'Relax, you're out with your auntie,' replied Babs, causing Nellie to smile.

As Babs excused her way down the row of seats a man came on stage in front of the curtains.

'For those of you who don't know me, I'm Mr Nisbit, the theatre manager,' he explained. This news was greeted by several catcalls.

'I can see I've got some fans in tonight,' he said, which

raised a laugh. 'As you're well aware, it's Friday night, therefore I'd like to introduce, for your entertainment, our guest singer Miss Moira Tinning. A big hand for Miss Tinning please, ladies and gentlemen!'

It had been so long since Nellie had been to the pictures she'd forgotten that at weekends in the larger town cinemas there was often a singer in the interval. It was a tradition that went back as long as she could remember.

'She's not bad,' said Babs rejoining Nellie and handing over a tub of ice cream.

Nellie agreed. Moira Tinning had a pleasant voice indeed.

'She's not a patch on you though.'

The idea came to Nellie like a thunderbolt from the blue. 'What did you just say Babs?'

'I said she's not a patch on you. I think you've got the best singing voice I've ever heard.'

Nellie leaned forward to stare at Moira Tinning with renewed interest, her mind suddenly churning with ideas.

It wasn't a bad idea at all, and certainly one worth thinking about she decided as, having concluded her spot, Moira Tinning walked offstage to a warm round of applause.

The lights dimmed and the second feature started. But Nellie's mind was elsewhere.

She lay in bed listening to Jim snore. Her bed was a fold-down one that she made up every night over by the window, which was about as far away from him as she could get in that room.

She hadn't shared a bed with him since he'd come home from hospital. Nor would she ever again.

Would she have the nerve to stand up in front of several hundred people and sing, she asked herself. She wasn't sure, but she thought so. Singing in front of people had certainly never bothered her in the past. But then, they had always been small groups, friends and relations.

140

Going out in front of a mass of strangers would be a different matter entirely.

For a start, Glasgow audiences could be downright vicious if they didn't like you. She could remember one poor woman being pelted with all manner of things and all because she'd gone off key. On the other hand, of course, if Glasgow audiences took to you there was no one like them for warmth and appreciation.

Money, she thought. How much did someone like that Tinning lassie get paid? It must be fairly decent, surely? Perhaps even enough to take her and Jim off the parish.

God how she loathed and detested having to report every week for her money. They always succeeded in making her feel like a beggar or a parasite. That contemptuous look of the man who handed the money over. The way he had of looking down his nose at her, as though she was a bad smell suddenly wafted in his direction.

And always, always the feeling that she was somehow trying to put one over on them. That she was lazy, work-shy. And that they were, self-righteously, having to support her because of it.

And she did have a good voice. No doubt about that. The voice of an angel her da had always said. She made up her mind. She would have a go at it. After all, what did she have to lose? Nothing at all.

In the morning she would go round to the music shop and buy some sheet music. She couldn't really afford to, mind you, but it would have to be done. The sort of songs she knew weren't at all what would be required. And if she was going to have a bash at this she might as well do it properly.

The other problem was that she literally didn't have anything decent to wear, not having bought anything new since Jim's losing streak started. She'd have a word with Babs. Babs might have something she could borrow, or even give her.

Her head was spinning with plans when she finally fell asleep.

*

She was despondent. This was the fifth picture house she'd been to and so far no one even bothered to listen to her.

'We're already fixed up, hen,' one of them had said. Two of them had said, 'Sorry,' and the fourth, had kept her waiting over half an hour before finally going off somewhere for the rest of the day, leaving her sitting there like a fool. Had he forgotten her, or was he just being nasty? She suspected the former, but she could be wrong.

'I'd like to see the manager please,' she said to a woman cleaner.

'Down that passage there and third door on the right,' the cleaner replied.

She knocked.

'Come in!'

He had a kind-looking face she thought. 'Are you the manager?' she asked.

He laid down his pen and studied her. 'I am. What can I do for you?'

'I'm looking for a job singing at the weekend intervals. Have you anything going?'

'Not at the moment.'

Her heart sank. Another blank.

'But I'll listen to you and if I like what I hear I'll take your name and address in case something comes up. I'm afraid that's the best I can do.'

Well, at least she was making some progress, she thought. He was the first to show even a flicker of interest.

'Will I sing here?' she asked.

'In a wee room like this?' he laughed. 'No, I want to make sure you can hit the back of the circle.'

Once out the room she followed him down the corridor to a door that took them into the auditorium. They walked down to the front row of the stalls where he indicated a flight of steps running up the side of the proscenium arch that would take her on to the stage.

'Give me a minute to get up to the circle. I'll shout from there when to start,' he said, and, turning, strode away.

Once on stage she put down her handbag, but kept hold of her music. That for confidence more than anything else. There obviously wasn't going to be a pianist to accompany her. But no matter, she was used to singing on her own.

She stared out over the huge expense of red plush, a sea of it she thought. The walls were cream and gilt, further adorned in places with murals of Far Eastern scenes. High above was a glass dome that looked like it needed a good clean.

But what impressed her most was the sheer size of the place. It was so huge from up here, a veritable cavern.

'Are you ready?' the manager's voice bellowed from the back of the circle.

'Yes!' she shouted back.

'On you go, then!'

The song she'd chosen, thinking it appropriate for the occasion, was a number called 'At The Moving Picture Ball'.

Nervously, she began to sing, her voice hesitating but sweet.

She watched a couple of cleaners come in at the back of the stalls, rattling buckets, mops and brooms and talking to one another.

One of the cleaners laughed, then the other, the second having just delivered the tag line of a joke.

God Almighty! Nellie thought. She was accustomed to rapt audiences, not this sort of treatment. Well, she'd better get used to it, she told herself. For there would be a lot of it if she landed a job as an interval singer.

When she was finished she took a bow the way Moira Tinning had done. Up at the very back of the circle the manager had the graciousness to clap. She appreciated that.

The cleaners were now going about their business of

sweeping between the seats. They hadn't once glanced in her direction.

She went back down into the auditorium and waited for the manager.

'Very good,' he said coming up to her. 'And clear as a bell.'

He ushered her back to his office where he sat behind his desk.

'Have you done this sort of thing before?' he asked.

'No.'

He raised an eyebrow. 'In that case you were even better than I thought. And you've got charisma. That counts for a lot.'

Nellie wondered what charisma was.

He took up his pen. 'Name and address?' he asked. Carefully writing it down when she gave it to him.

When he'd filed that in his drawer he rose and, leaning across the desk, shook her hand. 'If anything comes up, I'll be in touch.'

At the door she turned to thank him but he was already lost in a sheaf of papers he'd started to read.

She closed the door quietly behind her.

It was six weeks since she'd done the rounds of the town picture houses and she was still as short of a job as ever. She sat gazing morosely into the fire.

'How about a cup of tea?' Jim demanded from his bed.

He was becoming more and more demanding of late. And petulant, too. 'In a minute.'

She glanced at the clock. Six o'clock on a Saturday night. All the young people would be home getting dressed ready to go out. God, how she envied them.

It was so incredibly boring being stuck at home for most of the day. Housework, cooking, body rubs, emptying Jim's pot – it was driving her crazy.

It might not have been so bad if she'd been a reader. There was a library nearby. But books had never really interested her all that much. Nine times out of ten she never got past the first chapter.

She started when the knock on the door came. She hoped it was Babs come visiting.

But it wasn't. It was a lad about fifteen years old.

'Are you Mrs Biles?' he asked.

'Aye.'

'Mister McRae sent me. He wants to know if you'll do the night?'

She was lost. 'Who's Mister McRae and what does he want me to do?'

'Who's Mister McRae!' the boy exclaimed, rolling his eyes upwards. 'He's only the manager. And he wants you to sing.'

Excitement gripped her. It had happened. At long last it had happened!

'Manager of which picture house?' she asked patiently.

'The Kingsway in West Nile Street.'

The Kingsway. Her mind flew back. Of course! He was the nice man who'd been the first to ask her to sing. He'd sat at the back of the circle while those dreadful cleaners made such a racket. She'd never even found out his name. Up until now.

'Well, will you come?' the lad demanded.

'What time does he want me there?'

'As soon as you can make it. The first singing interval's at five past eight.'

'Tell Mister McRae I'm on my way,' she said.

'Do you want me to wait for you?'

'No, no. You go ahead. I'll have to change first.'

'Aye, well don't take too long about it.'

She indicated her pinny. 'You don't expect me to go on and sing in this do you?'

He gave her a cheeky grin. 'See you again shortly then,' he called running down the stairs.

For a moment or two she stood in the doorway, a dozen things tumbling through her mind at once.

'Who is it?' Jim shouted from the kitchen.

She ignored him. First thing to do was to get someone to look after him while she was out.

She hurried up the stairs, praying as she went that Myra Finlayson was home. From time to time, Myra had looked after Jim.

She rapped Myra's door and waited impatiently. She rapped again almost at once.

'Aye, what is it Nellie?' Myra's mother asked, opening the door.

Nellie quickly explained her mission and Myra's ma said yes, Myra was home and would be only too happy to look after Jim while Nellie went into town.

'She'll be down in a minute,' Myra's ma said to Nellie's already retreating back.

'Right!' Nellie called back up the stair.

'What the hell's going on?' Jim demanded querulously when she burst into the kitchen.

She told him in a few short, terse sentences as she pulled her dress off and quickly washed herself at the sink.

Jim knew about her trying to get a job as an interval singer, and in fact had been rather scathing about it, asking if she didn't think she wasn't getting a wee bit above herself? After all, you had to be good to stand up in front of all those folk. The implication being that she wasn't as good as she thought she was.

She was making up when Myra chapped the door. 'Come away in,' she said, ushering Myra through. She'd just managed to afford the make-up out of their meagre income. It had lain new and untouched in its box against this very moment.

When her make-up was complete, she slipped into the dress Babs had given her and which she'd virtually remade. It fitted well and looked a treat.

It was the work of a moment to put on her best pair of shoes and get into her coat. Picking up her music she stuffed it into her pocket.

'Will I do?' she asked.

'You look right smashing,' said Myra.

146

Jim grunted.

'I'm away then,' she said. 'Wish me luck!'

'All the best Nellie!' Myra called out as Nellie flew from the house. Jim remained silent.

Standing waiting for the tram Nellie thought of Myra Finlayson, or the daftie as some of the crueller children in the neighbourhood called her. She was a little mentally backward or eleven pence ha'penny in the shilling, as a neighbour had been heard to remark, but she was a good soul of whom Nellie was genuinely fond. Kind, warm hearted, nothing was ever too much trouble for Myra if you asked her to help you.

At nineteen, Myra was unemployed and had been since leaving school. Although she looked a lot simpler than she actually was, the natural slow way she had about her made employers reluctant to give her a job.

After all, why take a chance when there were far brighter sparks clamouring for work, any work, when it became available?

Nellie often thought of her as poor Myra upstairs.

'I'm glad you could make it, Mrs Biles,' Mr McRae said when she entered his office. A glance at his watch confirmed there was still plenty of time before the first singing interval.

'Were you let down by your regular?' she asked.

He picked up a letter from his desk and waved it at her. 'This came in this morning but I never got round to reading it until early evening. Says she's had a better offer from elsewhere and has to start there the night, which, of course, well and truly lumbered me. Till I remembered you, that is. Now how about a cup of tea before you go on?'

'Yes please,' she replied. She had butterflies in her stomach and her brain felt as though it had been partially anaesthetized. She kept thinking of the huge audience awaiting her in the auditorium. She knew it was huge because she'd seen the HOUSE FULL signs on the way in.

Mr McRae left her to order the tea, returning with a bespectacled man whom he introduced as Charlie, the pianist.

She shook Charlie's hand, noticing her own was trembling slightly, and handed over her music which he glanced at briefly.

'Just give me the nod when you're ready,' said Charlie. Adding kindly, 'And if you're a wee bit nervous don't worry. *I'll* be following *you*.'

'Thank you,' she said gratefully.

The tea came which she drank, glancing up at the clock on the wall every few seconds as she did so.

Charlie had gone off with her music leaving her with Mr McRae, who immediately became immersed in work at his desk. On the stroke of eight he looked up and smiled.

'Ready?'

Despite the tea her throat was parched dry. When she returned his smile her muscles were so tense she thought her face must surely crack. 'Ready,' she replied.

She followed him down the same red plush corridor that she remembered from her previous visit. Only this time instead of going into the auditorium he took her up some back stairs which eventually led them into the wings.

She stared up in awe at the enormous silver screen upon which the film's credits were rolling. Then the screen was blank and the red curtains were swishing closed.

'I'll introduce you. Your cue to come on stage being when I turn to face you and start clapping my hands. Got that?'

'Yes,' she whispered in reply.

'Good luck then.' Leaving her he strode on to the stage.

'Ladies and gentlemen. Tonight I have a special treat for you . . .'

Panic was going to engulf her she thought. She

suddenly wanted to turn and run. Jim was right, she was
mad thinking she could do this. It all looked so easy from
out front. But here, waiting to go on, it was a different
matter entirely.

And the audience, they terrified her. They were like
some great animal waiting to pounce and devour her once
she stepped on stage.

The insides of her legs had started to tremble and her
heart was beating nineteen to the dozen. She knew with
certainty that when she opened her mouth to sing nothing
would come.

And then, suddenly, the moment had arrived. Mr
McRae was clapping and smiling at her. Still she
hesitated, completely terrified. He was beckoning to her
now.

Forcing herself she put one step in front of the other,
smiling fixedly she headed for centre stage, she felt like
she was walking to her own execution.

There seemed to be millions of faces staring at her.
Some expectantly. Others bored. Others talking amongst
themselves.

And the heat! It hit her like a wave. Perspiration burst
on her head and back. She clasped her hands together so
that the audience wouldn't see how badly they were
shaking.

She glanced down at Charlie in the pit, giving him the
nod that she was ready. She opened her mouth and,
completely surprising her, words came out. She sang:

> 'I fetch his slippers,
> Fill up the pipe he smokes,
> Join up with gyppers,
> Laugh at his oldest jokes;
> Yet here I anchor –
> I might have had a banker –
> Boy! What love has done to me!'

*

149

She came off to find Mr McRae waiting for her. 'How was I?' she asked.

'Fine. Not bad at all.'

'Can I have the job then?'

'Let's go to my office and talk money.'

As they left the wings, the audience was still applauding.

That night in bed she couldn't sleep. At long, long last she had a job! And what she would be getting per week and for only working the Friday and Saturday nights, would be fractionally more than what she was getting now from the parish. Come Monday morning she would take the greatest delight in going round to see the buggers and telling them she didn't need their money any more.

She thought again of herself out on that stage, singing. Going on had been sheer murder but once started she couldn't remember enjoying anything more. Especially after the first number when she knew the audience was for her.

What had happened to her up on that stage was a strange feeling to describe. Like love, almost. Yes, that was it. Love.

A shiver ran through her. She hadn't experienced those sort of emotions since . . . since Frank.

She couldn't wait for next Friday night to come round so she could get back out there again.

'Boy! What love has done to me!' she sang softly in the darkness.

5

The moment she'd first clapped eyes on Brownlee, which was only ten minutes previously, she'd thought him a hard-eyed sod. What he was saying to her now confirmed that opinion.

'I'm sorry Mrs Biles, but that's it. A fortnight's notice as from tomorrow,' he said coldly.

Brownlee was sitting behind what, up until that week, had been Ronnie McRae's desk. Dear Ronnie who, three-and-a-half years ago, had hired her as an interval singer. Nor had she missed a Friday or Saturday since.

'I know you're very popular with the audiences,' Brownlee went on, 'but now that I've taken over, I feel it's time for a change. A fresh face and voice so to speak. I'm sure you'll have no trouble finding employment elsewhere.'

Ronnie McRae's transfer to the Odeon, Paisley, had been a surprise to them all, Ronnie included. But, as he himself had said, it was company policy to move their managers about and he had been at the Kingsway a long time.

He'd also said to Nellie that he'd happily give her a job at his new picture house, an offer she'd had to refuse as Paisley was just too far to travel.

The entire theatre staff had clubbed together to give Ronnie a going-away present. They'd all had enormous respect and liking for him. He'd been a gem.

151

'What about Charlie?' she asked. She was referring to Charlie Muchan, her accompanist.

'He'll be going as well,' Brownlee replied.

Nellie nodded to herself. An era had come to an end. Glancing up at the clock on the wall she saw it was time for her to get ready for her first spot. Muttering her excuses she left the room.

She went out onto the stage to rapturous applause. Over the years she'd become a great favourite. Later, when she came off, there were tears in her eyes.

'You got the bullet as well?' Charlie asked when they got together for their usual cup of tea between spots.

'Aye.'

Charlie offered her a cigarette and they both lit up. They'd become very friendly since that first night she'd appeared on the Kingsway stage. A number of times she'd been over to his house to have tea with his wife and weans.

'So what'll you do now?' he asked.

The thought of having to go back on the parish made her cringe inside. But that was what she'd have to do unless she found another job. The pound a week the Masons paid Jim from their Benevolent Committee, the award being made shortly after she'd started work at the Kingsway, was hardly enough for them to get by on.

'Start chapping doors again,' she replied morosely. 'I've got a fortnight so I can hope and pray I'll land something in that time.'

'One of the other town picture halls might have an opening for a singer?' Charlie suggested hopefully.

Nellie shook her head. 'They're all happily fixed up at the moment, I know that for fact.'

Nellie thought of Big Jessie, married and moved away to another part of Glasgow. With Jessie gone from the Bastille she could always try there again. But she doubted that would be any good. She'd been branded a bad worker. And that sort of thing wasn't forgotten.

Thinking of Harrison's made her think of Babs, also married, and very happily, to Phil Drummond. They had

152

a wee boy called Ian who was the spit of his da. She smiled to think how even yet Babs still referred to Phil on occasion as her *Fate*.

Charlie frowned and stroked the left leg of his spectacles, a gesture of his when thinking.

'I did hear something the other day which might interest you,' he said.

'Oh, aye?'

'Do you know the Palace Theatre down in Jamaica Street?'

She nodded.

'Well, they're opening a new show there shortly and I heard they'll be auditioning sometime soon for lassies who can sing and dance.'

'What do you mean by sometime soon?'

'Next week I would imagine.'

The Palace was a well-respected variety theatre which put on many of the country's best acts. Harry Lauder himself had played there.

Nellie had been to the Palace twice, both times years ago before she'd met Jim.

To go into the professional theatre was an attractive thought and one which very much appealed. The singing she could cope with, of that she had no doubt. But what about dancing? She had no experience of that whatever.

'What's the pay like?' she asked.

He shrugged. 'Fair I would think. Certainly more than you're getting here.'

Then that was another big plus in its favour. And her current wage at the Kingsway wasn't all that bad either. Ronnie McRae had upped her money four times since taking her on. Each time he'd done so, he'd said she was more than worth it as her presence nearly always guaranteed a full house.

She would certainly have a go she decided. After all, she had nothing to lose – and everything to gain.

'I'll make enquiries tomorrow,' she said, excitement in her voice. 'Now what about you?'

And over the rest of their tea they talked about Charlie's prospects.

She was nervous, but not to the point where she was shaking, as she entered the Palace's stage door. She was confronted by an empty cubicle.

What to do now, she wondered. Best wait. There was a board with papers tacked to it on the wall facing the cubicle, which she crossed to and idly started to read.

When there was a noise behind her she turned abruptly to bump into a tiny, bald-headed man who went spinning to crash against the cubicle.

She was appalled. 'Oh I'm awful sorry!' she said as the stage doorkeeper came dizzily to his feet having nearly fallen.

She put her arm round his shoulders, he was considerably smaller than she, and said, 'Are you all right?'

'I think so,' he replied, shaking his head.

'I am sorry.'

'Not your fault. Mine. I should have been looking where I was going,' he said taking her in for the first time, his eyes brown and warm.

He was wearing some sort of cologne Nellie decided, finding it strange and amusing. She'd never met a man before who wore cologne. In Govan that would've been thought of as jessie. A man wouldn't have dared wear it, even had he wanted to.

Oh well, she thought. This was the professional theatre. She was sure a man wearing cologne wouldn't be the only strange thing she'd come up against.

'Are you here for the auditions?' the man asked.

'Aye. The Palace Ladies.'

Reaching into the cubicle he picked up a sheet of paper which had a list of names on it. Against some of these names were tick marks.

'Name?' he asked.

'Nellie Biles.'

He looked up at her, smiling. 'You're early.'

'Better that than late.'

'True,' he said, replacing the piece of paper in the cubicle. 'I'm on my way past the stage. Will I take you through?'

'Please.'

Blonde and marvellous green eyes he thought. Unusual combination for this part of the country. Quite a looker, too. 'Follow me then,' he said, and led the way.

On arriving at wooden swing doors the doorkeeper stopped and, turning to her, said, 'Through these, through the doors facing those and if you go down left you'll find a boy called Sandy. He'll look after you.'

'Thank you very much.'

'Good luck.' Giving her a salute with his hand he went on his way.

The stage itself was far bigger than she'd imagined. There was clutter everywhere. And everything looked so grimy!

She made her way down left past several bits of scenery – and how tawdry they were up close – to where a young boy was standing beside some ropes which were tied off and running upwards to disappear behind a catwalk above. On stage, a girl was singing, but she couldn't see her because of the intervening scenery.

'I'm Nellie Biles,' she whispered to the boy.

He consulted a sheet of paper, a copy of the one in the stage doorkeeper's cubicle. 'You're early,' he said.

'Yes.'

He chewed on a finger before making up his mind. 'All right, I'll put you on next. Although you really should wait your turn.'

'Sorry,' she replied apologetically.

'That's all right,' he grinned.

The singing stopped and a male voice could now be heard on stage.

'That's the stage director, Roderique Mansell,' Sandy

155

said. He pronounced Mansell with two syllables, Man-sell.

Roderique? Nellie smiled to herself. She'd never heard of a man being called that before. He must be foreign, Spanish perhaps.

'You done this before?' Sandy asked.

She shook her head.

'That's good. They like new faces.'

There was the sound of dancing from the stage which went on for about a minute. Then Mansell's voice said, 'Fine dear. You'll do.'

'Thank you ever much, Mister Mansell,' a female voice answered. The girl came off smiling gratefully.

'Next!' Mansell bellowed.

The girl gave Nellie an encouraging smile as they walked past one another. 'Good luck,' she whispered.

Nellie went through a door in the scenery to emerge blinking into harsh white light which shone from above and out front.

'Name?' Mansell snapped.

'Nellie Biles.'

'Tell me, *briefly*, about yourself.'

Help, Nellie thought as she spoke. What sort of man was this?

Beside Roderique Mansell, a little cologne was nothing at all. His hair was dyed, and his face made-up. He stood staring at her, one hand on hip, the other dangling delicately by his side. When she'd finished speaking he came up close to her. 'Let me see your legs,' he said.

She pulled up her skirt to above the knee. 'Higher dearie. Don't waste my time,' he snapped.

She pulled her skirt up to mid-thigh.

'Hmmh!' he said, sounding none too pleased. There was something sly about him, something sly and calculating. And something else she couldn't put her finger on. Then, suddenly it hit her! Bitchiness. That was it. It was a look she'd seen on certain women but never on a man before.

Turning abruptly, Mansell jumped over the footlights into the auditorium. He strode up the aisle to a seat roughly halfway. 'Sing!' he commanded.

She didn't like him at all. And what's more, she was sure he didn't like her. But she put that from her mind as she sang, concentrating on where she was and why. When she finished she knew she'd never sung better.

Mansell sat staring at her for a few seconds, then, coming to his feet, he strode toward the stage. When he was standing beside her he held out his arms, indicating she should come into them.

'Waltz. You lead,' he said.

It confused her to dance without music, and even more because she had never led before. She did her best, however, surprised that she finished as well as she had.

Mansell stood, posing, regarding her. Finally he said, 'No. You're quite wrong, darling. Sorry.'

She was dismissed.

Sandy smiled apologetically when she rejoined him. 'Too bad,' he said.

She watched a dark-haired girl enter the same door she'd just come through. She couldn't believe she hadn't got the job. In her mind she'd convinced herself – oh so stupidly she could see now – that she had. It was a terrible disappointment that she hadn't.

At the stage doorkeeper's cubicle she stopped to light a cigarette. She would stand here and smoke it, until she calmed down and the threat of tears had passed.

'Well, did you get it?'

She turned to find the wee, bald-headed doorkeeper smiling at her. She shook her head.

His smile faded, replaced by a frown. 'Why not?'

'Mister Mansell said I was quite wrong.'

'And that was all?'

'Yes.'

He studied her afresh. She was a knockout. Mansell should have grabbed her. Not only beautiful but talented, too. He'd heard her singing from the back of the

157

auditorium. He knew then why Mansell had turned her down. He simply didn't want someone around who was prettier than he was.

It was time Mansell was taken down a peg or two. He had been getting far too big for his boots of late.

Suddenly he wasn't so nice and cuddly anymore. His eyes glinted as he said in a steely voice, 'What's your name again?'

'Nellie Biles.'

'You come with me, Nellie.'

She wondered what the doorkeeper wanted with her, but she followed him unquestioningly. It hadn't been a request. It had been an order.

Sandy, who'd been sitting, jumped to his feet the moment the doorkeeper and Nellie appeared.

'Sorry. You're not for us,' Mansell's voice said on stage.

The dark-haired girl who'd followed Nellie through the set door reappeared to shrug. 'Can't win them all,' she quipped in a tired, dispirited voice.

'Stay here,' the doorkeeper said to Nellie, and strode on to the set.

'You didn't say you knew him. Did you tell Mansell?' Sandy asked in a whisper.

'Know who?'

'Him. Mister Spira.'

'You mean the doorkeeper?'

Sandy grinned. 'He's not the doorkeeper. He *owns* the bloody place.'

'Oh!' was all Nellie could think of in reply.

On stage, Roderique Mansell was glowering at Baz Spira. 'She'll unbalance the line,' he said.

'Nonsense.'

'She's too different from the rest. She'll stick out like a sore thumb.'

'Then put her in the middle. Make a centrepiece of her.'

'Baz, I know my job –'

158

'And I know mine. What's more, I employ you. And you'll do as I say.'

'And if I don't?'

'There's a train leaves for Liverpool every evening. You can be on tonight's.'

Mansell winced. Though he came from Liverpool he much preferred having people believe he came from London.

Roderique Mansell swallowed hard and thought even harder. This was a good job and well paid. Jobs like this, even with his vast experience, weren't exactly ten a penny. And it suited him to stay in Glasgow for the time being. He'd found a 'friend' in one of the other shows whom he was dotty on.

'Well?' Baz Spira demanded.

'As you say, you're the boss.'

'And don't you ever forget it, Roderique,' Baz replied. 'That Biles girl is exactly the type to have in the show. She's got class, quality. A line consisting of a dozen like her would make the Palace Ladies the best in Scotland. Britain even.'

'I'll build the line round her then,' Mansell replied.

'Now you're talking.'

'She isn't a particularly good dancer.'

'Then teach her. What do you think I pay you for?' Mansell nodded. 'I'll do my best.'

'That's what I expect from you, same as everyone else in this theatre, including myself. Their best.'

Baz Spira strode off set to find Nellie waiting for him, eyes shining. She'd overheard every word.

'Thank you,' she said.

'That applies to you too,' he said, his eyes suddenly twinkling mischievously. 'Your best.'

She watched Baz Spira waddle away, then turned her attention to Sandy who was asking her address.

A few seconds later Mansell, his eyes blazing, brushed past. The look he gave her told her she'd made an enemy.

*

'That's marvellous news, Nellie,' said Myra Finlayson clapping her hands together.

Jim looked out sourly from the bed. 'And what about me? Who's going to look after me?' he demanded. 'For I sure as hell can't look after myself all day while you're rehearsing. Or at nights even while you're doing the show.'

It was a problem Nellie had already given considerable thought to. 'Myra,' she said, choosing her words carefully, 'how would you fancy the job of looking after Jim on a permanent basis? I couldn't pay you very much, but I'll give you what I can. And of course you'll eat here as you'll be cooking for Jim.'

Myra's homely features broke into a smile. She enjoyed looking after Jim. It made her feel useful.

'I'd like that fine,' she replied.

'Jim?'

'It's time for my back rub,' he grumbled.

'I'll do it,' said Myra quickly.

Nellie put the kettle on. It was settled.

Her call was for ten o'clock which was an awful late start she thought. But she certainly wasn't complaining. At the stage door she found the real doorkeeper in his cubicle.

'I'm here for rehearsals,' she said.

'Name?'

'Nellie Biles.'

He checked her name against his list, grunting when he found it. 'Away through to the green room,' he said.

The green room wasn't green at all and she wondered why it was called that. There were a number of easy chairs, one of which she sank into after greeting the other girls.

By one minute to ten the full dozen girls who would be

160

making up the Palace Ladies were present. On the stroke of ten Roderique Mansell breezed in.

He was dressed like something straight out of the pictures, Nellie thought. He might have been Ali Baba or Sinbad the Sailor.

Sandy was with Mansell. When he saw Nellie he gave her a fly wink.

Nellie was one of five new girls, the other seven having been in the previous show. Starting with a pretty, dark-haired girl called Liz, each of the dozen was asked to stand up and introduce herself. When that was completed Mansell spoke for a good ten minutes about the theatre, the forthcoming show and himself. But mainly about himself, continually preening and striking poses as he talked.

When he was finally finished he said, 'Right, we'll have coffee now and then up to the dressing rooms to change into rehearsal clothes. We'll be rehearsing on stage.'

Rehearsal clothes? Nobody had mentioned anything about those to her. What were they?

'Mister Mansell?'

He gave her an irritated look. 'Yes?'

'I'm afraid I haven't brought any special clothes to rehearse in. I wasn't told.'

He waved one hand in the air. 'Of course you weren't told, darling! One presumes you know. I mean, it's absolutely basic isn't it?'

'I'm sorry,' she mumbled. She could feel her face redden with embarrassment.

'I knew you were going to be trouble. It's written all over you.'

She wanted to snap back at him, but, wanting the job, decided to keep her mouth shut.

'Huh!' said Mansell, turning to the other girls who were milling round a tray of coffee that Sandy had brought in. 'Here's one doesn't even know enough to bring rehearsal clothes with her! Talk about amateur.'

161

Several of the girls tittered, and Nellie blushed even more. How could she not have thought of it?

Mansell was enjoying making Nellie squirm. 'If you didn't bring rehearsal clothes I don't suppose you thought to bring flats with you?' he asked maliciously.

She hadn't a clue what flats were. And seeing her expression Mansell guessed as much.

'Ballet flats, darling. For dancing.'

'No,' she said.

'Not much use to us then this morning are you, darling?'

She bit her lip.

'It's all right, Mister Mansell,' one of the girls piped up. 'I've got a spare set of clothes upstairs and her feet look about the same size as mine. She can borrow my old flats.'

Nellie flashed the girl a grateful smile.

Irritation crowded Mansell's face. His sport had been cut short. Snapping his fingers he said, 'On the green in five minutes,' and signalling to Sandy to follow, sauntered from the room.

Nellie crossed straightaway to the girl who'd saved her further embarrassment, and perhaps her job even. 'Thanks,' she said.

The girl stuck out a hand. 'I'm Margo, as you probably heard when I introduced myself.'

'And I'm Nellie, as you probably heard.'

'We'd better get upstairs and changed. When Roderique says five minutes he means just that.'

There were two dressing rooms, each long and narrow. Nellie chose a place beside Margo. From now on that would be her dressing table.

The rehearsal clothes turned out to be black tights and an old sweater. The flats were black leather with a very thin sole. As they changed Margo told her where she could buy flats of her own.

'He certainly seems to have got his knife into you,' Margo whispered, not wanting any of the other girls to overhear.

Nellie told her about the audition and the fact she'd been hired at Mr Spira's insistence.

'Nice man, Mister Spira,' Margo said. 'Not like that Mansell. I don't think he's got a soft spot in his body, unless it's his head.'

'What about the rest of the people in the show? When do they come along and rehearse?' Nellie asked Margo. It was lunchtime that day and they were sitting in a café having coffee and a sandwich.

'They don't rehearse. At least not with us,' Margo explained. 'They're all self-contained acts which come and go from week to week. You see, we, the Palace Ladies, are the only constant thing about the show. And even then we change our routines every month. An act will be booked for a week or a fortnight, perhaps, fulfil the engagement and then move on.'

'Oh, I understand.'

'The show will run for ten months and then the theatre will go dark for two.'

'Dark?'

'Close down. There's never any business in those two months which include the fair anyway.'

The Glasgow Fair was the fortnight when, apart from insurance offices, banks and food shops, the entire city closed down and went on holiday. For those who could afford holidays, that was.

Margo went on, 'Mister Spira usually goes away for the first month. When he comes back a new show is put together and the whole thing starts all over again.'

'How many shows have you been in?'

'This is my third. And I hope not my last.'

It was the opening night and five minutes had been called. Nellie was trembling with excitement. She couldn't wait to get out there.

'Nervous?' Margo asked.

'A little. But I'm looking forward to it.'

A natural performer, Margo thought. She'd come to that conclusion in rehearsals as, grudgingly, had Mansell. Not only was Nellie a natural, but she was also different, special in some way. She stood out from the rest of the line, not only because she was physically outstanding but also because she had, as Ronnie McRae had once told her, charisma.

They were in the wings waiting for the curtains, or the rag as Mansell called it, to open.

Nellie noticed a small man in baggy trousers, wearing an old coat and battered hat, with a pipe stuck in his mouth. His eyes were droopy, as though he was half asleep.

'Who's that?' she asked, nudging Margo. She'd never seen this man around before.

'Who?'

'Him over there.'

Margo glanced across at the man who gave her a wave. 'He's the top of the bill,' she said.

'Will Fyffe?'

'The same.'

Nellie stared in awe at the man who was a household name in Glasgow. Only Harry Lauder was bigger.

'He always stands in the wings for the first few minutes of every performance,' Margo said. 'He does it to get the feel of the audience before going on stage.'

'Go curtains!' a voice said.

Nellie took a deep breath as the curtains swung apart. Then she was on stage dancing, smiling – all teeth and tits darling, as Mansell put it – at the audience.

One of the differences between this and interval singing was that here the auditorium lights were off so she was staring into a black hole. On cue she started to sing, her voice soaring above the others. She was in her element.

*

'Very good, girls! Very good!' Baz Spira said, coming into the dressing room. He was carrying two bottles of champagne.

Several of the girls squealed with delight as a popped cork bounced off the ceiling. The second one flew across the room like a bullet.

It was the first time Nellie had tasted champagne. She liked it. There was an elegance about it which appealed.

'You did really well tonight,' Baz said to her. 'Justified my faith in you completely. But then, I knew you would.'

He moved on down the row of dressing tables, congratulating each girl in turn. Then he was gone.

Nellie cleansed her face of the heavy make-up, 'slap' Margo called it, then changed out of her costume into her street clothes.

Margo kept her make-up on but toned it down a little. 'Going out on the town with my chap,' she confided.

'Where to at this hour?' Nellie asked. It was well past pub closing time, and other places, like restaurants, would be shut as well. Glasgow was notorious for going to bed early.

'There are places. Clubs and the like. If you're in the know,' Margo replied.

'What sort of clubs?'

'Drinking. Gambling.'

Nellie was surprised. It was the first time she'd ever realized that type of establishment operated in Glasgow. It just showed, she reflected, how naïve and innocent she was about certain things.

'What about you?' Margo asked.

'Och, I'm away home to my bed.'

'Well, you've got a man to go back to after all.'

Nellie slowly lit a cigarette. She'd told Margo about Jim, and the fact that he was paralysed, but not that their marriage was a complete bust and she could hardly stand the sight of him.

What a relief it had been, these last few weeks, to be out of the house and away from him. She felt like she'd been

165

reborn after all those months of being with only Jim day in and day out, and all those nights in between.

'What does your boyfriend do?' she asked.

'He's a chartered accountant.'

Nellie was impressed. An accountant was awfully grand. 'Are you going to marry him?'

Instantly, Margo's face fell. 'We have a problem there. I'm a Catholic, you see, and he's not.'

That Margo was a Catholic surprised Nellie, she didn't look like one at all.

Involuntarily Nellie thought of Frank Connelly, experiencing the same dull ache she did every time she did so. 'Why don't you go abroad together?'

'We've thought of that, but it's not really possible. He's too well established here to give it up. And then there's the matter of qualifications wherever we went.'

Nellie took her friend's hand and held it gently. 'Do you love him?'

'Aye.'

'Then God help you.'

Later, at the stage door, Nellie met the boyfriend, a chap called Bob Copeland. He was in his late thirties and very well spoken. She liked him.

'Have a good time,' she said, waving them on their way.

Catholics and Protestants, she thought as she trudged toward the tram stop with her coat collar turned up against the drizzle. The foundation of all her own problems. How much heartbreak had that bigoted division caused? She hated to think.

Poor Margo, she could have cried for her.

It was one night several months later that she was standing at the tram stop when a car drew up. The window rolled down and a voice said, 'Nellie?'

'Hello, Mister Spira,' she replied in surprise.

'Can I give you a lift?'

166

'I'm going to Govan.'

The door swung open. 'That's not too far out of my way.'

She got into the car, which smelled deliciously of polish and leather. 'This is awful kind of you.'

'Nonsense. It's a pleasure.'

They drove toward Eglinton Street, turning right for the Paisley Road. 'How are you enjoying being in the theatre then?' he asked, breaking the awkward silence.

'I'm loving it.'

'Aye. That comes across.'

'I take it that's a compliment.'

'Oh indeed!' he laughed.

'Have you owned the Palace long?' she asked.

'A little over twenty years. And to be quite accurate I don't actually own it. My wife does. The twenty years is how long we've been married.' He stared intently at the road ahead. 'The theatre was part of her dowry,' he added.

'Pardon?'

He smiled in the darkness. 'We come from old families and keep our old customs. We still believe in dowries and arranged marriages.'

Nellie was intrigued. 'Was your marriage arranged, then?' she asked shyly.

'Yes.'

'And didn't you mind?'

'No. Why should I? It's the custom. Besides, I was getting a theatre which was something I'd always wanted. I've always been in the theatre, you see. Started off backstage at twelve and graduated to about every job there is. Flyman, dayman, I've even operated the limes. I've also worked as a booker down in London to get to know that side of things. Good job it was, too. I thoroughly enjoyed it.'

'You make your marriage sound so . . .' She stopped herself, thinking she might well be going over the mark.

'Go on.'

'You might think it cheeky, especially coming from an employee.'

'Go on anyway. I'm interested in what you have to say.'

She said hesitatingly, 'You make it sound rather clinical if you don't mind my saying so. A bit cut and dried.'

'And it is,' he replied. 'But as I told you, that's our way. At least for some of us.'

There was silence for a while and then he said, 'Are you really so shocked?'

'I suppose I am.'

'You believe the only good marriages are those based on love?'

'Yes,' she said.

He chuckled. 'Love's a transient thing. It comes. It goes. And when it's gone you may well be left with someone totally unsuitable. Our way, well . . . you work at it. To begin with you work at respecting your partner and with that respect love often comes later. A love built on solid, secure, foundations that will endure to the grave.'

'And what happens if that love doesn't come?'

'Then you have the respect to fall back on. And that in itself can make a worthwhile marriage. Believe you me.'

She was dying to ask him if he'd come to love his wife, but did not dare. 'And if there's no respect?' she asked, thinking of Jim.

Baz shrugged, glancing sideways at her. 'Then you make the best of what you've got, I suppose.'

Nellie couldn't help wondering what Babs – and surely there was no bigger romantic than her with her *Mr Right* and *Fate* – would have made of this conversation. Been completely scandalized, no doubt.

Again they drove in silence, she lost in thought.

'A penny for them?' he said eventually.

She roused herself. 'Oh, no, I couldn't!'

'Come on. I won't be offended.'

'Are you sure?'

'Certain,' he replied, laughter in his voice.

'If you got the theatre as part of your wife's dowry, then what did she get in return?'

'Good practical question,' he said. 'You know, you Scots and we Jews have a great deal in common. We're both very practical people. What did she get? Two things. I come from a better family than she, although a poor one as opposed to her rich one, so she was improving herself and any family we had together. She was also getting someone who could run her theatre for her. And when I say run it, I mean make a success of it. As I've done, I think I might say.'

'So you have some families who have better –' she groped for the right word.

'Ancestry?'

'Yes. Ancestry than others?'

'That's correct. My wife marrying me was the same as, well, you marrying someone of the landed gentry.' He added suddenly, 'I hope that hasn't offended *you*?'

'Not at all,' she laughed. 'I'm working class through and through. Rough as they come.'

'Working class, maybe. But not rough,' he said quietly.

She smiled. And then started to give directions for her turning.

Baz Spira slipped into the back of the auditorium just in time to catch the end of the vent, or ventriloquist, act which he could tell right away the audience hadn't enjoyed.

It was a new act that he'd booked in for a week. Well, good as the act was, and he knew it was artistically good, it seemed Glasgow audiences just didn't like it. The man wouldn't be getting an extension or a return engagement.

Then the vent was off and the Palace Ladies were on. And immediately the whole atmosphere changed.

Where minutes before the audience had been muted,

restless, they were now alive, leaning forward in their seats to hear and see just that little bit better.

The girls were good, Baz thought. But no better than previous lines. What was different about this particular line was one girl in particular: Nellie Biles.

No doubt about it. She had magic on stage. As soon as she stepped on the boards she lit up, creating an aura, an electricity about her. She had the ability that all great artistes must have, to draw the audience to her, to empathize with them.

She shone in the middle of the line like a jewel, her dazzle so strong, she completely dimmed the glamour of those around her. It was high time he promoted her. Brought her on a bit. Not too quickly – which could destroy her – but at the right pace.

He had a potential moneymaker here. He knew that with certainty. All his theatrical instincts and hard-won knowledge screamed it.

He would give Roderique Mansell his instructions after the show.

'I've never known any girl get as many flowers as you,' said Margo. The curtain was just down a few minutes and the line had returned to their dressing rooms to change into their street clothes.

Nellie shook her head in amazement at the huge bunch of red roses she now held in her hand, which had been waiting for her on her dressing table.

'Who's it from?' Margo asked eagerly.

There was a card upon which was written: Please accept this small token of my esteem. Humbly yours, Edward Tallis.

'Never heard of him,' said Nellie.

'Well he must be worth a bit if he can send you red roses,' said Margo.

'I suppose I'll have to take them home,' said Nellie. There were already four bunches of flowers in vases on her dressing table, all handed in backstage by admirers.

She laid the roses to one side and started to remove her slap. It had started not long after the show had opened. flowers, presents, invitations out.

The flowers and gifts she accepted, but never the invitations. The truth was, she didn't really want to know about men. Jim Biles was more than enough.

Nightly she thanked God he was paralysed and unable to come to her. Just thinking of what she'd had to endure at those hands – those terrible hands – was enough to make her skin crawl.

She might have gone out with them if she'd thought it would have stopped at conversation, a few drinks, a meal. But men were never content with just that. They always wanted more. And so she refused them all.

A few catty comments were made about the roses by several of the other girls, the ones who were jealous of her popularity, but she ignored them as she always did.

When she and Margo were ready they made their way down to the stage door where, as was often the case, they found a number of men waiting for a chance to speak to the particular girl who'd caught their eye. Of the six men there, five wanted to speak to Nellie. One of them was Edward Tallis.

Nellie, as she always did, had a quick word with each of them.

'Thank you for these beautiful flowers,' she said to Edward Tallis, a tallish, handsome man in his early thirties. The cut and style of his clothes, not to mention his accent, confirmed what Margo had guessed. He wouldn't be worrying where his next meal was coming from.

'I was wondering if I could possibly take you out tonight? Or if not tonight another night?' he asked hopefully.

Nellie smiled shyly. He seemed a nice sort of chap – and for a second she wished that things were different. 'I'm afraid I'm married,' she replied.

His face fell. 'Oh!'

'I'm sorry,' she said softly, and with Margo by her side moved on, leaving the five men staring after her.

'He wasn't bad at all,' commented Margo. 'Now, if that had been me he'd been asking, I'd have been tempted.'

'Get away with you. You're happy with the man you've got.'

'Aye,' sighed Margo. 'I suppose I am.'

'Be thankful. Believe me, be thankful.'

Margo looked at her quickly, surprised by the passion in her voice.

They parted, for Margo's tram stop was a different one to Nellie's and round the corner.

'Nellie, like a lift?'

Baz Spira didn't always give Nellie a lift. Some nights he wasn't in the theatre or went home early; others he worked on after the show was over. But at least once or twice a week, he waited for her.

'It went well tonight,' he said when she was seated beside him and they were on their way.

'I thought so, too.'

'Our audiences have really taken to you, you know.'

She smiled. 'Thank you.'

'Credit where it's due. That's what I always say.'

She decided she would give the roses to Myra Finlayson. Myra would go potty over them.

And, thinking of Myra, sighing to herself, she wondered just how long it was going to be before she heard that Jim's turn had come up for an institution bed. Still, they had warned her it could drag on.

'I had a word with Roderique Mansell before leaving tonight,' Baz said.

Nellie roused herself from her thoughts about Jim. 'Oh, yes?'

'As you know, the line starts rehearsals Monday for the monthly change of routines. Well, I've decided I'm going to feature you.'

A sense of joy and jubilation – and even of vindication –

172

welled through Nellie. Lately, being on stage had come to mean a great deal more to her than just a job. To begin with, there had been the sheer pleasure of performing, but now the first buds of ambition had begun to grow. She had just begun to worry about what her next step up the theatrical ladder should be. Well, it seemed that step had been taken for her.

'That's . . . that's just marvellous,' she managed to say at last.

'I knew you'd be pleased.'

And she was. Oh how she was!

'Will it mean more money?' she asked.

He laughed. 'I was right about you Scots. Always the practical question. I'll put your wages up to twenty-two-and-six a week.'

Nellie thought of the roses lying on the back seat and the countless other bunches of flowers she'd received over the past months. Proof of how popular, as Baz had said only a minute ago, she'd become. Now, a man like Baz Spira didn't give something unless he was going to get a good return on it. Twenty-two-and-six sounded a lot, and it was, but if she was bringing in people just to see *her* now, and she knew she was, then how many more might she bring in when featured? That was what Baz was counting on and was why he was offering to feature her.

He was no mug Baz Spira. But, then, neither was she. And anyway what did she have to lose? For it was most unlikely he'd sack her. Fee haggling was part and parcel of this game she'd come to learn.

'Make it thirty bob and we'll shake hands on it,' she said.

He gave her a shrewd look and then nodded his head. 'Done,' he replied, extending a hand from the wheel.

This would be only the start if she had anything to do with it, she promised herself.

Only the start.

*

173

'But I've told you, I can't sing in that key,' Nellie said through gritted teeth.

'Try, darling,' Mansell replied.

'It hurts my throat.'

'Nonsense. You're just being difficult.'

The rest of the line stood watching the interchange. It had been like this ever since they'd started rehearsing the new routines three days ago.

Nellie ran a hand over her forehead, which was slick with sweat. She was almost at the end of her tether and knew it. If only he'd give her half a chance. But no. Whatever she did was wrong. Whatever was natural to her he changed. And he was revelling in it. She could tell that from the occasional smirking glint that crept into his eyes.

She was shaking inside from rage, her stomach hot and sour, an iron band of frustration gripping her chest.

She tried not to glare at him. That wouldn't improve matters, but only antagonize him more.

'From the top, sweetie,' said Mansell, shooting her a smile that was in itself an insult.

She sang:

> 'Fantasy in olden days
> In varying and different ways,
> Was very much in vogue,
> Columbine and Pantaloon,
> A wistful Pierrot 'neath the moon,
> And Harlequin a rogue.'

'Stop! Stop!' cried Mansell waving his hands in front of him. 'My God, darling, you sound like some dreadful screeching cat in a back alley!'

She fought to keep her temper under control. 'I'm aware of that, Mister Mansell,' she said sweetly.

'Oh, you are, are you. Well at least that's something. And would you mind, if it's not too much trouble, that is, telling me what you're going to do about it?'

'There's nothing I can do about it while I'm forced to sing in this key.'

'Perhaps it's the piano that's at fault as well?' he asked pleasantly.

'I keep telling you. The key is wrong for me.'

He raised an eyebrow. 'Are you now saying you know more about this than I do?'

'Of course not.'

'Well I'm glad about that,' he replied, and laughed.

She threw a despairing glance at Margo who gave her a sympathetic one in return. The man was impossible!

'I shall decide what is the correct key for you, darling. I after all, have been in the business a considerable amount of years. And this is your first professional job, isn't it?'

'Yes.'

'And what was it you were before again? Do remind us. I, for one, have forgotten.'

The majority of the line, including several of the girls who'd occasionally been jealous of Nellie, failed to respond. Like Margo, they were entirely sympathetic towards her. Mansell's behaviour, always peculiar, had become totally outrageous. Not only that but, it was making life more difficult for everyone. They were having to spend far more time in rehearsing these new routines than they would have done normally.

'I was an interval singer at the Kingsway picture house,' Nellie replied, clearly.

Mansell snapped his fingers. 'Of course! How could I possibly have forgotten that!'

Nellie was seething, her hands clenched into fists, her nails jabbing into her flesh. Whatever happened, she promised herself, she wouldn't cry. God and all his angels would descend first before she gave Mansell the satisfaction of that.

Because that was what he was after – or at least one of the things he was after. To have her in floods of tears would delight him. If she broke down that way, then he'd be one step closer to what he ultimately had in mind: to break her completely.

Mansell went on, 'So, what little you know about singing you learned amidst the rustle of sweetie papers and scraping of ice cream cartons? Not to mention the constant hum of chat. Very illuminating, darling.'

'They didn't chat while I was singing,' Nellie snapped back hotly.

'Oh, you were that brilliant were you? I see.'

'They just listened, that's all.'

'So you say, darling. So you say.'

'Are you calling me a liar?' she asked, her voice little above a whisper.

'Heaven forbid, darling! I'm sure every word you've told us is gospel.' Having said that, he turned his back on her and tittered.

'Mister Mansell?' she asked.

He put his hand to his mouth before facing her. 'Yes?'

'Are you trying to make a fool of me?'

'I don't have to, darling,' he laughed. 'You do it so marvellously all on your own!'

The end of the tether had suddenly been reached. She could take no more of this dreadful man. The anger rose from the pit of her belly to engulf her in a red mist. Reason fled as she advanced on him, her hands extended as talons. There were a few moments when it was Big Jessie's face she saw instead of his.

His laughter died when he saw the look in her eyes. Starting to back off, he had only gone several paces when she leapt at him. He shrieked as her nails raked his cheeks.

Catching her on the chin, he sent her sprawling. 'You witch!' he howled, frantically trying to staunch the flow of blood from his lacerated cheeks with a fancy cotton handkerchief. 'I'll have you fired for this!'

She lay, exhausted on the stage where she had fallen, knowing it was true. You couldn't do what she'd done and expect to get away with it. Despair replaced her anger. She should have been able to control herself, but

176

the provocation had just been too great. She stared up at Mansell, contempt and loathing written across her face. She wanted to come up with some stunning reply. Some shaft of wit that would leave him completely speechless.

She couldn't think of a single thing.

'She just attacked me for no reason at all. The girl's completely mad!' Mansell said, his voice rising hysterically.

Baz Spira was sitting at his desk, where he had been doing some paperwork when Mansell burst into his office. He eased himself back in his chair to stare at Mansell. 'Go on,' he said quietly, a small frown creasing his forehead.

'We were in the middle of rehearsals and I had been telling her how dreadful she was when suddenly she launched herself at me. Doing this with her nails.' He came closer so Baz could get a better view of his damaged cheeks. 'Vicious bitch!'

'Nasty,' said Baz. This didn't sound at all like the Nellie he knew. 'And there was no provocation?'

'None at all. Just can't take direction that's all. Thinks she knows better than anyone else. And her not five minutes in the business either. I tell you, Baz, she's got to go, and today. It's either her or me.'

'Yes I can see that,' said Baz quietly. He sighed. 'Well, you'd better send her in.'

Mansell hurried off to the green room where all the girls were waiting. 'The big boss wants you,' he said to Nellie, smirking. Then, clapping his hands, 'Come on girls, back to work. The fun's over and we've a lot to do today if we're to make up lost time.'

'Enter!' Baz shouted when she timidly knocked at his door.

She came in to stand before him. There was defiance in her eyes and her mouth was set with determination.

'Sit down,' he said, and when she'd done so, offered her

a cigarette. 'Now tell me about it, Nellie,' he said when they'd both lit up.

He listened in silence, his eyes never leaving hers. He was certain, even before she was halfway through her story, that she was telling him the truth: that Mansell had been making life hell for her in rehearsals.

Nellie ended up by saying, 'But don't just take my word for it. Ask the girls.'

'Good idea,' he replied. 'Verification puts it beyond doubt.'

'I'm sorry about this, Baz. I feel I've let you down.'

'Wait in your dressing room and I'll send for you again shortly. In the meantime, ask Bunty to pop along and see me.'

Bunty was the oldest girl in the line, and one of the best liked.

She found the line rehearsing on stage. Coldly she said to Mansell, 'Mister Spira wants to speak to Bunty right away.' Without waiting for a reply, she made her way to the dressing room where she sat morosely staring into her mirror and playing with the rabbit's foot Margo had given her to dust off facial powder.

Bunty confirmed everything that Nellie had told Baz. As did Liz, Hannah and Margo. He didn't see the need to interview any more girls; the evidence against Mansell was overwhelming.

Mansell entered the office rubbing his hands and smiling. Both his cheeks had plasters on them. 'Yes, Baz?' he asked breezily.

'You lied to me,' Baz said bluntly.

'I beg your pardon?'

'You've been riding that girl unmercifully ever since rehearsals started.'

'That's just not true! Are you taking her word over mine?'

'Yes,' replied Baz quietly.

178

'This is preposterous!'

'No, you are, Roderique,' somehow making the word Roderique sound completely ridiculous. 'You said yourself, either she goes or you do.'

Mansell's eyes were suddenly veiled. He hadn't expected this at all.

'I want you out of the theatre within the next fifteen minutes. And if you report to the stage door tonight at the half hour I'll ensure your money is there waiting for you.'

Mansell was rocked. He had fired people often enough, but this was the first time it had happened to him. It wasn't a pleasant sensation at all.

'You won't find a better stage director than me,' he said.

'Balls!' shouted Baz. 'My instructions to you were to polish Nellie's technique and you interpret that as trying to destroy her. You call that being a good stage director?'

'What technique?' sneered Mansell. 'She doesn't know what she's doing half the time or why she's doing it.'

'A good stage director would have tried to teach her. Not carry out a vendetta against her.'

'Is that what she said?'

'That's what *everyone* said.'

Mansell reached up to touch one of his torn cheeks. 'I should have known you'd take her side,' he spat.

'Please close the door behind you on your way out, Mister Mansell,' Baz said, managing to get a wealth of meaningful innuendo into the word mister.

Mansell slammed the door. Baz chuckled.

'You're wanted on the green,' Margo said to Nellie.

'Who by?' although she knew. It was time to be given the sack.

'Mister Spira. And guess what?'

'What?'

'Mansell's been given the heave-ho.'

Nellie's face lit up. That was something at least. She

179

rose from her dressing table and slipped her arm through Margo's. 'Well come on, let's get it over with.'

Baz had decided he would take the rehearsals himself, continuing to do so until the new routines had been worked into the show. The replacement stage director would take rehearsals for the new routines the month after.

'Right,' he said when Nellie and Margo appeared. 'Let's get on with it.'

Nellie stared at him.

'Something wrong, lass?' he asked.

'Me, too?'

'Yes.'

If the other girls hadn't been present she'd have taken him in her arms and given him a big hug. God Almighty! At the sweetie factory even to lay your hands on someone, no matter what the rights and wrongs of it were, meant instant dismissal. She'd come to think very highly of Baz Spira since he'd hired her. But now she positively worshipped him.

'You were rehearsing this particular song I believe?' said Baz, holding up some sheet music.

'That's right.'

'Then we'll take it from the top in the key Mansell wanted you to do it in.'

She stared at him, unable to believe her ears.

'Well? What are you waiting for?'

She sang, genuinely doing her best, but it was hopeless.

'Hmmhh!' he said thoughtfully when she'd finished. 'You know Mansell was right. You do sound like a cat wailing in a back alley. Quite dreadful.' He suddenly burst out laughing. 'So shall we do it properly then?'

Nellie joined in the laughter with the other girls.

For a moment there he'd really had her going.

*

On the opening night of the new routines Nellie and the rest of the line – but Nellie in particular – were a huge success. Baz Spira wasn't surprised at all.

Making his way backstage after the show had rung down, he was thinking that Mansell had been right about one thing. Nellie's singing was magnificent. But if she was to go further, she would have to have lessons. A natural singing voice was one thing, fine for occasional use, but if she was going to hammer it night after night after night, then she needed to learn how to use it properly so that she didn't damage it.

He was fulsome in his congratulations to the line. When he had a chance he beckoned Nellie outside into the corridor.

'You were absolutely splendid,' he said, holding both her hands.

'You wouldn't lie?'

'In your case, Nellie, there's never any need to because you're never less than excellent. Now listen to me closely. I have a proposition I want to make to you.' He put his arm round her shoulders and walked her a little further down the corridor. 'I've been giving a lot of thought to you since I took over the rehearsals,' he went on. 'And I've decided to offer you a three-year contract. Apart from the guaranteed work, the advantages to you are twofold: first, I'll pay you when the theatre's dark, the same wages as when you're working; second, I will pay for singing lessons with a woman I know in the West End. What do you say?'

'How about yes?'

He smiled. 'That's what I'd hoped you'd say. I have other plans for you, but those will come in time. When I think you're ready. All right?'

She kissed him on the cheek. 'Thank you. I appreciate this.'

He smiled at her with more than his usual kindness. 'You're going to go far, Nellie. I sensed it the first time you auditioned. And I'm rarely wrong about these things.'

She closed her eyes, thinking how marvellous it would be to be up there, top of the bill. That was something she was coming to want more and more. Top of the bill. Number one. The very thought sent thrills racing up and down her spine.

'Now,' he said, heading her back to the dressing room, 'how about you and I celebrating by going out and having a little supper together?'

She tensed instantly, instinctively.

'Why are you suddenly looking at me like that?'

Supper one night, and then another – and then what would be expected of her?

'I have to get home to my husband,' she mumbled, suddenly feeling gauche and awkward.

'It was only an invitation to supper. Nothing else, Nellie,' Baz said quietly.

'Of course. I didn't think otherwise.'

What a strange one she was, he thought. She must be very much in love with this husband of hers although, from what he had heard, the man never came backstage or to any of the shows. A complete mystery man by all accounts.

'Perhaps another night,' he said, and giving her a curt nod walked away.

Nellie bit her lip as she watched him go. She knew he'd felt slighted, put down. And after him being so good to her.

'Oh hell,' she muttered to herself.

She ought to have been on top of the world, but having had to rebuff Baz had somehow soured the evening for her.

She slid her hatpin into position and then patted a stray hair into place. She was off to Miss McLeish for her Thursday lesson. She went twice a week, Tuesdays and Thursdays.

'Everything's all right now, Myra?' she asked *en route* to the door.

'Oh, aye, Mrs Biles. You don't have to worry about me,' Myra replied cheerily.

Jim was sitting up in bed sipping tea. 'This you off gallivanting again?' he asked.

'I'm going for my lesson.' As well he knew.

'That's what I said. Gallivanting.'

'You wouldn't call it that if you had Miss McLeish putting you through it.'

'Nor would Miss McLeish,' he replied quickly. The look in his eye leaving no doubt about exactly what he meant.

She looked at Myra but it was way over Myra's head.

It amazed her that Myra could voluntarily put up with Jim, who with every passing month became more whining and petty. It was time to write about the institution again she thought. Surely something must be coming up soon! She prayed it would, for she'd never rest happy in this house till Jim Biles was out of it for the last time.

'I'm off then,' she said, giving Myra a final wave.

Outside she made her way to the tram stop. She enjoyed her lesson days. She'd learned a great deal in the four months she'd been taught by Miss McLeish who was a thin, bony stick of a woman with iron-grey hair and a will to match.

To begin with it had been a rude awakening to learn there was a great deal more to singing than just opening your mouth and letting the sound come out. She was thankful to Baz for suggesting the lessons. She could see now that if she'd gone on the way she had been, she might well have had no voice left in a few years' time.

She hadn't seen all that much of Baz since the night she'd refused his supper invitation. He was pleasant enough to her when they did meet. Always a smile and a kindly word. But not once had he brought her home after the show in his car.

*

Nellie tapped Baz's door. She was presenting herself as instructed.

'Come in!'

She found him smoking a cigar, almost hidden by a pall of blue fug.

'Sit down, Nellie,' he said, half rising. When she was settled comfortably he offered her a cigarette.

'You've had me dying with curiosity all afternoon,' she said.

He laughed. 'I thought I might.'

'So what's this all about then?'

'Your featured spots are doing very well. But of course you know that.'

She sat studying him, waiting.

'I've been keeping an eye on you and I must say I'm impressed. You just get better and better.'

'Thank you.'

'Now, the thing is, we're coming up to the end of the season when the theatre goes dark for two months. Nellie, when the new season opens, how would you feel about doing solo spots?'

Slowly, she took a deep breath. It was exactly what she'd been praying for.

'Miss McLeish assures me you're up to it. And I think so too,' he said. He went on, 'What I envisage is this. In the past only the Palace Ladies have been the permanent fixture in the show. Right?'

She nodded.

'What I'm thinking of now are you and them, sometimes working alone and sometimes together, as two permanent fixtures. So, in some spots you would be on your own. In others with them. And in yet others they would be on their own.'

It was perfect, she thought. Absolutely perfect. 'What about billing?' she asked.

'Nellie Biles and the Palace Ladies,' he replied. Then grimaced. 'We're going to have to do something about Biles. It's a dreadful name.'

She couldn't have agreed more. 'That's all right as long as my name is in bigger type than Palace Ladies,' she bargained.

He pretended to consider that, but it was precisely the billing he'd always intended. 'Deal,' he said.

'What about my material?'

'You and I will choose it together. And I will rehearse all your solo spots with you. That is, if you don't object?'

'Not at all. I couldn't ask for better.'

'Now – money,' he said, chuckling inwardly when he saw the gleam come into her eye. 'Fifteen pounds a week and I won't haggle.'

Fifteen pounds! she thought. It was a fortune!

'And I mean it when I say I won't haggle. That's my first and final offer.'

'Then that's what it'll be.'

He sat back in his chair. 'Now, what about a name?' he mused aloud.

'Thompson's my maiden one,' she suggested.

He shook his head. 'Too ordinary. We want something with a bit of zing, a bit of stardust in it. A name that's different, which makes *you* different.'

Nothing different was coming into Nellie's mind at all. The only names she could think of were very ordinary ones, the names of Glasgow folk she knew and had grown up with.

Baz considered all sorts of possibilities, rejecting each in turn. What he really needed he decided was something that fitted Nellie's own personality. Something instantly identifiable with her.

Blonde? Green eyes? A sort of wildness about her. Although often very placid in appearance, when on stage, or emotionally aroused, there was a wildness about her which was unmistakeably attractive.

On the other hand, there was that childlike quality about her which made you want to protect her from the harshness of the world.

A curious combination, he thought. And suddenly he

185

had it. 'Nellie Wildchild,' he said, puffing smoke at her.

'Wildchild? What sort of name's that?'

'Theatrically, a damned good one,' he replied.

'Nellie Wildchild,' she said aloud, tasting it in her mouth and testing the sound of it on her ears. Well, it was certainly different, she couldn't deny that. And it would look good up on a bill. The sort of name to make people stop and stare and wonder.

'I like it,' she said.

So did Baz Spira. It had a money sound about it.

The theatre had been dark for two weeks and Nellie was bored to tears. How she missed the Palace and the other girls. But most of all she missed the audience: the rapport she had with them; the love they gave her.

Baz was abroad with his wife and family and wouldn't be back for another fortnight. She was missing him, too, in a strange and unexpected way.

She was still attending Miss McLeish twice weekly, which made the only break in the long dreary days.

She stared out of the window. The sun was bursting the skies and Glasgow was sweltering. It was funny, she thought, Glasgow just never looked right when the sun was shining on it. Glasgow was a dark city, built for rain, smoke and bitter cold. Sunshine made it look unnatural, almost obscene.

'Here we go then,' said Myra, pushing a wheelchair through the door. They'd had the wheelchair a few months now, and Myra often took Jim out and about. They kept it in the hallway where Myra and Nellie were for ever falling over it.

Jim glared at the wheelchair. 'I'm not getting in that damned thing again,' he declared stubbornly.

'It's beautiful out,' coaxed Myra.

'I don't care.'

'It'll do you good to get some sun about you. Look at your face. I've never seen anything so peely wally.'

'The wheelchair hurts me,' complained Jim.

Myra glanced across at Nellie. This was an allegation he'd made before, but one which they could neither prove nor disprove.

'But you always feel so much better after, despite what you say,' Myra said reasonably.

'It's a torture device, that's what it is. A torture device,' said Jim, eyeing the wheelchair with hostility.

The patience Myra had with Jim continually amazed Nellie. Myra put up with a lot more than she'd have been able to. 'I'm having no arguments,' said Nellie in her best matter-of-fact tone. 'You're going out for a breath of air, and that's an end to it.'

'I hate going out! I hate it!' Jim protested.

'But why? You always come back in a much better mood.'

'Because –' he glared at her. 'You wouldn't understand.'

'Try me,' Nellie urged him gently.

'I can't stand the pitying stares and comments that are made,' Jim burst out sullenly.

Both women paused to look at him.

Jim wiped his forehead with his one good hand. 'I mean, look at me, the state I'm in compared to what I used to be like. It's bad enough for me to have to see myself. But for them to see me as well is just too much. "Poor man", they say. And "Isn't it a shame?" "To think what he used to be like, such a big strapping fellow".'

'I know full well what it's like for folk to say things about you,' Nellie said softly. 'It's not nice at all. But you learn to live with it. You have to. What else is there?'

'For me there's an alternative. I don't have to go out.'

'Ach, why cut off your nose to spite your face? You enjoy being outside. I know that. So if they bother you just forget about the people out there. Ignore them if you have to.'

'And if they want to stop and talk?'

'Myra can tell them you're in a hurry, or that you're not

up to it. You don't have to talk if you don't want to.'

His eyes took on a faraway look and he turned to Myra. 'Would you take me down to the river? I'd love to see the Clyde again.'

'Then that's where we'll go,' she said, getting his things ready.

'And can we stay there a wee while and watch the big ships go up and down. I'd like that fine.'

Nellie and Myra exchanged a look and a smile. So much had she hardened her heart against Jim that it surprised her when he did or said something that moved her. 'You two have a nice walk,' she said as she left the room, brushing just the smallest trace of moisture from her eye.

'Baz, how are you!' she yelled, and rushed into his arms.

He responded by squeezing her tight and then planting a wet kiss on her cheek.

He pushed her out to arms' length and swept his eyes over her. 'The break has done you good. You look raring to go.'

'And I am! God, I've been so bored!'

'I also. But don't tell anyone. You're not meant to be bored with your family.'

She laughed. It was marvellous seeing him again, and being back in the theatre. Smelling once more the now so familiar smells. Greasepaint, paint, size, ropes; the hundred and one odours which combined make the one peculiar to the backstage of a threatre.

Arm in arm, they went through to the green room where the other girls and Robert McLaughlin, the new stage director, were waiting.

McLaughlin would be rehearsing the line for those routines it did on its own. Baz would be rehearsing those it did with Nellie, as well as Nellie on her own.

Everyone had coffee and chatted, the new girls in the line being introduced and made to feel welcome. Margo was back, which pleased Nellie, but Bunty had left to get married. Liz had decamped to try her luck down south.

'All right girls, on the green!' called Baz. It was time to start work.

On their way to the stage, he said to Nellie, 'Know all your songs?'

'Backwards.'

He laughed. 'I'll bet you do.'

And in that mood they started rehearsing the new show, Nellie's second – and first as a solo artiste.

A few days later Baz sat halfway up the stalls, listening to Nellie go through one of her numbers which she was attacking with verve and gusto, his thoughts wandering. While abroad he'd missed her tremendously, spending much of his time daydreaming about her. By the end of the holiday he knew he'd come under her spell completely. Hook, line and sinker.

Through all the years of his marriage, he had never been unfaithful to his wife. He had toyed with the idea several times, but in the end no attraction had ever been strong enough to tempt him fatally.

Nellie, however, was a different matter. It wasn't simply her body that he wanted; it was her. The person inside. He actually cared for her.

Wildchild, it suited her perfectly he thought. His wild child. His. But that was only as far as business was concerned. Every night she returned to this husband to whom she was so loyal. So what chance did he have? A small, fat, balding middle-aged man? None at all. He was old enough to be her father – and that was the way he should think of her.

But he doubted he'd be able to.

Nellie had them in the palm of her hand and knew it. Her voice rose, soaring like an eagle. A crashing wave of sound one moment; a silken caress the next.

In this particular number the words were immaterial. It was the music that was important. A shrewd choice by Baz, she now realized, as it showed her off superbly.

Also something of a gamble as it wasn't at all the usual sort of fare for a Palace audience. But if the one on this opening night was anything to go by, that gamble was going to pay off: they were lapping it up as cats do cream.

When she came to the end of the number she raised her hands, holding that position for a few seconds while the thunder of applause grew, then very slowly curtsied, hands coming down to her sides as she did so. The applause became an uproar; people standing, whistling, shouting 'encore!'.

She rose and blew them a kiss, then turning on her heel, ran into the wings.

But they wouldn't let her go. Again and again they called her back to take bow after bow.

Even the old pros said they'd never seen anything like it.

The opening show was over. Nellie sat numbly at her dressing table staring into the mirror. She couldn't believe what had happened tonight was real.

She touched her face. Was this the same Nellie who'd worked at the sweetie factory? Who'd lived for so many years in grey despair because she'd been unable to get a job? The same Nellie who was just like any other Glasgow lassie?

Well she was, and she wasn't. She was the same person, but only to a certain extent. For since coming into the theatre she had changed: imperceptibly at first; more so of late.

Tonight she'd stepped out from amongst the ranks to become somebody, somebody important. From now on Glasgow was going to hear a lot more of Nellie Wildchild. She knew that was a certainty; she could feel it in the pounding of her heart.

'Come in!' she called out when there was a knock on the door.

Baz entered, his eyes shining. 'What can I say that the audience didn't? You were superlative, Nellie. Superlative! Real alpha plus.'

'It's thanks to you Baz. It was inspired of you to choose the operetta number.'

'It pleases me I had a little hand in it. But that doesn't detract in the least from you, my girl. The talent, presence, looks are all yours.'

'Thank you,' she said softly, finding herself blushing.

He took her hand and kissed the back of it. 'To a long and successful working relationship together.'

Before Nellie could reply there was more knocking at the door. 'It's open!' she shouted.

In burst Margo and some of the other girls in the line, come to offer their congratulations and be congratulated in return. Bob Copeland, Margo's boyfriend, was with them, waving an opened bottle of champagne.

Thinking something of a party was about to develop Baz made his excuses and left. He had other people in the show to call upon.

During the space of the next half hour more people came and went, till finally Nellie was left on her own. Margo and Bob had gone on somewhere, as had several of the other girls and their boyfriends. Suddenly it was all very anti-climactic. The champagne bubbles had burst. The elation died.

Slowly she started removing her slap, staring at herself in the glass. When her face was clean, she slowly began to comb her hair.

Everyone else was out having fun with someone they cared for, making their plans and swapping their dreams. All she had to go home to was Jim. Jim and her memories.

She started when there was a tap on the door. 'Come in!'

Baz poked his head round the door. 'Still here? I thought you'd be long gone by now.'

'I usually am, but tonight . . . well, I just fancied a little sit on.'

Immediately he was concerned. 'Everything all right?'

'Fine. Couldn't be better.'

'Husband in tonight?'

'No.'

Queer he thought. Definitely queer. 'Aren't you going out anywhere?'

She shook her head, suddenly feeling tearful. Probably the aftermath of the evening's excitement.

He smiled kindly. 'Still all keyed-up. Is that it?'

'I suppose so.'

He looked undecided for a few moments, and then seemed to come to a decision. 'Rachel, my wife, was supposed to be coming tonight but had to cry off at the last minute with a migraine. Suffers terribly from them, you know.'

'No, I didn't.'

'She regularly gets shocking heads. Often has to shut herself away in a darkened room for two, sometimes even three, days and nights. A dreadful business. Anyway, the point is that she and I were intending to go out for a meal after the show. A little private club I know where I'm a member. Now the thing is, the table's booked. How about you joining me?'

She remembered the last time she'd rebuffed him. How upset he'd been.

And, in truth, she desperately wanted to go on somewhere. To complete the evening. Not just go home to Jim's whining and her bed by the window.

'Won't Rachel mind?' she asked.

'Not in the least. She'll be only too happy that I didn't waste the booking.'

'But shouldn't you be getting back to her?'

'When she's got one of her migraines no one's allowed near her. All she wants is absolute peace and quiet with no disturbance, and that includes me.'

Nellie laid down her brush, her mind made up. 'I'm

game if you are,' she said. Then added quickly, 'One thing, Baz.'

'What's that?'

'No strings?'

'None at all, Nellie. You're just going out for a meal with your uncle Basil.'

'Basil!' she exclaimed. 'I never knew that's what Baz was short for!'

'Well now you know.'

'But why Baz! Childhood name?'

'No. my own invention. For survival.'

She frowned. He'd lost her.

'Could you imagine being called Basil in Glasgow? My life would have been a continual misery if I hadn't had the bright idea to disguise it.'

Nellie laughed, relaxing for the first time in weeks.

'How long will you be?' he asked.

'Give me ten?'

'You've got five.'

She took fifteen.

She had never been in a club like this before. It was extremely opulent, exclusive and discreetly expensive.

The table they were ushered to was lit by a candle in a crystal holder. The cutlery was King's and silver. The tablecloth crisp, creamy and best Irish linen. To say Nellie was impressed would be an understatement.

Baz ordered champagne, Krug, snapping at the wine waiter to go ahead and pour when the man asked if he'd care to taste it.

'Pretentious nonsense that,' he said when the waiter had gone.

'I thought it was the done thing to taste wine before accepting it?'

He smiled. 'You shouldn't have to taste. Your eyes should tell you what's what. First, look at the clarity of the wine. If it looks right then ninety-nine times out of a hundred it is. Secondly, when the first glass is poured look at its level. If the bottle's been corked you'll see bits of the cork floating around. That bottle you have a right to send back.'

Nellie was fascinated. 'Do the bits of cork make all that much difference?'

Baz laughed. 'Not really. But at the prices you pay in a place like this, you may as well get what you're shelling out for. At home, I wouldn't bother too much about the cork. Mind you, I'm only a simple imbiber of wine. The real connoisseurs I'm sure wouldn't agree with me.'

Nellie stared around her. She couldn't help but compare the sophisticated, genteel atmosphere of the room they were in with Govan where she'd been born and bred. Govan of the dirt and grime and violence which had a permanent smell about it. An unwashed, acrid smell.

Not that she was ashamed of Govan in any way. Not at all. She was proud to come from there. But a place like this showed her how much more there was in the world. What better things there were to be had than what she had been taught to expect.

She ordered a veal dish which came covered in the most gorgeous, rich cream sauce. Brought up on the simplest of cooking, she wouldn't have believed that food could taste like this.

'Like it?' Baz asked.

She closed her eyes. 'Hmmh!'

It pleased him that she was pleased. It also gave him a great deal of pleasure to be able to entertain her this way. It took no brains to guess that this sort of lifestyle was completely new to her.

They finished the champagne and he ordered another, despite her protests. 'I'm the one who's got to be careful because he's driving,' he argued.

Nellie was relaxed and thoroughly enjoying herself thanks to a combination of the alcohol and Baz's witty, and very clever, conversation. He would've made a marvellous comedian. It had been a long time since she had laughed like this. Since she had had any fun.

'What's wrong Nellie? You've suddenly gone quiet,' he said.

'Just thinking about someone.'

'Your husband?' he asked shrewdly.

She gave him an astonished glance. 'Do you read minds as well?'

'Not quite.'

She lit a cigarette while he trimmed and lit a cigar. He regarded her through blue smoke.

'Want to talk about it?' he asked quietly.

'He's paralysed down one side and he's lost half his leg on the other. He was hit by a motorbike.'

'I'm sorry, Nellie. I had no idea,' Baz said, reaching across and touching her hand.

'I suppose you, like the girls, have been wondering why he never picks me up or comes to see the show. Well now you know.'

She saw the sympathetic look on his face and gave a half smile. 'Don't think I'm cut up about it in any way. I'm not. He's been a right sod all the time we've been married. He means nothing at all to me, Baz. Less than nothing.'

'You must have loved him when you married him surely?'

'Love? No. He got me on the rebound, and I thought he was a decent fellow. I thought I could make something of a go of it. But it's true when they say you don't know a person till you're married to them. I found that out to my cost.'

She didn't know why she was telling Baz all this. Except that, for some reason, she wanted to. It felt right somehow to confide in him.

'And who did your husband get you on the rebound from?'

She told him then about Frank Connelly, although not mentioning Frank by name, and how her father had forced her to break off their engagement.

195

Her voice was low and level as she recounted how Frank had then run off abroad before she'd been able to get word to him that she'd wait for him till he was time served and they could elope.

She told Baz of Jim and how he'd seemed such a decent chap. Till the wedding day itself when she'd found him with her cousin Marj. And how that night in the hotel room, filled with drink, he had raped her.

Baz sat very still while Nellie told him about herself. He'd known there was something. He'd sensed it. And now here it was all coming out. It hurt him deeply to hear what she'd been through.

'And when I saw it was Jessie he was with I just blew up and ran at them,' Nellie said a little later. 'She saw me coming and took to her heels. Jim stayed long enough to knock me into the gutter and then he went after her. But it was foggy and he wasn't looking where he was going. Neither was the motorcyclist.'

He wanted to take her in his arms and comfort her. Her eyes had taken on a hollow, far-away look that tugged at his heart. In that look he could see quite plainly the years of despair behind her.

She looked so vulnerable he thought. But he knew that underneath the vulnerability there was tempered steel. Forged there by herself for survival.

When she was finished he called for brandies which they sat drinking in silence.

Finally she said, 'Sorry if I've spoiled your evening.'

He shook his head. 'You haven't, Nellie. I'm glad you told me all this.'

'It just seemed the right thing to do.'

'I'm flattered. But tell me, won't this Myra worry that you're late home?'

'She knows I'll be all right. That I can take care of myself. She mind the extra time looking after Jim? She'd happily do it twenty-four hours a day if asked.'

He parked outside the grey, stone tenement where she lived. 'I enjoyed our little supper,' he said.

196

'I enjoyed it also.'

They paused to listen to seagulls screeching overhead. An unusual occurrence late at night. Something must have disturbed them.

'Good night Baz,' she said, opening the door, but on an impulse, leaned back and kissed him on the cheek.

'Good night,' he said as she banged the door shut behind her.

He watched her vanish up the gas-lit close. A slim, blonde-haired figure, young enough to be his daughter.

He stared in distaste at the tenement, at the dirt and graffitti and greyness of it.

He was going to have to do something about where she stayed, he decided. She certainly couldn't go on living here. Although he'd seen worse, and lived in it. In the old days in Russia. One day the family had been rich. The next, all they had were the clothes on their backs and a few small items they'd managed to pick up as they ran. And they'd been the lucky ones. For they'd escaped with their lives.

Even now, and though he'd been so young at the time, he could vividly remember the Cossacks descending on their village. The screams, the shouts of fear, of agony. The fires, the milling horses, the man with no head. The woman speared to a tree. The mangled mess that was a child who'd been trampled to death. The long march out of Russia into Germany where they'd lived for a few years before moving on to Scotland because there was no work in Germany and his father had the promise of a job in Glasgow.

Dear Glasgow. In Russia they'd never even heard of it. But to Glasgow they'd eventually come and here they'd settled.

Although hardly the prettiest city in the world, he had come to have enormous affection for Glasgow. It had great character.

He put these thoughts from his mind as he brought his

197

attention back to Nellie. Knowing her better now, he felt even more for her than he had before.

Nellie was approachable. He was certain of it. But it would have to be done very, very carefully if he was going to succeed. She was repressed, frightened of men. He would have to nurse and coax her out of herself. A little at a time until the closed flower was fully open again.

She liked him. He knew that. But fancied him? Well he was certainly no oil painting but he did have a lot to offer, not the least of which was the power he held over her career. And, as he well knew, power is one of the greatest aphrodisiacs there has ever been.

Nellie found Myra and Jim playing snap. 'Sorry to be so late,' she apologized.

'How did it go?' Myra asked anxiously.

'Marvellously. Couldn't have been better.'

'Oh, Nellie!' said Myra clapping her hands together. 'I'm so pleased for you.'

'Where have you been to this hour?' demanded Jim.

'Mister Spira's wife was taken ill before the show. He'd booked a table to take her out, and as she couldn't make it he asked me instead.'

'That was nice of him,' said Myra.

'I thought so, too.'

'I'll bet he's after you,' snarled Jim.

Nellie swung on him. 'Don't judge everyone by your own low standards,' she replied coldly.

'I'll away, then. See you in the morning. Usual time,' said Myra, and hurried out of the house to run upstairs.

Jim watched Nellie while she undressed. 'I don't want you to go out with this Spira fellow again,' he said.

Nellie stopped to turn and stare at him. 'What did you say?'

'You heard. I don't want you going out with him again.'

'I'll go out with whom I please.'

'I'll have you remember you're still a married woman,' he hissed angrily.

The sheer hypocrisy and audacity of the man made her want to laugh out loud. She regarded him in amazement. 'Being married didn't stop you seeing whoever you wished as I recall,' she said.

His eyes blazed with both anger and frustration. His face had gone red and blotchy.

'Are you sleeping with him?'

'No. Not that it's any of your business.'

'I don't believe you.'

'I don't give a damn whether you believe me or not.' She turned her back to him.

Hungrily he stared at her, desperately wanting her.

He felt so useless lying here. So utterly and totally useless. What had happened to him just wasn't fair, he screamed inside his head for what might well have been the millionth time. God, to be doomed to be like this for the rest of his life. There could be another forty, even fifty years like this; trapped inside this paralysed husk. Still wanting, and capable of having, a woman.

Get a grip Jim, he told himself. Just get by day to day. Don't contemplate the future. For there was madness in that. Insanity.

He stared at this woman he'd married. It was still difficult to believe that she'd gone on the stage; that she was making such a success of it. Who would have credited it? His Nellie.

He'd tried to imagine her on stage, but couldn't. The image just wouldn't come somehow. Perhaps he just didn't want it to.

And the money she was making! That was incredible. Way and above anything he'd have been able to bring home if he'd still been working.

Mind you, he might have been making something like it had he succeeded in getting his own shop. And who knows? He might have done by now. There was no telling.

But now he'd never own a shop. Or go to work again.

He was reliant on her for everything: the food he ate, what clothes he wore, the roof over his head, the fire in the grate.

He should have been thankful but all he felt was resentment.

She was in her nightclothes now, turning her bed down, her hair a cascade of yellow dancing on her shoulders.

Going on the stage had changed her, he thought. Given her more self-confidence, assurance. Not only that but her tastes had changed. Clothes, make-up, conversation even, all altered. She'd also acquired poise to compliment her natural elegance, an elegance that was in itself greatly enhanced of late.

Nellie paused in the process of lighting her last cigarette of the day. His eyes were fastened on her, malevolent with hate. He'd come to hate her as much as she hated him.

'I'll suggest to Myra she take you out for a hurl in your wheelchair tomorrow,' she said.

'It's your wheelchair. You bought it,' he replied.

'For you.'

He turned his face away. 'I don't want it.'

He was becoming more and more petty, she thought, but what else could you expect with him cooped up like this day after day.

'I'll buy you –' she started to say.

'I don't want you to buy me anything!' he yelled back. 'Not a damn thing!'

She shrugged. 'Suit yourself. It's no skin off my nose.'

'The sooner you get me into an institution the better.'

'Well don't think I'm not trying. You'll be in just as soon as there's a bed available for you. I promise.'

'I can't wait.'

Me neither she thought. When she'd finished her cigarette she put out the light and crawled into bed. She was just drifting off when he spoke again.

'Nellie?'

'What?'

'Please?'

She didn't reply.

'Nellie?'

She squeezed her eyes tightly shut. If somehow she could have switched off her ears she would have done so.

Suddenly Jim lost his temper, furious with himself and humiliated at having pleaded with her. 'You're a rotten bitch of a woman!' he roared. 'The worst woman I ever had. Why if I wasn't lying here like this I wouldn't even spit on you!'

He ranted and raved, his voice ringing round the room while she lay with her hands covering her ears.

In her cold, narrow bed, Nellie wept silently.

'And this, Nellie, is my wife Rachel.'

The two women shook hands, Rachel saying, 'I've heard so much about you, Nellie, I feel I've known you for years already.'

Rachel Spira was a short woman, although still taller than Baz, in her early forties. Her figure was plump and matronly while at her chin several jowls wobbled. The overall impression was one of flesh.

'It's a great pleasure to meet you, Mrs Spira,' Nellie replied.

'Rachel, please. We don't stand on ceremony in this house.'

'And this is my son, Daniel,' said Baz proudly. Daniel was a strapping lad of about nineteen.

'And my second son, Joseph.' Joseph was a few years younger than his brother.

'And my daughter, Sarah.' Sarah was about twelve with large, doe eyes and jet-black hair.

Nellie shook hands with all three of them, thinking to herself what good-looking children they were. The girl especially. There was no doubt she would grow up to be a beauty.

'Allow me to get you a drink, Miss Wildchild,' Daniel said. 'What would you like?'

Miss Wildchild. If only it was true. 'It's Mrs actually,' she replied. And was secretly amused to see disappointment flash across his face. It seemed she'd made a conquest. 'I'll have a glass of wine, please,' she said.

Baz had asked her to this party the previous week, saying she could come on after the show was down for the night. He'd sent his car with a driver to pick her up.

Trying not to be too obvious, she stared about her. What a beautiful place it was. Certainly by far and away the grandest home she'd ever been in.

The carpet underfoot was fitted and inches thick; the furniture covered in gold velvet. But what impressed her most was the chandelier that hung overhead.

Her entrance into the room had created a stir. Heads, mostly male, were turned in her direction.

'Baz tells me you are a big success in the show,' Rachel said, returning to Nellie's side, having been gone for a minute to receive another late guest.

'It's very kind of him to say so.'

'He says you have the most marvellous voice. I must come myself one night and hear you.'

'Introduce us, Rachel,' a man said, having strode over to join them. He was of average height, thin, with carrot-red hair. He wasn't nearly as smartly dressed as the other men present. His cheeks were gaunt, the bones above them prominent. There was an overall air of intensity about him.

'Nellie, I'd like you to meet Geoff Carson. One of Glasgow's foremost painters,' Rachel said.

'Not one of, but *the*,' Carson put in swiftly.

Nellie smiled. 'Modest with it, too, I see.'

'He doesn't know the meaning of the word,' Rachel said, a mischievous glint in her eye.

Carson was staring at Nellie like a hungry predator. She found his gaze uncomfortable.

'What do you think of McIan?' he demanded suddenly.

'Never heard of him.'

'Ah!' he said and gave a brief, wolfish smile.

'McIan's an Edinburgh painter and Geoff's main rival,' explained Rachel.

'Rival! Nonsense! The man's a no-talented phoney. He doesn't even begin to compare with me!'

'Not McIan again!' another man said, joining their little group. 'You're obsessed with him, Geoff.'

Carson glared at the man who smiled back rather patronizingly.

'What would you know about art anyway?' Carson demanded. 'You're nothing more than a businessman,' saying the last word as though it were something disgusting.

'Nellie, this is Murray Ventre,' Rachel said.

Ventre gave the tiniest of bows. 'At your service, Miss Wildchild.'

She was about to correct him, but decided against it. Let them think of her as an unmarried woman. At least for the moment.

The evening progressed, during the course of which Nellie met a great many interesting people from all walks of life, including a knight of the realm, a charming man down from Perthshire, where he had an estate not far from Pitlochry.

Nellie was thoroughly enjoying herself finding all these new and interesting acquaintances absolutely fascinating.

She was coming out of the toilet when she was suddenly accosted by Geoff Carson who came straight up to her and pinned her against the wall.

'I've been looking everywhere for you,' he breathed. 'I wanted to get you alone.'

He ran his glance over her. It was obvious enough what was going on in his mind. 'I thought I might take you home when you're ready.'

There was something about the expression on his face which reminded her of Jim. 'I don't think so,' she replied, trying to keep the contempt out of her voice.

'I want to paint you. Will you come to my studio tomorrow?'

'I have a rehearsal.'

'The next day, then?'

'I'm rehearsing then also.'

'When you're not rehearsing then?' he said, angry now.

'I don't want my picture painted, thank you very much,' she said. 'And now will you please let me pass?'

He came closer his breath thick with alcohol. 'I don't think you realize that it's an honour, a great privilege to be asked by me to sit.'

'Thank you for the honour, but I decline.' She tried to push him aside, but came up short when his hand covered her breast. 'What do you think you're doing?' she hissed.

'You're lovely. The best-looking woman here tonight.'

'Do you mind taking your hand off me?'

As though she hadn't spoken, he began to fondle her.

She was outraged and ashamed. But how could she get rid of him without creating a scene? Without cheapening herself?

'Geoff, I think you're wanted in the other room,' Baz said quietly, suddenly appearing behind Carson. His voice was low and full of authority. The voice of a man used to giving orders and being obeyed.

The hand was removed instantly. 'Just talking to Nellie here,' Carson said with a grin.

Baz looked from Carson to Nellie and then back again. Carson wilted a little as Baz's eyes bored into him.

'I'll go away through then,' Carson said, moving off.

'You all right?' Baz asked anxiously when the painter was gone.

'Yes, thanks. No harm done.'

'He's had too much to drink, I'm afraid. The old Glasgow problem of not knowing when to stop.'

She rushed a wisp of hair away from her face. Dear Baz, she thought, trust him to be on hand to sort things out. Just like him. Always there when he was needed.

'I wanted to have a word with you anyway,' he said.

'About the show?'

'No. Something else. I have a surprise for you.'

'What?' she demanded eagerly.

A smile turned the corners of his mouth gently upward. 'If I told you it wouldn't be a surprise.'

'Beast!'

'Can you spare about an hour, maybe longer, after rehearsals tomorrow?'

'Of course.'

'I'll take you to your surprise then.'

'Take me to it?'

'That's right.'

She frowned, desperately trying to work out what this surprise could be.'

'You'll never guess so there's no use trying,' he laughed, knowing full well that would only make her try the harder. 'Now shall we join the others?'

'Baz—?'

'And no questions about it. Because I'm not saying.'

Nor did he, despite the many times she tried to worm it out of him.

'Ready?' he asked.

She had changed out of rehearsal clothes into her outdoor ones. A last check at her mirror confirmed that her make-up was satisfactory. She was bubbling with anticipation inside, dying to find out what the surprise was.

'Let's go.'

He took her by the arm and guided her downstairs. Once outside they made their way to where his car was parked.

It was a cold, crisp, clear day, the air sharp and stinging.

'I liked your wife very much,' Nellie said once they were underway.

He gave her a sideways glance. 'And she liked you. In fact the whole family did. Daniel in particular.'

'I think he fancied me,' she said in a mock stage whisper.

'He wasn't the only one.'

She thought of Geoff Carson. 'So it seemed.'

But Baz wasn't thinking of the artist.

'Where are we going?' she asked.

'Wait and see.'

'You're not giving anything away are you?'

'Whoever heard of a businessman giving something away!' he replied, pulling a face as though horrified at even the suggestion.

Nellie laughed. She liked men who made her laugh.

They drove along the Great Western Road until at last the urban sore that was Glasgow was left behind them. The countryside was beautiful, very green with occasional purple and yellow splashes. It made a heart-lifting contrast to the seemingly never ending Glasgow grey.

Nellie sighed and leaned back in her seat. 'This is the life,' she said languorously.

A little further on Baz turned off the road to motor along a leafy lane. Presently he stopped in front of a largish house which was fronted by a wild, overgrown garden.

'Come on,' he said, helping her from the car.

'Where are we?'

'Just outside the village of Bishopton,' he replied, and opening the garden gate ushered her through.

'Who lives here?'

'A woman I know,' he replied mysteriously.

At the door he produced a key which opened it. Smiling he beckoned her inside.

The house hadn't been empty long. She could tell that from the excellent condition it was in. Why there wasn't even more than a few days' dust on the window ledges.

He showed her round downstairs where there were four rooms with a kitchen and adjoining w.c. Upstairs there were three more rooms, a toilet and bathroom.

Nellie stood in what was obviously the master bed-

206

room, staring out of a large window. As far as she could see there was greenery, and there, between two clumps of trees, the glint of water which was the Clyde.

'Like it?' Baz asked.

'Marvellous,' she replied. Then turning to him, 'So who's this female friend of yours who lives here?'

'Her name's Nellie Wildchild.'

She blinked and stared at him. 'I beg your pardon?'

'The place is yours.'

She shook her head. 'I don't understand?'

'Nellie, you can't continue living in a Govan slum. It's just not on now that you're becoming a name.'

'But I can't afford this!'

'You don't have to. It's a gift from me.'

She stared around her in wonder. What a wonderful house. Precisely the sort she'd always dreamed about. 'I can't accept it from you, Baz,' she said sorrowfully.

'Why ever not?'

'It just wouldn't be right.'

'Look, it didn't cost all that much. I swear it. Not that I bought it on the open market. It came to me in lieu of a debt I was owed. I was already looking for a place for you anyway and so when this came up I thought it ideal.'

'It is. It is,' she replied. 'But I can't accept it as a present. It's far too much.'

'Let's talk about it,' he said, taking her by the arm and guiding her back downstairs.

Nellie was in love with the house, just aching to live in it. She thought how lovely it would be to wake up every morning in the country as opposed to the filthy squalor of Govan.

Baz took her out to the back where they found many fruit trees and bushes overgrown and running wild.

'The previous owner didn't go in much for gardening it seems,' he said. 'But this and the front garden wouldn't take long to get back in shape. Especially if you got someone in.'

There was a garage which he said they'd look at in a

minute or two. After the matter of the house had been resolved.

'It's absolutely perfect,' Nellie said, eyes shining, staring up at the rear of the house.

'Then accept it from me.'

'I can't.'

'I'll make you change your mind somehow.'

'No you won't.'

'You're a stubborn woman, Nellie.'

'I thought you already knew that.'

They strolled round the side of the house. She was thinking she could put Jim downstairs in a room of his own, and, next door to him, Myra. That would leave her the entire upper area for herself. Her heart leapt at the thought of the freedom that would entail.

'How much did the person owe you?' she asked.

'Three-fifty.'

She didn't know much about house prices but was sure it was a snip for that.

'Why? What are you thinking?' he asked.

'That I would buy it off you. If you'd let me pay it up weekly that is.'

'But I want to *give* it to you!'

She shook her head. 'I buy or nothing.'

'You're mad, woman!'

'No Baz. Just keeping my independence.'

'All right, we'll work it out that I dock your wages every week. Two or three years and you'll have paid it off.'

Her head was suddenly full of plans for the place. There was so much she was going to need in the way of furniture and furnishings.

'It's a lovely surprise, Baz. Thank you very, very much,' she said, and, stooping, kissed his cheek.

'Now you're sure this is how you want to do it?' he asked.

'Absolutely positive.'

He clicked his tongue and waved his hands in a gesture of reluctant acceptance. 'So, if I can't give you the house will you take a house-warming present? It is traditional you know.'

'All right,' she laughed.

'Come then,' he said, taking her by the hand and leading her to the garage.

It was a bull-nosed Morris in black and maroon. It had been polished till it shone.

'Now don't give me any shtik about not being able to accept it,' said Baz. 'Living out here you'll need a car to get to and from the theatre.'

'But I can't drive!'

'*Yet*, Nellie. *Yet*. I'll fix you up with some lessons. You'll soon get the hang of it. It isn't difficult, I promise you.' He caressed the bonnet of the car with his hand. 'She's not new, but a lovely little machine none the less. You'll get a lot of good use out of her.'

A house and a car in the same day. It was too much to take in at once. 'It's beautiful Baz, truly.'

He beamed. 'You being happy makes me happy. It's also good for the show. Now come on, sit in her. Let me see how you look.'

'A picture,' he pronounced when she was behind the wheel.

'How about you giving me a lesson right now?' she asked.

'Why not! I'd enjoy that.'

The next half hour was a mixture of laughter and curses as for the first time in her life she came to grips with the internal combustion engine.

'Live in the country!' exclaimed Myra. 'That would be wonderful, Nellie.'

'Wait till you see it, Myra. It'll bowl you over.'

'I can hardly wait. And I'm to have my own room?'

'*And* I'll put your money up, of course. That seems only fair.'

Jim glowered from the bed. 'I think the idea stinks.'

'Oh, Jim, you'll love it. Just think of all that good, fresh air,' Myra coaxed.

'I was born and bred in Govan. Leaving it is the last thing I want,' grumbled Jim.

Nellie sat by the fire, regarding him thoughtfully. 'You've no option but to come,' she said finally. 'You certainly can't stay here on your own.'

'I'll have Myra to look after me.'

'Oh, aye? And who's going to pay the bills then, if I'm not here to do so?'

'I wondered how long it would take you to throw your money in my face.'

'I'm not doing that at all, Jim.'

'Sounds hellishly like it to me.'

There was nothing she could do that was right.

'I won't go,' he stated flatly.

'You'll do as you're told, and that's the end of it.'

'Don't I have any say in the matter?' he demanded.

'None at all.'

'I would have bought a house one day if it hadn't been for the accident,' he said defiantly. 'My luck was on the turn. I was coming up to the winning streak to end all winning streaks. I could feel it at the time.'

Nellie didn't answer. She'd heard it all before. It had bored her then as it did now. She let him ramble on about all the things he'd planned to do with his winnings. When he'd finally finished she said, 'Another thing. I now own a car.'

Myra gawped at her. Only real toffs owned cars.

'You're buying a house *and* a car?' Jim demanded.

'I'm buying the house. The car was a present.'

'From whom?'

'None of your business.'

'Your boss, Spira, I'll bet. You *are* having it off with him!'

'I am not. I told you.'

'Men don't give you cars for nothing. He must be getting something in return.'

'He is. My friendship.'

Jim guffawed. 'Don't be so bloody naïve! He wants inside your knickers. Don't you kid yourself he doesn't.'

She regarded him with distaste. Trust him to put it so crudely.

She threw what remained of her cigarette into the grate. 'I'll make a cup of tea,' she said.

Using the sharp end of an orange stick she put a dot of red on each of the inside junctures of her eyes. The lights out front would pick up the red, making her eyes appear larger and brighter.

When that job was done to her satisfaction she sat back in her chair and studied herself in her dressing-table mirror. The curtain wasn't long up and she would shortly be called for her first cue.

She thought back to the party at Baz's house. She had enjoyed that. Tremendously. She'd been nervous beforehand thinking she might be out of place – the proverbial square peg faced with a round hole – but she hadn't been. On the contrary, she'd felt completely at ease and at home.

Such interesting people had been there. Civilized people used to gracious living. The good things in life. Well-mannered, if you disregarded Geoff Carson. Softspoken. Cultured.

She'd thought that they might look down their noses at her because she spoke 'broad', but that hadn't been the case either. Not once had she even detected a hint of condescension or patronage because of her accent.

Still, that was something else she'd have to see to. At the moment there were singing lessons and driving lessons. When the driving ones were completed she would replace them with ones for speech.

She used the rabbit's foot Margo had given her to smooth in some powder that had become a little streaked, thinking about what Jim had said about Baz.

211

Jim was right, of course, Baz did fancy her. She'd known that for some time. The question she had to ask herself was what she was going to do when he did something about it. There was no doubt in her mind that she'd become tremendously fond of him since coming to the Palace – his kindness, his thoughtfulness.

But could she actually bring herself to sleep with him? That was something else entirely.

What she mustn't forget was that he ran the Palace, and as such could exercise tremendous influence over her career. A career that was blossoming more all the time.

There was nothing to stop her going to other theatres and appearing there, once her contract with Baz had expired, but why make life difficult when she had everything she could ask for at the Palace – and more? For a management to be so totally on her side wasn't something that should be discarded, or even interfered with, lightly.

Her thoughts were interrupted by a tap on the door. 'Come in!' she called out.

Sandy entered. 'This arrived by hand after the half so I thought I'd bring it up to you personally. I was coming this way anyway,' he said, handing her a letter.

She thanked him and they exchanged some good-natured banter before he left. Then she ripped open the envelope.

What she read brought a smile to her face. The letter was a request from one of the daily newspapers asking if one of their journalists could interview her with a view to doing a feature spread.

Well, well, well! She certainly was coming on, she thought. A newspaper article all about *her*! The prospect was thrilling.

Nellie held the high note, pure and golden. On and on it went, seemingly forever, till at last she killed it to finish the song.

Baz sighed with pleasure, enraptured. Miss McLeish nodded her approval. Nellie's voice had improved beyond measure since coming under her tutelage. Now Nellie was the master of the instrument instead of the other way around.

A glance at his watch told Baz the lesson was over which disappointed him. He could have sat all day listening to Nellie sing.

Nellie and Miss McLeish had a last few words, then Nellie slipped into her coat. She and Baz were now off to the salerooms to look at second-hand furniture for the house at Bishopton.

'I think I'll come up and listen to your lessons more often,' Baz said when they were underway. 'And, afterwards, if neither of us was rushing off anywhere, we could take tea together. What do you say?'

'I'd love that. But Baz?'

'Yes?'

'If you and I are seen too often together won't it get back to Rachel? For such a big city, you know how small Glasgow can be.'

His face clouded. It was a thought that had crossed his mind before now. 'It's not as though we were doing anything wrong, is it?' he replied with a grin.

'There's still bound to be talk.'

He *would* have to be a bit more careful. He loved Rachel, and though it was a different love than that which he felt for Nellie, he didn't want to cause her pain or upset.

It would be a lot easier when the house at Bishopton was habitable, for then he wouldn't have to be seen out with Nellie nearly so much.

'It's best you buy second-hand for the moment,' he said. 'And then you can replace with new, providing you want to that is, as you go along. There's some very nice pine on sale today.'

For the rest of the drive to the showrooms, the subject of themselves put aside, he told her what was coming up for auction, having been to view himself beforehand.

213

*

Nellie was dog-tired. It was Saturday night, the end of the week. A week that had been harder than usual, because of getting the new house into shape on top of the show.

She said good night to Myra and then put the kettle on for a cup of tea. Jim was lying in bed watching her, the morning's paper spread before him.

'Pretty picture of you,' he said.

'Oh, you liked it then?'

'And a good article. Fair tugs the strings of your heart, the bit about the husband lying at home paralysed.'

'Does that upset you?'

'No. Why should it? It's true after all.'

Nellie put the tea by to mask. She'd considered it carefully before admitting to the journalist that she was married and that her husband was paralysed. If she'd thought she would have gotten away with saying she was single she would have done so, but she was too well known in Govan. Somebody would have told the papers what she was trying to hide. It was better this way; open and above board.

Besides, as Baz had pointed out, it wasn't such a bad thing being a married woman. It lent you a certain respectability and 'weight'. And as for Jim being paralysed, nothing but sympathy would come her way because of that.

'So that's Baz Spira, your boss,' Jim sneered, holding up the paper with his good hand. 'A right sugar daddy he looks.'

'It's not a particularly good photo of him,' Nellie replied.

'Good or not, it doesn't hide the fact he's bloody ancient.'

'He's not *that* old.'

'Gordon Highlanders, he looks older than your da! And bald to boot. Not to mention the size of him.

214

Tuppence ha'penny's worth right enough. He doesn't even come up to your shoulders.'

'He may be wee, but he's kind and considerate and all the things you never were!' she retorted hotly.

'I might have been more kind and considerate if you'd been the same to me.'

'What did you expect after our wedding night? And me a virgin? Can you even begin to imagine what it was like?'

'You made far too much of it.'

'What, my virginity?'

'No. Our wedding night.'

'You don't understand,' she said shaking her head. 'You just don't understand.'

'I was due my rights and I took them. That's all there was to it,' he said in a surly voice.

'You consider you were due *your* rights after what I'd caught you doing to my cousin Marj at the reception?'

'That meant nothing at all. I told you that after.'

'It meant something to me!'

'All those months of me wanting you, Nellie, and you saying no, not till the wedding night. If I was seeing Marj, then you've only yourself to blame for denying me. I'm only a man, after all, and you were driving me nuts with wanting you.'

'Oh, so it was all my fault, was it?'

'There are two sides to every story, Nellie. And you never took mine into account.'

There was a certain amount of truth in what he said. She had been denying him. But it had been so important to her – so important to her dreams of marriage and of love. But how could she possibly have given into him when she hadn't to Frank? Frank whom she'd so desperately loved.

'How can you do it with a Jew?' Jim went on. 'They're a filthy people, Nellie. Filthy.'

'There's nothing filthy about them.'

'They're even worse than Catholics. And that's saying something.'

215

She thought of Baz, always so immaculately turned out. Even when he was wandering around backstage in his old cardy, he looked like he'd just stepped from the bath. And as for his house, why it had been beautiful inside, so clean she felt she could have eaten off the floor.

'I'll tell you for the last time. I'm not sleeping with him.'

His look told her he didn't believe her.

She poured herself a cup of tea and lit a cigarette. She couldn't wait to move into Bishopton and not have to face Jim every night. In Bishopton he would be tucked out of sight and, as much as possible anyway, out of mind.

'Nellie Wildchild,' said Jim scornfully. 'It's a bloody daft name.'

She put out the light and sat in the darkness finishing her tea and cigarette.

When he spoke several times more she didn't bother replying. She pretended he didn't exist.

'That's just about it,' said Baz glancing around. Outside, the van that had brought the last of the sale furniture was moving away.

They were in Nellie's bedroom. The double bed had been the last item brought up.

Nellie tucked the sheets in and then the blankets. She'd bought them new that very morning. From now on she didn't want to sleep in any of the bedding associated with the Govan house.

'You're bringing them tomorrow?' Baz asked, studying Nellie while she went about making the bed.

'Yes.'

He watched the shape of her backside press against her skirt. It was all he could do to stop himself from reaching out and touching her.

She came upright and wiped the hair from her face. Her cheeks were flushed and there were beads of perspiration on her forehead.

'I love you, Nellie,' Baz said quietly.

She stopped to turn and stare at him. The truth of his statement was written quite plainly on his face.

'I know,' she replied softly.

He came to her and took her in his arms.

'What about Rachel?' she whispered.

'Rachel's my wife and I'll never leave her. I wouldn't, I couldn't break up the family. And there's the theatre – I couldn't give that up either.'

He drew her head down to him and kissed her, a gentle kiss, full of feeling.

'The last thing I want to do is hurt you in any way,' he whispered.

She was trembling, a leaf in the wind. She'd wondered how she'd feel when this moment came. And now she knew. Secure. That was it. Secure.

She was nervous, all right, but she didn't have the urge to run away screaming as she had every time Jim laid his hands on her.

'I never thought this would ever happen to me,' said Baz, pulling her down to the bed so that they were both in a sitting position.

'You once said this sort of love was transient,' Nellie replied.

He frowned, regretting having spoken those words. But they'd been spoken by a man who'd never experienced what it was like to be physically in love. The way he was with Nellie. He'd babbled on about love arising out of respect – true as far as it went. But that was a love totally unlike to the all-consuming passion he felt now.

She closed her eyes as he undid her buttons, shivering as the dress fell away from her. Baz stroked her hair, her shoulder.

'If we're going to do this, then let's do it properly,' she said. Rising from his half embrace she allowed her dress to slip to the floor where it was soon joined by the rest of her clothes.

'Promise not to laugh? I'm hardly a male model.'

'I won't laugh,' she replied, touched.

They lay down together and he took her in his arms. He could feel how tense she was, almost rigid. 'There, there,' he crooned, stroking her thigh.

She closed her eyes, trying to relax, but the spring inside her just wouldn't uncoil.

'There's no rush. No rush at all,' he whispered, all the while stroking and ever so gently massaging.

Ages passed before he moved on top of and into her. Despite herself she gasped. It had been so long, she'd forgotten what an intrusion it was. She put her arms round him and held him as he moved, curiously detached, as though it were happening to someone else. She was getting no sensation at all from what he was doing, but she tried to give the impression that she was.

When it was over they again lay side by side. 'Thank you, Nellie,' he said.

'Hold me close, Baz. Cuddle me,' she whispered.

And he did till it was time for Nellie to get up and make herself ready for the theatre.

The taxi driver helped Myra and Nellie get Jim out of the cab and into his wheelchair where Myra immediately covered him with a rug.

He stared up at the house and sniffed, his eyes rheumy and his mouth set in a downward, disapproving slant. 'So this is it.'

'It looks grand,' said Myra.

'Wait till you see the inside. And the view,' said Nellie.

'I'm cold,' Jim whined. He'd hated the journey. Especially the degredation of being manhandled in and out of the taxi.

'Bring the cases,' Nellie told the driver, and led the way in.

Myra was thrilled with her room and effusive in saying so. After the taxi driver had been paid off and told to return later to take Nellie to the theatre, she and Myra got

218

Jim into his new bed, a second cocoon affair that the hospital people had constructed for him.

She left Myra to get herself and Jim sorted out while she went upstairs to unpack those items of hers that had been brought in the taxi. The bulk of her wardrobe and personal effects had already been installed during the past few weeks.

She stood at the window, lit a cigarette, and stared out over greenery to that glint of the Clyde in the far distance. From now on there would be no more having to sleep in the same room as Jim. And the relief was profound.

She smoked her cigarette through to the end and then carefully stubbed it out. Then she lay spreadeagled on the bed where Baz had made love to her.

What a loving, gentle man he was, how considerate and kind. He'd taken infinite care not to hurt her or rush her.

She thought about Baz's body which had fascinated her because of its softness. Rather like a baby's, and so different to Jim's which had been lean, hard and rough. Being made love to by Baz wasn't going to be a difficult thing to endure at all. She liked the cuddles. That and the feeling of security that went with him.

She gazed round the room. He'd come back here often. They'd discussed and agreed that.

Jim would make a fuss, of course. But she'd see he kept his mouth shut and out of the way when Baz was around. She held all the ace cards, after all.

For the first time since marrying Jim Biles she felt free.

6

Nellie heard the commotion on the stairs followed by the sound of raised voices, one of which she recognized as the stage doorkeeper's. Seconds later there was a thundering on her dressing-room door.

'Miss Wildchild, can I please see you?' a strange voice boomed.

She snatched up her dressing gown and put it on. 'Who is it?'

'Ian McIan.'

She didn't know anyone of that name. 'I'm not decent. And, anyway, I'm going on in a few minutes.' Neither statement was true. It was a good twenty minutes before her first cue.

'I won't take up much of your time. I promise!' McIan shouted. This was followed by more scuffling noises.

'I'm sorry, Miss Wildchild. He burst right past me!' the stage doorkeeper called out.

She opened the door to be confronted by a giant of a man sporting a huge, bushy beard above which were ropelike moustaches. So big was he, she felt like a doll beside him.

'I'm awfully sorry, Miss Wildchild,' the stage door-keeper repeated.

'I can see why you had trouble keeping him out,' she replied drily. Which caused McIan to roar with laughter. The stage doorkeeper was old, small and painfully thin.

220

'What can I do for you?' she turned to McIan.

'Can I come in and sit a wee while? I won't get in your way.'

'Are you safe?'

He looked shocked at the suggestion that he wasn't. 'As houses, I can assure you.' Then with a wink, 'At least till I get to know you better.'

She decided to leave the door open. Just in case. She told the stage doorkeeper she'd look after McIan whom she ushered inside where he perched his enormous frame into a rickety wooden chair which squeaked its protest.

'I can see what attracted him,' McIan said, peering at Nellie's face.

'Attracted whom?'

'Yon idiot and charlatan Carson.'

Suddenly it all clicked into place. This McIan must be the same one she'd been told about the night of Baz and Rachel's party. The Edinburgh man who was Geoff Carson's main rival.

'You're a painter,' she stated.

'Aye, that's right. Or at least I like to kid myself I am. Turn your head a wee bit to the left, will you?'

She did and he grunted, running his fingers through his beard and then scratching underneath.

'I heard Carson asked you to sit for him and you refused. Is that right?'

She nodded.

'Why did you do that?'

'Because I didn't like him.'

McIan's face lit up in a smile. 'Well that's something we agree on anyway,' he said. He rose from his chair and prowled first to the left and then to the right, his gaze never leaving Nellie's face.

'I can well see what the attraction was. For once yon bampot's shown a bit of taste,' McIan said.

Nellie was fascinated by this huge man with the magnetic eyes and slight lilt of a Highland accent. When

221

she asked him if he was born in Edinburgh he replied no, he came from up north. Edinburgh was his adopted home.

'They're all phonies though there you understand,' he growled. 'Would-be artists and would-be intellectuals. Phoney through and through.'

'So why do you live there?'

'I like the city itself. I get something from it. Rather the same way Gauguin got something from the South Seas.'

'You mean it inspires you?'

'You could put it that way I suppose. Although inspire, or inspiration, aren't words I like to use myself. I think they're overused and abused. Especially in Edinburgh.'

'I take your meaning,' she replied with a smile.

'I'm going to be totally honest with you,' he said. 'I came up here the night wanting to paint you for no other reason than to spite Carson, whom I can't stand at any price. You turned him down so I thought I'd put his nose out of joint by asking you to let me do you. But now I've seen you to hell with Carson and all that bloody nonsense! I want to paint you because . . . there's something about your face that's crying out to be put on canvas. And I'm the man to do it. If you'll let me.'

Nellie wasn't sure. She'd never really thought of herself in this particular light before. Carson's request had been denied out of hand because of her dislike for the man.

'What happens to the painting when it's complete?' she asked.

'I'm having an exhibition through in Edinburgh later on this year. I'll make it the exhibition's focal point.'

That idea appealed. 'How much of my time would actually be taken up in sitting for you?' she asked.

He gazed about him, taking in the dressing room, thinking. 'I'll want to do you in a theatrical setting because that's where I feel you belong. So I'll tell you what. How about if you don't sit for me at all in the conventional sense? Let me come backstage to watch you and sketch, and I'll do it all from that.'

'I'll have to ask Mister Spira's permission first. It's not usual for people to wander about backstage.'

'I won't get in anyone's way. I'll just tuck myself up in some wee corner. And as long as there's enough light for me to see by, I'll get down on paper what I need. Now, what do you say?'

Why not? It certainly couldn't do any harm. And she'd taken a liking to this big painter.

'Leave me your address and I'll drop you a line after I've had a word with Mister Spira.'

McIan beamed. 'It's going to be a work of art!' he declared.

'And now you must go. I've got to get into my first costume.'

He took her hand and with a great flourish kissed it. 'Your devoted slave, Miss Wildchild,' he said.

Nellie laughed after he'd gone. Slave indeed!

For a week McIan haunted backstage. Sketchbook and pencil in hand, he was to be found lurking in various well-lit vantage points from where he could observe Nellie when she was on. True to his word, he was never any bother and never got in anyone's way.

During the second week McIan never came near the theatre. Then on the third he reappeared to do more sketching.

On the Wednesday of that week Nellie went out to do her second solo, a semi-novelty number. Confident and relaxed, she began to sing.

She was about to launch into the second verse when a face in the front row caught her attention. At first she couldn't place him. And then the penny dropped. He would glance at her, and then his head would dip as though he were reading something on his lap. Not reading she told herself, sketching. The man in the front row was Geoff Carson.

She came to the end of the number, with an effort

concentrating on the song. As usual, the applause was almost deafening. She made her curtsy while the audience rose to her. When she was finally allowed off she signalled McIan to follow her out into the corridor.

When she told him Carson was in the front row sketching her, his face suffused with anger. 'Of all the lowdown, underhand rats!' he exclaimed vehemently. He clenched his right hand and the pencil in it snapped in two.

'He must have heard you were going to paint me,' she said.

He nodded and tugged his beard. He glanced across at the stage where an eccentric comedian was doing his stuff. 'How long till the interval?'

'About fifteen minutes.'

He tugged his beard again. 'Right. I'll settle Mister Geoff Carson's hash for him,' he said ominously, his eyes flashing like two black diamonds.

Nellie shivered, saying it was best she got back to her dressing room. But once there she decided she couldn't leave matters as they were and sent for Sandy. When he arrived she told him what had happened and asked him to find Mr Spira and explain the situation to him.

The interval came and went.

When she came off she found Baz waiting for her and together they went up to her dressing room. 'What happened?' she asked eagerly.

'McIan got to Carson before we got to him and half-killed him.'

'You mean there was an actual fight?'

'More of a massacre, as McIan's twice Carson's size. The iron was no sooner down than McIan went storming into the auditorium to confront Carson. Words were exchanged, the outcome of which was that McIan took Carson's sketches off him and tore the things up. Then Carson took a swing at McIan who promptly floored him.'

'Is he hurt badly?'

'He'll live. Although he's going to have an awful sore face for a few weeks to come.'

'And what about the customers?'

'Oh, they loved it. Thought it was great.'

Nellie laughed. 'Trust a Glasgow audience. So what happened then?'

'The police arrived. Don't ask me where from. It was like magic. And off McIan and Carson went to the station, the pair of them arrested for brawling in a public place.'

Nellie had been changing her costume while they'd been talking. She now paused as a thought struck her. 'Baz? I wonder if we could use this?' she said.

'How?'

'Remember that journalist who interviewed me before? He might think this was a good story. And if he printed it, it would be more publicity for the Palace.'

Baz raised his eyebrows. She definitely had something. And why just the one journalist? Why not all the dailies? A glance at his watch told him it was ten o'clock. First editions of the morning papers would be being put together even now.

'I'll make a few phone calls,' he said.

It was the following night and Nellie and Baz were lying on her bed drinking champagne. Copies of the morning's papers lay strewn around.

Baz brought himself up onto one elbow to stare at her. 'You just couldn't buy publicity like that,' he said. He glanced across to the nearest paper where the page three leader was, 'The Woman The Scottish Art World Is Fighting Over'. Below was a photograph of Nellie followed by a fifteen-paragraph story about her, McIan and Geoff Carson.

'You know what this means don't you?' he said.

'What?'

'You're not only a sensation. You're an overnight

225

celebrity. From now on everyone in Scotland will know the name Nellie Wildchild.'

She closed her eyes and smiled. 'Do I get to be top of the bill now?' she asked.

He wasn't only in love with her. He was besotted by her. He knew the trouble she was having with their lovemaking but that would right itself in time. In the meantime, he would have to work at it; breaking down and erasing the damage her husband had done to her.

'Next season, top of the bill,' he promised.

'Oh!' she whispered.

'I've got half an hour then I'll have to go,' he said. He reached out to fondle her, kneading her flesh, then caressing it. 'As you know the theatre goes dark soon. What are you going to do with your time off?'

She liked it when he touched her this way. It made her think of herself as a cat. 'I've nothing specific planned.'

'Then how about coming away with me?'

Her eyes snapped open. 'Say that again?'

'Would you like to go on holiday with me?'

'What about Rachel and the children?'

'Daniel and Joe have planned to go off on their own anyway. Sarah was going to come with us but now she can go with her cousins. She'll much prefer that to being alone with me.'

'And Rachel?'

'Has just discovered a place down in Wiltshire where they claim they can cure migraines. Apparently the cure is all tied up with diet and exercise. And the course lasts six weeks. She's already been in touch with them and the only time they can fit her in is when we were supposed to be going on holiday. So now I'm going on my own. Or at least, that's what she'll believe.'

Excitement bubbled in Nellie. This was tremendous. 'Where had you planned to go?' she demanded eagerly.

'France. Belgium. Perhaps up into Germany. We can go where we like, really, I'll be taking the car.'

Nellie had never been out of Scotland before and the

prospect thrilled her. She thought about Jim and Myra. There was no reason she could think of why they couldn't get on on their own for a while.

'Well?' he asked softly, his hand moving slowly in a cupped position between her legs.

'I can hardly wait.' She accepted him into her arms.

While he made love to her she imagined, behind closed eyes, all the places she was going to visit and the things they could do while there.

'What are you thinking about?' Nellie asked, curious. She'd found Jim in his wheelchair out in the back garden where Myra had left him to get some fresh air while she got on with a few chores.

Jim's eyes swung slowly round to fasten on to Nellie's. 'Things, people, places,' he replied.

'What people?'

'Oh, the wifeys who used to come into the shop for their butcher meat. I used to have a good crack with some of them. One or two were right comedians.' His gaze left hers to stare at a nearby bramble bush. 'I never really noticed things until this happened to me. I mean, have you ever had a really good look at a blackbird?'

She shook her head.

'There was one here up until a few moments ago. Absolutely fascinating. And caterpillars, I could watch them for hours. Truly amazing creatures.'

This was a side to Jim that Nellie had never seen before. She almost felt some sympathy for him. Almost.

'When the season finishes, I'm going on holiday for a few weeks,' she said.

'Oh?'

'You and Myra will be all right here on your own, won't you?'

He gave a lopsided, leering smile. 'And what if I said we wouldn't be?'

'You'd be lying.'

'True. True. We'll get by, I suppose.'

'Right, then,' she replied, and made to turn away.

He stopped her by saying, 'Where are you going?'

'Abroad.'

'Very nice. No doon ra watter for our big star, eh? Nothing but the best for her.'

'I deserve it,' Nellie snapped in reply.

He smiled again, as though laughing inwardly at some private joke. 'Going alone?' he asked.

'Yes.'

The smile widened. 'I don't think so. Not you,' he whispered.

'And even if I was going with someone it's certainly none of your business,' she said coldly.

'I'm still your husband.'

'Which you were when you were sleeping with Big Jessie and God knows who else.'

'You're going with the Jew, aren't you?'

She bit off her reply.

'At least I always stuck with my own kind.'

'I find him a lot more my kind than you.'

His eyes became hard and vicious. 'Whore!' he hissed. 'I hate you.'

'Coooeee!' Myra called out, appearing at the rear of the house with a steaming mug of coffee for Jim.

'Not nearly as much as I hate you,' Nellie retorted.

'Go rot in hell!' he shouted after her as she strode away.

'Blackbirds and caterpillars!' she exclaimed out loud. Who would have thought it?

The last night of the show they had a party on stage. Baz laid on whisky, beer and wine together with a buffet of cold meats, sausage rolls and sandwiches.

After a while the musicians played and everyone danced with everyone else. Sandy got drunk and swore undying love for Nellie who, not unkindly, told him to

228

come back when he was more used to wearing long pants.

Rachel was there, and she and Nellie had a long chat about the place she was off to in a few days' time down in Wiltshire. She could hardly wait. Migraines had been the bane of her life since puberty. Nellie wished her well and said she would keep her fingers crossed that the cure was successful.

Since the night of the party in the Spira home Nellie and Rachel had met a number of times, and, indeed, had become fairly good friends.

Nellie was never quite sure whether Rachel knew or not about her and Baz. She suspected she did. But no hint was ever given.

Nellie had come to the conclusion that as long as things continued the way they were, which is to say the Spira family wasn't directly threatened, then Rachel would continue to turn a blind eye. On the other hand, she might be quite wrong and Rachel might know nothing at all about her relationship with Baz. But she was only too well aware that wives have a way of finding these things out.

The party lasted into the small hours and finally ended when Edith, one of the girls in the line, nearly killed herself by falling into the orchestra pit – only saved at the last second by the Great Zampato, Magician.

Nellie drove home alone. Parking her car in the garage she went into the house and upstairs where she found a small supper laid out by her bedside, as it was every night, by Myra.

On the tray containing her supper was a letter. Her stomach gave a little lurch when she read the letter's contents. At last, at long last it had come! A bed was now available for Jim in an institution situated on the outskirts of the city. She lit a cigarette with trembling fingers. Then she read the letter through again.

Jim stared at Nellie, aghast. The threat of being institutionalized had been hanging over him for so long that

229

he'd been lulled into believing it would never actually happen.

'It's all settled,' Nellie said. 'There will be an ambulance here for you later on today.' She'd just come downstairs having made the arrangements by telephone.

Myra stuffed her pinny into her face and started to cry, her eyes wide with horror.

Jim was staring at Nellie but what he was actually seeing was what he imagined the institution would be like. And the vision his mind conjured up caused him to quake inside.

'You can't do this to me,' he bullied.

Nellie was about to reply when suddenly she remembered that scene she'd had with Jim long, long ago. She'd bumped into Mr Sanderson, his old boss at the butcher's shop, and confided in Sanderson, asking him to have a word with Jim. Only Sanderson had made a mess of it by telling Jim that she'd spoken to him, and that night, after work, Jim had come home and beaten her. And after the beating she'd said, just as he had now, 'You can't do this to me.'

His reply rang in her ears. He'd shown no compassion, pity or feeling at all for her then. She'd show none of these things for him now.

'Who can't? I've just done it haven't I?' she said, echoing his reply of long ago.

He seemed to crumble in on himself, as though, at long last, his spirit had been broken. He hung his head to stare dully at the floor.

Myra came to him and gathered him to her breast, her tears splashing down on to his head.

'Oh God! Oh God!' he whispered over and over again.

Nellie stood fully framed in her bedroom window watching the ambulancemen carry Jim out on a stretcher to their waiting vehicle.

Myra walked beside the stretcher looking as distraught

230

as a human being can. All morning she'd been alternately keening and wailing. She was silent now that the moment of parting had arrived.

Nellie had already decided that when Myra was more herself she would offer her the position of housekeeper.

The stretcher was loaded into the ambulance and the rear doors shut. One man had stayed with Jim. The other now climbed into the front of the ambulance and started the engine.

In celebration of having finally got Jim Biles out of her life Nellie painted her nails an exotic shade from a new bottle she'd been saving for a special occasion.

Nellie and Baz spent three weeks in the South of France then motored north into Belgium. After a few days there they decided to go on to Germany where, he told her, he and his family had once lived for a few years after they'd fled from Russia.

Nellie loved the German countryside: the thick pine forests, the clear blue lakes, the golden sun which blazed down day after glorious day.

They drove westward to Leipzig where they turned south again heading for Nürnberg and beyond that Regensburg which Baz remembered from his childhood.

They arrived in Regensburg early in the afternoon, booking into a small *Gasthaus* where they were shown to a large double room. As they'd done since coming on holiday, they registered as Mr and Mrs Spira.

'Everything is so clean,' said Nellie sinking into a large chair by the window which opened out on to a small balcony.

'Makes a change from Glasgow, eh?'

She raised an eyebrow. 'You can certainly say that again.' Even the most fanatically loyal Glaswegian had to admit that the words dirt and Glasgow were synonymous as far as the city's inner areas were concerned.

Nellie was bronzed and, despite the constant driving,

feeling very fit. She was eating well and sleeping a lot. Her holiday was doing her the world of good.

A maid brought them a jug of coffee over which they planned their evening. It was decided that after eating they'd go out and explore the town, going where the fancy took them.

For supper they had chicken, sausages and sauerkraut. They washed it down with an excellent Rheinwein, indulging themselves by drinking two bottles between them.

The meal over, they strolled outside into a warm, balmy night. Arm in arm they crossed a square and into a cluster of small streets beyond. For over an hour they meandered, gradually making their way in a circle which would bring them back to their starting point. Outside a *Bierkeller* they stopped to listen to the accordion music coming from within.

'Shall we?' Baz asked.

The *Bierkeller* was busy with many flaxen-haired waitresses dressed in traditional clothes flying hither and yon, serving tankards and steins of foaming beer. There was also food to be had but not too many people were eating. It was the beer the majority of the customers were interested in.

They sat at a wooden table and Nellie lit a cigarette while Baz tried to catch the eye of one of the waitresses.

When she spoke to Baz in English she was aware of curious glances being shot in their direction. She also felt a subtle change in the atmosphere, which wasn't as friendly any more.

The girl who finally condescended to serve them did so with bad grace. She was hard-eyed and unsmiling.

'*Juden*,' a voice muttered in the background, causing Baz to look up. His good-humoured expression faded a little when the word was repeated with more hostility.

Nellie glanced around her. The men she saw were big and fleshy, many with red faces and eyes moist from drink. '*Engländer*,' she heard. And then '*Juden*' again.

Tiny prickles of fear raced up and down her back.

'When we've finished this we'll go,' Baz said, attempting a smile which didn't quite come off.

'Why wait?' she replied, and started to rise. She was stopped by him placing his hand on hers.

'We finish our drink, *then* we go,' he said.

There was a group of Brown Shirts over in one corner. They wore jackboots and peaked pillarbox hats. On their left arms each sported a swastika.

Baz followed the line of her gaze. '*Sturmabteilung* or storm troopers to you and I,' he muttered. 'Otherwise known as the SA.'

One of the Brown Shirts caught Nellie staring at him and his companions. He smiled, no doubt mistaking her for a German because of the colour of her hair. The smile became a glower when he saw Baz.

The accordionist launched into another tune and as he did the Brown Shirts began to sing. A rousing number which they sang with enormous passion.

'"The Horst Wessel song",' Baz said very quietly so that only Nellie could hear.

The atmosphere was ugly now, jagged and shot through with undertones. The singing rang loudly and raucously bouncing off the walls and ceiling to reverberate round and round the room.

She and Baz were the only ones not singing. His lips were compressed into a thin, slash of a line.

The accordionist again changed tune, the new one being '*Deutschland Über Alles*'. Several of the singers flashed looks of triumph, and hate, in Baz's and Nellie's direction.

One of the Brown Shirts jumped to his feet to raise his arm in the Nazi salute. Every one of his companions immediately followed suit. '*Heil Hitler! Heil Hitler!*' they chanted, while the rest of the singers continued with '*Deutschland Über Alles*.'

The clamour was deafening as Baz coolly finished his beer. He took some marks from his wallet and placed them under the stein. 'Shall we?' he said to Nellie.

There was cold sweat on her forehead and the insides of her thighs were trembling as she came to her feet, but she kept her face devoid of all emotion as she followed Baz to the stairs.

Once outside in the warm night air she took hold of his arm. 'That was terrible,' she said, feeling faint now that it was all over.

Baz shook his head. 'Such hate. And why?'

'Let's head back for France tomorrow?' she suggested. 'What happened down there has sickened me of Germany.'

'Trust me to walk into a den of Nazis,' Baz said, chuckling. The next moment he gave a cry and pitched forward to the ground as he was struck from behind.

There were four of them. Nellie recognized them as the Brown Shirts from the *Bierkeller*.

One of them took hold of her and flung her against a nearby wall. The other three started punching and kicking Baz.

'Stop it!' she screamed. 'Stop it!!' She struggled, trying to break free of the Brown Shirt who was holding her against the wall. But he was far too strong for her.

Coughing blood, Baz tried to come to his feet. His intention was to make a fight of it but he had no hope against the three hulking men surrounding him.

A hand chopped to send him spinning again to the ground, where the feet and fists started in on him again.

And then, as suddenly as it had started, it was all over. Nellie found herself released as the four figures hurried off into the darkness to disappear around a corner.

She ran and knelt beside the moaning Baz. She helped him into a sitting position, sickened and pained by his blood-covered face.

Carefully, he prodded himself all over. 'I don't think there's anything broken,' he mumbled. He held out his arm for her to take hold of, and she helped him to his feet, where he stood swaying.

234

'We'll have to call the police,' she said.

He shook his head. 'No police, no doctor. I'll be all right.'

'But Baz –'

'No buts, Nellie. I know what I'm doing.' He laughed, low and cynically. 'What makes you think the police would be any different from that lot there? Once in their cells they might well have another go at me. It's my fault for being stupid enough to come to Germany.'

With her supporting him he limped down the road in the direction of their *Gasthaus*. 'And tomorrow we *will* head back for France,' he said, squeezing her.

In the *Gasthaus* they made their way up to their room without being seen by anyone. There Nellie stretched Baz out on the bed and stripped him.

His plump body was ripped in several places, a few largish gashes in particular down his back. She insisted they call a doctor, but he was emphatic that they didn't.

Using a flannel soaked in hot water and some antiseptic, she washed him, gently removing the clotted and dried blood from round the gashes and his face.

Already his body was beginning to discolour. By morning he would be a mass of black and blue marks.

When she had washed him as best she could, she patted him dry with a towel. Returning from the bathroom, having rehung the towel, she found him silently crying.

'Baz?'

He turned his head away from her.

She sat on the bed and gently stroked him the way he had so often stroked her.

'Baz?' she said again.

The tears ran down the side of his face to fall on to the pillow where they were immediately absorbed. His eyes were distorted with pain and rage.

'I feel completely humiliated,' he choked in a small voice.

'There were four of them. Far too many for you.'

'I didn't even get in one punch. Not one.'

She could see the hurt was far more than physical. His pride had been wounded, and deeply. Her heart went out to him. She wanted to take him to her and comfort him like a child.

'It's a wonderful thing being a Jew,' he said. 'It can also be terrible. Tonight, well there were nights like this in Russia. Dreadful things have been done to my people, Nellie. Dreadful. And tonight I saw it starting to happen all over again. I'm crying not only for myself, but for Jews everywhere. Especially those in Germany. God help us all.'

She was crying now, too, the tears streaming down her face.

Somehow, it was right to make love at that moment. She knew that with an absolute certainty. With the tears still rolling down her face she stood and stripped. Inside she was a jumble of emotions, but the dominant one was the need to comfort Baz.

She sat by him and used her hand to arouse him, then knelt across him and very gently lowered herself on to him.

Her hair hung down over her face and her breasts fell against him as she moved. After a while she could feel his senses rising to meet her.

Perhaps it was because for the first time when having sex she was giving rather than being taken, but she began to experience sensations where there had never been any before.

Her breath became short and laboured as these new-found feelings forced her to move faster and faster. Part of her mind was filled with wonder and surprise, part given over to the urgency of the moment.

Baz came, a hot gush that she could feel quite clearly shooting up inside her. 'No!' she moaned. And then it happened. A shock wave of sheer pleasure exploded inside her. She screamed, a tearing sound that came from deep in the back of her throat. Her whole body was alive, each nerve end tingling, for the first time in her life. She screamed again as a second shock wave radiated through her.

The walls built up by Jim came tumbling and crashing down. The chains that had bound her broke and were shattered. The damage Jim had done to her had at long last been vanquished and overcome. She was whole again.

It was the first day of rehearsals and they'd just been called on stage from the green room. Beside Nellie and the line, which had half as many girls again as in previous years, there were also a dozen acts which would be making up the bill. The fact that those acts were called for rehearsal was unusual in the extreme. As was the fact that they'd been booked for the entire season rather than the normal week or fortnight.

Robert McLaughlin, the stage director, was there, as was Sandy and Baz, who would be directing the entire show.

'Gather round, ladies and gentlemen, and I'll explain to you what this is all about,' said Baz. He waited for silence before going on. 'Up until now the Palace has presented the normal type of variety, or music hall as it's called in England. Acts coming and going with a continual change over. Then last year I introduced the idea of having something constant in the show, or I should say, someone. Nellie here was that person. And most successful she and the idea proved, too.

'Well, this year I'm going to take that idea a lot further. I'm going to build an entire show, which will remain the same till the end of the season, round Nellie. That show will be called the Palace Follies.'

He waited until the excited buzz had died down before continuing.

'As you know, this sort of thing hasn't been done before in Scotland, so we're all going to be in at the start of something new. And I think very exciting. Any questions?'

237

'I always knew you'd make it big,' Margo whispered to Nellie, squeezing her arm.

Nellie awoke to find herself gummy-eyed and with a foul taste in her mouth. She swung her feet out of bed, but had to grab hold of the side of the bed to steady herself. Her head swam round and round and she felt distinctly nauseous.

Must be a cold or the flu coming on, she told herself. That was the last thing she needed slap bang in what were proving to be the most arduous rehearsals she'd ever known.

Baz was working her harder than she'd ever been worked before. But it was going to be worth it. There was no doubt in anyone's mind that the show would be a winner. It had had that feel about it right from the first day.

She'd gone with Baz to the workshops to have a look at some completed scenery. That in itself was going to be a knockout, being grander and far more spectacular than anything yet seen on the Glasgow, and Scottish come to that, stage.

And then there were the costumes. A fortune had been spent on those. Every penny worth it, Baz had declared on viewing the first ones ready. Her reaction had been one of sheer incredulity, followed swiftly by delight. She hadn't thought so much dazzle and sparkle possible.

The dry retch caught her completely unawares. Gagging, she stumbled through to the bathroom. She thought she was going to throw up, but, gradually, the feeling subsided.

She returned to the bedroom to sit on the bed. She had an hour before being due at rehearsals. She reached for her blouse and skirt.

The skirt wouldn't do up. Impossible she thought as she tugged at it. The damn thing had fitted her perfectly before. Finally she gave up and crossed to the wardrobe

238

where she had a skirt which had always been a little bit loose on her. When she put that on she found it tight round the waist.

Suddenly all the pieces clicked together. Reaching up she touched her breasts which tingled beneath her fingers. She could feel they were fuller.

'Oh my God!' She ran a hand over her face. Pregnant.

She didn't know why she should be so shocked at discovering she was pregnant. She'd never taken any precautions after all! Nor had Baz, or Jim before him.

Somehow, over the years, she'd come to believe she'd never get pregnant. That, perhaps, she was incapable of it. There was absolutely no foundation for her believing this, other than the fact that it simply hadn't happened.

Well, now she knew differently. She was pregnant. Up the spout. In the club. A bun in the oven. And the show, which was totally geared round, and dependent on, her due to open in less than a fortnight.

She put her head in her hands. What a mess! Beside this, flu or a cold paled into insignificance.

Keeping it, she knew without thinking, was completely out of the question. Not only because of her, but because of Rachel and Baz as well.

But an abortion. She'd heard so many stories about what could happen, and often did. Lassies bleeding to death. Dying of blood poisoning. Always remembering.

Shaking her head, she put these thoughts from her mind. She would have to go through with it: the sooner the better.

Without talking about it, or thinking about it.

She wouldn't tell Baz till it was all over.

Betty answered the chap on the door to find Nellie smiling hesitantly at her. 'Help, my God! Come away in, hen,' she said.

'Is he still at his work?'

'Aye.'

She kissed her mother on the cheek and went into the kitchen. She stared around. Everything was more or less just as she remembered it.

'A long time, lass,' said Betty.

'Aye, Ma. It is that.'

'You're looking well.'

'And so are you.' Which was a lie. Betty was looking older, and there was a frailness about her that hadn't been there before.

There was a photograph of her brother Roddy on the mantelpiece above the fire. She wouldn't have recognized him, he'd grown up so much. He was in uniform.

'He joined the Army a few months back,' Betty said proudly. 'He's in the HLI.' The Highland Light Infantry was Glasgow's most famous regiment.

'Time flies,' said Nellie. 'I still think of him as a wee boy.'

'It's a long time since he's been that,' replied Betty, putting the kettle on and getting out a tin of shortie. 'I hear you're doing right well at the Palace.'

'I'm top of the bill in the new show.'

'Fancy that. Our Nellie top of the bill,' said Betty, shaking her head in wonder.

'If you want to come and see me sometime, I'll get tickets for you.'

'Does that invitation include your da?'

'The tickets will be for you, Ma. If you want to take him with you then that's your affair. Just don't bring him backstage to see me that's all.'

'Will you never forgive him Nellie?'

'Never,' Nellie replied grimly. Defiantly she lit a cigarette, remembering the countless times she'd been dying for a fag in this room and not been allowed to light up.

'How's Jim?'

'Ma, I'm pregnant and I need your help,' Nellie stated bluntly.

Betty stared hard at her daughter, then sat down at the

table. 'It's not your husband's then, I take it?' she said.

'It doesn't matter whose it is. I need to lose it.'

'Are you sure Nellie? Killing a wean is an awful thing,' Betty said softly.

A little of her bravado left her then. White-faced, she sat looking at her mother. 'I know, Ma. But it has to be done. There's no other way. Believe me, I'd keep this baby if I could. But it just isn't possible.'

'It's dangerous.'

'I know that.'

'And it's never certain that it'll work.'

'I know that as well.'

Betty sighed, rising when the kettle began to sing.

'Will you help me, Ma?' Nellie pleaded, her mother's little girl again.

'Aye, lass. I will. How far gone are you?'

'I'm not sure. Seven, maybe eight weeks. I missed my last period and the next should've been any day now.'

'You're certain you're pregnant?'

'Positive. I've got all the classic symptoms.'

'It'll cost about a tenner, Nellie.'

'That's no problem.'

Betty laid a cup of tea and some shortie in front of her daughter. 'Come back the same time tomorrow and I'll let you know what's what,' she said.

'The sooner the better, Ma.'

'Aye,' replied Betty. 'The sooner the better.'

The abortion was arranged for three days later. Nellie met up with Betty and together they made their way to an out-of-the-way part of Govan where Mrs Gourlay lived. Mrs Gourlay was the finest in the entire south side, Betty had assured her daughter. Nellie prayed that it was so.

The tenement they arrived at was an old one, broken down and crumbling. On its roof a chimney pot had become detached and was whirring round and round in the fierce wind that had sprung up. Side by side, the two women went into the close and up the stairs. Stairs that couldn't have seen a scrubbing brush in years.

Mrs Gourlay was old with white hair and a friendly smile. She looked like a kindly, much loved granny.

'Come in, come in,' she said, ushering them through to the kitchen where things were already laid out in readiness. There was a roaring fire with a blanket spread in front of it. There was a pan of boiling water on the stove with an assortment of instruments in it.

Nellie was suddenly very afraid. For two beans she would've turned and fled. She reminded herself sternly that she had to go through with it. There was too much at stake for her not to.

'Do you want to stay here, or wait in the other room?' Mrs Gourlay asked Betty.

Betty glanced at Nellie. 'You go through, Ma,' Nellie said.

Betty nodded, relief plainly written across her face. 'Good luck lass,' she said gently.

'If you'll just take your coat, skirt and knickers off and lie down there,' Mrs Gourlay said, pointing to the blanket.

Nellie's hands were shaking as she partially undressed herself. She lay down as instructed, watching fearfully as Mrs Gourlay took the sterilized instruments off the stove.

'I'll have to examine you first,' said Mrs Gourlay squatting beside her.

'Will it hurt?' Nellie asked fearfully.

'Och, just a wee bit, hen. But I'll be as quick and gentle as I can.'

Nellie was in a cold sweat and her heart was hammering in her chest. Her flesh was a mass of goose bumps. Her buttocks and stomach tensed as the instrument touched her.

'Easy, lass. Easy.' Mrs Goulay crooned.

Nellie chewed her lip to keep her mind from what was happening. From the bottom of her eye she could see Mrs Gourlay's white head bent over her.

242

Mrs Gourlay began singing in a cracked, reedy voice. She sang soft and low about a mining disaster. The sound of her voice sent prickles up and down Nellie's spine.

Minutes the length of years passed, until it seemed to her it would never end. She felt as though someone had taken their fist and hit her between the legs again and again and again.

The singing finally stopped and Mrs Gourlay rose to her feet to smile down at Nellie. 'That's it,' she said simply.

Nellie rolled on to her elbow and tucked her legs up under her. That position relieved the aching a little. 'Is it gone?'

'Not yet. That'll take a few hours. What I've done, hopefully, is loosen the foetus. The next thing is for the body to reject it. I suggest you go home and into your bed. Let it happen there.'

Nellie came to her feet. Then, sitting on a nearby chair, she started to pull on her knickers. Stopping in horror when she saw one of the instruments which had been used lying on the blanket. A knitting needle! There was no mistaking it. She'd always believed that knitting needles used for abortions were an old wives' tale.

Betty entered the room white-faced, her eyes immed-iately seeking out Nellie's. 'How did it go?' she asked, her voice trembling.

'We'll know in a few hours,' Mrs Gourlay replied. 'But I'm very hopeful.'

Betty helped Nellie into her coat.

'Ten pounds,' said Mrs Gourlay.

Nellie paid over two fivers, and then, her mother giving her support, they made their way downstairs to where her car was parked.

'Are you sure you're all right to drive?' Betty asked.

Nellie nodded. 'She said you should come home with me. Can you do that?'

'Of course. Your da can get his own tea for once. Won't do him any harm.'

Halfway back to Bishopton Nellie felt her temperature start to rise. Soon she was sweating badly. By the time they arrived she was slightly delirious.

She didn't bother putting the car in the garage as she normally did, but parked it in front of the house. With Betty supporting her, she made her way upstairs to collapse on to her bed.

Betty stripped her and got her into a clean nightgown. 'Hold my hand, Ma,' Nellie whispered.

Nellie dreamt then. A series of nightmares, which, afterwards, she couldn't remember anything about, except that at the time they had terrified her.

For five hours Nellie waited for something to happen, all this time sweating profusely and replenishing the liquid by gulping down cupful after cupful of water which Betty fetched from the bathroom.

'It's going to come, Ma,' she gasped suddenly, as a new pain racked her.

'Jesus!' she whimpered. The pain was almost unbearable. And then it was over.

Betty had seen the garden out back. 'I won't be long,' she said, and left the room.

Nellie was filled with an enormous sense of loss. Difficult to describe, it felt as though part of her very being had somehow been taken away from her.

She was still crying later when Betty returned. Betty sat on the bed and held her close. Mother and daughter wept together softly, no words needed.

When Betty finally left, she had made a firm promise that from then on in she would be a regular visitor to the house in Bishopton. The horror of the abortion had rekindled the natural closeness that had always existed between them but which had faded since Nellie's marriage and her leaving home.

The next morning Nellie presented herself at rehearsal promptly at ten o'clock, her call time. She looked dreadful. She was drawn and haggard, and there were dark bags under her eyes.

'What's wrong with you?' Baz exclaimed when he saw her. He told her to sit down and shouted to Sandy to get some coffee.

She didn't want to tell him yet. She would do that later at a more appropriate time. 'Flu I think,' she mumbled.

'Perhaps you should go home –'

'No!' She shook her head. Lying in bed thinking about what she'd been through the previous night was the last thing she wanted. 'If you just let me take it easy for a couple of days I'll get by all right.'

Baz wasn't so certain of that. She really did look terrible. But Nellie was adamant. She would continue with rehearsals.

She had never known an atmosphere backstage like it. Even the normally phlegmatic stagehands were looking nervous.

'Five minutes,' whispered Sandy, giving her a reassuring wink.

Normally she wouldn't have been ready and backstage this early, but tonight was extra special. Tonight was the opening night of the Follies.

'Good luck,' whispered Margo.

'And you,' Nellie whispered back.

They kissed each other on the cheek, then Margo joined the rest of the line who were in position now, ready to go on.

Baz appeared, dressed in an evening suit, looking as nervous as any of them. He took Nellie's hand and squeezed it. 'You're going to be marvellous,' he said. 'Just do it as you did in rehearsal and you can't go wrong. I promise you.'

'Good luck,' she whispered in reply.

'Break a leg.' He patted her on the arm, gave her what

he hoped was a confident smile, and then left her to cross to the line.

'Beginners!' Sandy called quite unnecessarily as everyone was already in position waiting for the rag to open. It was that sort of night.

Nellie went up on her toes, an old pro's trick that helped you relax. With one hand on her diaphragm and the other on the side of her ribcage, she did some breathing exercises the way Miss McLeish had taught her.

Out front the music struck up and the atmosphere became electric. Robert McLaughlin, who, for that night only, was running the corner, looked across at Nellie and smiled. He then gave her the thumbs up sign.

There was the swish of the curtains opening, followed instantly by a round of applause. 'Go line!' instructed McLaughlin. The applause intensified as the line danced on stage.

The line danced and sang its way through the number; then it was time for Nellie's first entrance.

She came on, atop a built-up level of platforms, to thunderous acclaim. The stage lights had been dimmed, the two limes from out front holding her in a cone of brilliant light. Smiling, she began to descend the flight of steps that would take her on to the stage.

She started to sing, and as she did so the applause faded to an absolute hush. The proverbial dropping pin could have been heard.

> 'Somehow by fate misguided,
> A buttercup resided
> In the Mandarin's Orchid Garden –
> A buttercup that did not grace
> The loveliness of such a place.
> And so it simply shrivelled up
> And begged each orchid's pardon.
> Poor little buttercup in The Orchid Garden.'

McIan was in the front row, an enraptured expression

on his face. Every few seconds his chest heaved in a silent sigh.

She'd been confident when she came on but that confidence grew with every passing second. Soon she knew she could do no wrong. They were hers. Every last one of them.

At the end of her first song they rose to her, cheering and clapping, McIan at the front like some giant conductor leading the applause.

It went like that all night. An entire half hour was added to the show's running time because of applause.

She got eighteen curtain calls and one man, quite overcome, tried to crawl up on stage only to be hauled off by McIan.

Glasgow had never seen the like before.

Nellie's dressing room, the largest the theatre could provide, was chock-a-block with other artistes and well-wishers. Baz had laid on two crates of champagne and McIan had appeared waving a jeroboam of the stuff above his head, most of which, thanks to his treatment of it, ended up on the floor.

'I'm going to do an entire series of paintings of you,' McIan declared, having finally managed to collar Nellie on her own. 'And when they're finished, we'll have the Nellie Wildchild exhibition. Every picture of you. Nobody else. Just you. A feast of you! What do you say?'

Nellie laughed. She was feeling marvellous. Absolutely glorious. The show had been a success beyond her wildest imaginings.

'Well?' he demanded, his face flushed with excitement and drink.

'Why not?' she said.

'Why not indeed!' he roared. 'Why not indeed!'

She was still in her slap and walk-down costume, not having had time to change before her dressing room had been invaded. She sipped champagne and then puffed reflectively at her cigarette. She wanted this moment to go on and on. Never to stop.

'Miss Wildchild?'

She came out of her reverie to find the stage doorkeeper standing beside her.

'A man asked me to give this to you. He said I should bring it right up.'

'Have you time for a drink?' she asked.

His eyes flicked across to where Baz was standing. 'That's awful kind of you, but I think not,' he replied.

She took two half-crowns from the top of her dressing table and gave them to him. 'Have a dram on me then when you get the chance,' she said.

'You're a right toff, Miss Wildchild,' he replied, making the half-crowns disappear into his trouser pocket.

Nellie was about to read the note when one of the acts approached her asking if he could introduce his niece. She laid the note on top of her dressing table, and promptly forgot about it.

It was a good hour later before the party started to break up. Baz had already gone off to his office, having told Nellie he'd return to take her home. The rambunctious McIan, with one of the new girls from the line hanging on to his arm and his every word, was the last to go.

A little bit tipsy from the champagne, Nellie sat at her dressing table and carefully removed her make-up. Then she changed into her street clothes.

She was about to put out the light when she saw the note the stage doorkeeper had handed in earlier. Picking it up she glanced at its contents.

Dear Nellie,

Remember me? Thought you were terrific tonight. I'll hang around outside the stage door for ten minutes as I'd love to have a word. But if you're too busy to see me, I'll understand perfectly.

Frank Connelly

'Oh no!' At the sight of that signature her heart nearly burst. Her Frank had been to see the show!

Whirling she ran from the dressing room, frantically clattering downstairs as she raced for the stage door.

'Good night Miss Wildchild!' the stage doorkeeper called out to her as she went haring past him. She never heard a word.

Through the stage door, into the night beyond. But the area was deserted, as she'd known in her heart of hearts it would be.

'Frank! Oh Frank!' she whispered. Her face suddenly awash with scalding tears. If only she'd read that note when it had been handed to her. And to think she was upstairs guzzling champagne while he was down here waiting for her.

She staggered and put her hand against the theatre wall for support.

'Are you all right, Miss? I thought you looked funny as you went past,' a voice said.

She turned to find herself staring at the stage doorkeeper. Why did his face keep going round and round? Somewhere at the back of her mind it dawned on her that it wasn't only him but the whole world.

'Oh!' she said as the blackness closed in and she pitched forward in a dead faint into the stage doorkeeper's arms.

She came to in Baz's office to find herself stretched out on his day bed. He was hovering anxiously over her, holding a glass of water. There was a wet towel across her forehead.

'You fainted,' he said, and putting his arm under her shoulders lifted her up a bit so she could swallow some of the water.

'Will I call a doctor?' he asked.

She shook her head. 'No. That won't be necessary.'

He perched himself on the edge of the bed and chaffed

her hand. 'You haven't been looking at all well since you had the flu. I've been dreadfully worried about you.'

She didn't want to tell him the real cause of her fainting. 'It wasn't flu I had. It was an abortion,' she said slowly.

Baz blinked. 'What?'

'We were halfway through rehearsals before I realised I was pregnant.'

He rose and crossed to his desk where he kept a bottle of brandy, pouring himself a liberal measure, which he drank neat.

'You should have said, Nellie.'

'Would it have made any difference? The result would have been the same, Baz. There was too much at stake for both of us. At least this way I spared you the extra worry and pressure.'

She fumbled in her pocket for cigarettes.

'Our child,' he said, staring into his now empty glass.

'I suppose the excitement tonight, not to mention the champagne, was just too much on top of everything else,' she lied.

He came to her then and took her in his arms. And they remained like that for some time, neither of them speaking.

He was thinking of her and their lost child. She was thinking of Frank Connelly.

Eighteen months passed, during which the first Follies season closed – a resounding success – and the second one opened to just as much acclaim. Nellie was now firmly established as the foremost female Scottish star, fêted by the public, the newspapers and fellow artistes alike.

As he'd promised he would, McIan, who'd become a great and close friend of hers and Baz's, had been beavering away doing a series of paintings with her as the subject. For months he'd haunted backstage making interminable sketches. One night he failed to turn up, and word reached them that he was now busy in his

Edinburgh studio, translating his sketches on to canvas.

On Tuesday morning Nellie left Bishopton to drive into Sauchiehall Street where she was scheduled to open McIan's Nellie Wildchild exhibition. Normally he exhibited first in Edinburgh, but in this case, because his subject was so identified with Glasgow, he'd decided to have the opening there.

Nellie was in a good humour as she drove into town. After all, it wasn't every day you had this sort of honour. She was thinking of the forthcoming speech she would have to make, the press were to be in full attendance, when, absentmindedly, she noted the vaguely familiar face of a passer-by.

She was a hundred yards down the road when she suddenly realized who that person was. Uttering a muffled exclamation, she slammed on the brakes and came to an abrupt halt. Swivelling in her seat, she saw the man's back disappear up a side street.

She whipped the car into gear and, nearly causing an accident, did a U turn. She gunned the engine to go screeching round the corner in pursuit. The man was halfway up the hill when she brought the car to a shuddering halt beside him.

He looked down in surprise and she saw that the face was a lot older than she remembered it.

'Hello, Frank,' she said.

There was a cynical, quizzical look on his face. 'Nellie.'

She swung the passenger door open for him. When he was seated she stared at him, drinking him in. 'You've put on weight,' she said.

'You've changed as well. But nothing that doesn't suit you,' he said nervously.

She wanted to reach out and touch him. To hold him. 'That night you sent up the note. I never got to read it till well over an hour later, by which time you were gone.'

He smiled, but didn't speak.

'I came the moment I did read it.'

'And how are you? Married?'

251

'Yes.'

'And you?'

'I never did. Lots of women, mind you. But nothing permanent.'

There was so much she had to explain. So much to say. All the misunderstandings that had to be cleared up. She was already late for the opening of the exhibition.

'I've got to see you and talk to you properly, Frank,' she said. 'But I have to rush off just now. Believe me, I wouldn't if I didn't have to, but I do. When can we meet?'

He shrugged. 'Name a time. I'm my own boss so I can fit in with you.'

She named a time and a place. 'Can you meet me there for lunch?' she asked.

'I'll be there.'

On a sudden impulse she leaned across and kissed him on the cheek. 'It's so good to see you again, Frank. You've no idea.'

He got out of the car and closed the door behind him. 'Till later then,' he said, and immediately continued on his way.

She tooted her horn as she passed him and he waved back. She watched him in the mirror till she turned out of sight.

She'd met up again with Frank after all these years. He wasn't married. And she was having lunch with him.

She felt like shouting her exultation to the skies!

She might have been a young lassie going out on her first date. Her insides were fluttering and she kept having the most ridiculous urge to giggle. She'd also been to the toilet four times in the past hour, which was something of a record for her.

On arriving at the rendezvous point she found him already there standing staring into space. His expression was thoughtful, withdrawn.

'Hello, again,' she said coming to his side.

252

'You're early.'

'So are you.'

The moment they'd sat down she blurted out the story she had been waiting so long to tell him. 'I never wanted to break off our engagement. It was my da who made me. He threatened to have you killed if I didn't do as he said.'

Frank rocked back in his seat, staring at her in amazement.

'I planned getting word to you later saying that I would wait for you till you were time served and I was eighteen. Then we could have run off together. But I didn't know where you lived to send a letter or who your friends were even. So by the time I did find someone who could've passed on a message for me you'd already gone abroad.'

The waitress came and they placed their orders, neither particularly interested in what that order was.

'I didn't go abroad,' Frank said quietly. 'I went to London.'

'Your mates at the Yard seemed to think you'd gone off to Canada or New Zealand. South Africa someone even said later.'

'Your da threatened to kill me?'

'He'd have *had* it done. He wouldn't have done it personally.'

'And you broke off our engagement to save my life?'

Suddenly there was a huge lump in her throat. 'Yes,' she whispered.

Frank ran a hand across his face and then closed his eyes. When he opened them again he said, 'What a fool I was.'

'I never dreamt you'd run away like that. The thought just never entered my mind.'

'And your da was listening to our conversation?'

'Through the plate-glass window. You probably never even saw him.'

Frank shook his head in disbelief.

'I never stopped loving you,' Nellie stated in a whisper.

253

'But you got married?'

She gave a bitter smile. Then she told him all about Jim Biles.

He listened grimly, occasionally interrupting to ask a question or to have some point clarified. When she was finally finished he said, 'And what about now, Nellie? Who's your man now?'

She hung her head. Somehow he knew that she had a man other than Jim. She wouldn't lie to him, nor would she keep anything back. 'He's made me what I am,' she said. And told Frank all about Baz and how Baz had built her into a star.

'Do you love him?' Frank asked at last.

'I'm very fond of him.'

'That's not what I asked.'

'No. I don't. You're the only man I've ever loved.'

Frank called the waitress over and ordered himself a large whisky. Nellie declined to have a drink.

'And what about you?' she asked quietly. 'What happened after you left Glasgow?'

'Well, to begin with it wasn't easy. As you can imagine,' he said slowly. 'I took the train down to London, arriving there knowing not a soul. I slept rough for a couple of nights and then landed myself a job in a Covent Garden café.'

'What did you do in the café?' she asked, fascinated.

He smiled at the memory. 'As you probably know Covent Garden is where the fruit and veg arrive in London from all over England, and the world. The traders who buy there have to have their purchases back in their shops before normal trading hours begin so that means a very early start indeed for those who work in the Garden. My own start was half past three, filling the coffee urn and slicing bread for sandwiches. The door was opened at four, by which time I'd been joined by the couple who owned the café. The rest of the working day, which was till 1 p.m., I spent behind the counter, clearing the tables, sweeping up, washing-up, drying. I never cooked though, the couple insisted on doing that themselves.'

'Half past three start,' said Nellie. And gave a tiny whistle. 'And I used to think the sweetie factory was bad. But go on, what did you work at after the café?' She indicated the smart suit he was wearing. 'I take it you're not still there?'

'No, I moved on. I went to work for a couple of Italian importers, brothers called Giovanni, or Johnny, as he's known, and Carlo Maestri. They're a fairly large organization which I've worked my way up in to an executive level.'

There was a slight pause. Then she said softly. 'So what brings you back to Glasgow? Holidays?'

'I'm here on business, Nellie. When I came to your opening night of the Follies I was up for a week. I had various people to see and reports to compile. Now the Maestris have sent me up again.'

'How long for this time?' she asked, unable to keep the eagerness out of her voice.

'That depends. Could be a month, a year, for ever even. It all hinges on the decision they eventually take on whether or not to open up a Glasgow end to their business.'

'You're obviously doing very well for yourself.'

'As are you,' he acknowledged with a grin. He shook his head. 'That night I came to see the Follies, I had no idea you were Nellie Wildchild. I nearly died when I recognized you.'

'Were you alone?' she asked coyly.

'No, I was with a business associate. It was he who provided the tickets.'

'And you never married, Frank?'

'Nope.'

'Can I ask why?'

'You know why.'

Warmth engulfed her. She felt suddenly weak and lightheaded. 'Tell me anyway,' she whispered.

'I never found anyone to replace you. And perhaps I never really wanted to.'

She reached out and took his hand, holding it clasped in hers. 'All those years wasted,' she said.

'But *can* we pick up where we left off?' he asked, studying her face.

'I want to try.' She stared down at the table. 'Do you?'

There was a moment of silence. Then, from far away, his voice said, 'Yes.'

It was one of the nights Baz wasn't in the theatre, being home with Rachel and the family. When the show was over Nellie changed in record time, not even bothering with her make-up. She would attend to that at home.

She was one of the first out of the stage door. A most unusual occurrence as she normally liked to linger for a while. He was under a standard lamp, waiting patiently.

'We're down early. Have you been here long?' she asked.

'Only a few minutes.'

'Have you got a car?'

'I left it at the hotel, knowing you've got one.'

She put her arm in his and guided him towards where hers was parked. 'How about the Roxy Saturday night?' she asked.

He laughed. 'God, do you remember?'

'I've never forgotten a moment of any of those times.'

'And we used to come into town so we wouldn't be seen together,' he said.

'Going home in the same tram and you following me into the back close.'

'You had a friend . . . ?'

'Babs. She's married now. A nice chap. They're very happy.'

'Do you still see her?'

'Oh, aye. She and some of my other pals from the sweetie factory come over from time to time. I see Babs

256

more than the others. We usually meet up in the town and have afternoon tea.'

'And what about your da?'

Her face clouded over. 'Ma thinks I should forgive him for what he did to me, and you, but I never will. Hell will freeze over first.'

'I'm sure he thought he was doing it all for your own good.'

'That's what Ma says, but whichever way you look at it, I was the one who lost you and then had to live with Jim. Small consolation, knowing it was for my own good.'

During the drive to Bishopton they talked, she occasionally reaching out to touch his thigh, as though to reassure herself that he really was there and not a mirage.

He stood looking up at the house while she parked the car in the garage. 'Very nice,' he said when she joined him.

'Bought and paid for. And everything in it. I earn quite a bit now since the Follies opened. And this year more than last.'

She took him inside and up to her bedroom. There he produced a bottle of whisky from his coat pocket, saying he hadn't come empty handed. The usual tray of supper was there from Myra, but she wasn't hungry. Nor was he.

She put on the gramophone while he poured more drinks. Then they sat back to look at one another. Neither was in a hurry.

'Tell me about your life in London.'

'Do you mean my life, or the women who've been in it?'

She laughed. 'Both.'

'I have a small flat in Islington overlooking the canal. From my back window you can watch the narrow boats chug up and down. I like that.'

'And the women?'

'They come and they go. All sorts really.'

'But nothing serious?'

'No,' he smiled.

She sipped her whisky and studied him. He'd become

very self-contained. There was a strength about him which she found exciting.

He'd always had strength of character, of course – that had always been a feature of his – but he had grown considerably, matured, in the intervening years.

Those same years had also added creases and crinkles to his face – and the tiniest of scars above his left eyebrow.

He got up and crossed to the gramophone and changed the record. His movements were also different. Before there had been the slight awkwardness of the young man. Now he moved with a tightly controlled assurance.

'Dance?' he asked. He'd put on a waltz.

She came into his arms feeling as though she fitted there. That it was the most natural place in the world for her to be. Like coming home.

They waltzed slowly, bodies hard against one another. She knew he was wanting her just as badly as she was wanting him. They danced to four records and then she said she'd had enough. She lit another cigarette while he topped up her drink.

'To us!' he toasted.

'Nellie?'

'Yes?'

'Let's go to bed.'

He was already in bed when she returned from the bathroom. He was up on one elbow, drinking whisky. The look he gave her made her shiver.

She slipped in beside him and they stared at one another. She was suddenly nervous. Feeling terribly virginal.

'This sure beats the back close,' he said, as nervous as she was. Reaching out she drew him to her. Breast to chest, she could feel the thudding of his heart.

Their lovemaking was over fairly quickly. Because it meant so much to each of them, they'd been a little shy, reserved. But it was true love they'd made, and because of that the experience was memorable. Forever etched in both their minds.

Nellie curled up against Frank holding him close; wishing it was in her power to melt her flesh into his.

Jim had debased and defiled her. Baz had made her whole again. But Frank had lifted her into an entirely new world.

When she heard the knock on her dressing room door she knew who it was and why he was there. It was a moment she'd been dreading. 'Come in Baz!' she called out.

The smile on his face belied the hurt, quizzical expression in his eyes. 'Can I sit?' he asked.

'Of course.'

The half had been called. She was in her robe, putting on her make-up, concentrating on making the black lines which swept across her lower eyelids like a bird in flight.

'What's wrong Nellie? Have I done something?' he asked hesitatingly.

It had been ten days now since he'd been home with her. During that time she'd pleaded every excuse imaginable from headaches to period pains.

'No, you've done nothing,' she replied, sadness heavy within her. She was about to hurt dreadfully this man who'd been so kind to her. Inevitable as it was, it was the last thing she wanted to do.

'Then why do you keep putting me off?' he asked.

She laid down her eye brush and looked at him in the mirror, feeling about two inches tall. 'Do you remember I once told you that my husband got me on the rebound?' she asked.

Baz nodded.

'And then I told you about the chap he'd got me on the rebound from. Well that chap's name was, is Frank Connelly.'

Baz sat very still, his eyes glued to Nellie's in the mirror.

'You've been marvellous to me, Baz. I couldn't have met a sweeter, nicer man. Patient, too.' She made a gesture that took in not only the dressing room but the theatre as a whole. 'Then there's all this. Nellie Wildchild, star of the Follies. I owe it all to you. Even the name was your creation.'

'Are you saying it's all over between us?' he asked slowly.

'Frank came back. And I love him just as much as I ever did. I wouldn't break us up for any other man, Baz. You've got to believe that. But Frank and I, well, it's something made in heaven.'

Baz took out a small leather case from which he extracted a cigar, taking his time in lighting it. 'Are you and Frank going to get married?'

'If he asks me. I'll have to get divorced first from Jim, of course.'

'Will he ask you?'

'I hope so.'

'But he's Catholic, isn't he?'

'That doesn't bother me in the least.'

'And where will you live?'

'Glasgow, London, wherever his job takes him.'

'You'll give up the theatre then?'

She hadn't really thought that through and said so, adding, 'But I will if I have to. He's more important to me, and always has been, than anything else.'

'I see,' said Baz behind a cloud of blue smoke.

'I'm sorry,' she said.

He smiled bitterly. 'So am I.' He rose and crossed to the door. 'I've come to love you as much as you say you love him.' Still smiling, Baz closed the door behind him.

That night after the show Frank met Nellie and she drove them back to Bishopton. 'Baz came to see me just after the half. He wanted to know what was what. So I told him.'

'How did he take it?'

'It cut him up pretty badly. He said he was in love with me as much as I am with you.'

They drove a little while in silence, each with their

separate thoughts. 'Now that's sorted out, do you want to move in with me?' she asked suddenly.

He glanced at her, then reached out to place his hand on her shoulder. 'I can't think of anything I'd like more,' he replied. 'Besides, the Scot in me hates like hell having to pay out for a hotel room I'm only changing my clothes in.'

Nellie and Frank lay on what was now their bed, glistening with sweat.

Each time they made love it got better and better as they relaxed and learned how best to please the other. As Frank joked, practice made perfect. They believed in lots of practice.

They'd been four days apart while Frank had been down to London talking to the Maestri brothers. They'd been pleased with what he'd had to report, telling him to consider himself based in Glasgow indefinitely. Nellie had been ecstatic to hear that; she could now continue at the Palace.

Frank had only been home from London a little over an hour.

'Oh, I've got something for you!' he exclaimed, and, getting up, crossed to where his suit had been thrown carelessly over a chair. He fished in the pockets till he found what he was looking for, returning to Nellie with one hand behind his back.

'Close your eyes,' he said. He took hold of her left hand and slipped a ring on to her wedding finger. 'You can look now.'

She opened her eyes to find herself staring at an engagement ring that was strangely familiar.

'Recognize it?'

'It's not – ?'

'It is,' laughing at the expression of incredulity on her face.

She touched the ring, remembering it from all those

years ago when he'd first given it to her; when she'd returned it to him that day in the shop entranceway in Sauchiehall Street.

'You kept it all this time,' she said, amazed.

'I suppose, at the beginning, I thought I might give it to someone else eventually. But of course I never did. I never dreamt I'd be giving it back to you, though.'

She raised the ring to her lips and kissed it, her eyes gleaming with tears.

'I had to wait till I went back to London before I could pick it up,' he said. 'And now that you've got it, will you marry me?'

The tears became a flood. 'For the second time, yes,' she sobbed.

He held her and kissed her till the tears had stopped. 'Before you can marry me you'll have to get divorced,' he said.

'I can't think of anything I'd rather do. I'll see a solicitor in the morning,' she replied.

'I'll come with you.'

'I'd like that. And you know what else I'd like?'

Her expression told him what it was she wanted. He was only too willing to oblige.

7

The next few months for Nellie were idyllic. Each day was an absolute joy to wake up to, now that she had Frank.

The Follies were packing them in and it was rare enough to cause comment when a performance wasn't a sell-out.

Baz had been the perfect gentleman in accepting the situation between her and Frank, and although he was deeply hurt, there was never any bad feeling on his part toward either of them.

It was getting on for the end of the season when Nellie received a letter from the Press Club informing her she'd been voted Scottish Personality of the Year and asking her to attend a party they were throwing in her honour.

The night of the party, Frank picked her up after the show and they drove to the Press Club in his new car, a sleek Riley. They were both in a frivolous mood as they entered the club where Nellie was immediately given a standing ovation.

Drinks were pressed on them, and, after a short while, they were led through to a large room where rows of tables had been set out ready for a meal.

After the meal speeches were made, the final one by Nellie which was short, very funny and consisted mainly of her thanking the press for being so kind to her over the last few years. That done, everyone retired to the bar where the beer and whisky were soon flowing liberally.

McIan, voted Personality of the Year himself in the past, was also at the function. His Nellie Wildchild exhibition had been widely acclaimed and, indeed, had a great deal to do with Nellie receiving that year's award and accolade.

McIan and Frank were at the bar treating one another when Nellie was approached by a suspicious looking, beady-eyed man who walked with a limp.

The man stopped beside Nellie, who was chatting to a cartoonist called Neil Mungo, and stared at her, taking her in from head to toe.

Aware of this, she was suddenly uncomfortable. There was something repulsive about the man.

'So you're Nellie Wildchild!' he said, interrupting her conversation with Mungo.

She smiled at him and offered her hand. 'That's right. I don't believe we've met.'

He ignored the proffered hand. 'Well, I certainly don't think you're anywhere near as good-looking as you're reputed to be,' he continued.

Nellie's smile became strained. She glanced to Mungo for help.

'Robin Carson,' Mungo said. 'Writes for the *Daily Post*.'

'I've seen you perform, or should I say I've had the *misfortune* to see you perform, and you certainly didn't get my vote for the award. As a so-called star, I think you're decidedly lacking in twinkle.' Then he laughed at his own joke.

'Well, you're entitled to your opinion,' Nellie replied quietly. 'But it certainly doesn't seem to be one shared by the vast majority of the people who come to see the show.'

The eyes became even beadier as they bored into Nellie, who had no doubts whatever that she was facing an enemy.

Those within earshot of this exchange had fallen silent causing a soundless oasis amidst the surrounding babble. A number of men glanced sympathetically, and a few anxiously, in Nellie's direction. But none moved to intervene.

'Robin has a reputation for acid wit,' Mungo explained. 'I'm afraid we've all suffered from it in the past.'

Nellie suddenly realized that Neil Mungo, as were the others listening in, was scared of Robin Carson. And as for the name Carson, it wasn't a particularly common one in Glasgow. In fact she'd only ever come across it once before.

'Are you by any chance related to Geoff Carson, the painter?' she asked.

'My brother.'

'Ah yes!' she replied. 'I thought I saw a similarity. You've both got atrocious manners.'

Robin Carson bared his teeth. 'Coming from the gutter as you have, I'm surprised you even know what manners are,' he said, his voice dripping spite and venom.

'I'm sure the gutter is something you know a great deal about,' she retorted instantly.

One of the onlookers tittered, stopping immediately when Carson flashed him a filthy look.

'And how is Geoff?' Nellie went on. 'Is he doing well?' She knew from McIan that he wasn't.

'You're becoming impertinent,' Carson snapped.

'Then that's something we'll have in common.'

'Are you trying to make a fool of me?'

'I don't have to, Mister Carson. You do that admirably enough yourself.'

The oasis of quiet had widened considerably now. Somewhere in its ranks there was a sharp, barking laugh followed by a guffaw.

Carson glared but couldn't see who the culprits were. He brought his attention back to Nellie. 'I've heard you slept your way to the top. Any comment?' he asked.

'What sort of question is that to ask a lady?' she replied.

His smile matched hers. Only there was a nasty, razor-like quality about his. 'I wouldn't ask it of a lady,' he said.

She'd left herself wide open on that one, she told herself.

Suddenly she wasn't so sure she could handle Carson.

'Who's the creep?' a voice said. She looked round to find Frank by her side.

'Robin Carson. He writes for the *Daily Post*.'

'I've read some of your muck,' Frank said, though he had never heard of the man before. 'And muck is certainly the right name for it.'

'I didn't catch *your* name?' Carson said.

'Frank Connelly. Miss Wildchild's fiancé.'

'Ah! And you imagine, I suppose, that you've come galloping to her rescue. Saving lady fair. Only, as has already been said, this one's no lady.' He swung his attention back to Nellie. 'Again, I ask you, have you any comment on the accusation that you slept your way to the top?'

'Take it easy, Robin,' Neil Mungo said somewhat half-heartedly. He was rewarded with a withering look which caused him to smile nervously and glance away.

'I'm waiting for an answer!'

'You really are a horrible little creep, aren't you,' Frank said, diverting his attention away from Nellie.

Carson tapped the floor with his rubber-tipped stick. The entire room had gone quiet now. 'You're beginning to annoy me, Connelly.'

'*Mister* Connelly to you.'

'Indeed!' said Carson, and laughed. He glanced around. '*Mister*,' he said sarcastically and with great emphasis. He laughed again.

'I suggest if you want an interview with Miss Wildchild then you write asking for one,' Frank said. 'That's the normal procedure.'

'Are you trying to tell me how to do my job?' Carson asked ominously.

Frank raised an eyebrow, but didn't reply.

Carson looked Frank up and down, the way he had done Nellie a few minutes earlier. Frank waited till Carson had completed his visual examination, then did exactly the same thing to Carson.

Carson was furious and showed it.

Frank smiled, a nasty smile that was both dismissive and full of contempt, to infuriate Carson further.

'Why don't you run along and play your silly games elsewhere,' Frank said.

Breath hissed from Carson's mouth. Slowly, he brought the tip of his stick up to jab Frank lightly in the chest with it. 'Connelly,' he said. 'I'm not going to forget that name.'

'Let's go home Frank,' said Nellie.

'Embarrassed or scared to answer my questions?' Carson asked her.

'Not in the least.'

'I'd say you were.'

'There's nothing I've ever done that I'd be ashamed to admit to.'

'A paragon eh?' Carson said, and chuckled, having regained his composure.

'Hardly that –'

'Tell me,' he interrupted. 'Is it true you used to work in a sweetie factory?'

'Yes.'

'And that you once brawled in the street with a co-worker?'

Where in the hell had he got that from, Nellie wondered.

'No answer, eh?'

Frank decided this had gone far enough. 'I've met men like you before,' he said. 'Bitter, twisted men who've become as deformed in their minds as they are in their bodies.'

'How dare you!' Carson spluttered.

'And how dare *you*!' Frank retorted. 'Now hobble off, before I'm tempted to flush you away.'

With a screech of rage Carson flew at Frank, managing to strike him several times about the face and shoulders with his stick before Frank was able to get his arms round him and hold him.

Carson struggled in his arms, trying to get free. It

suddenly came to Frank what he should do. If he couldn't hit the man, then he'd humiliate him. In two swift movements he sank to the floor on one knee, Carson over his upright leg. With great gusto, he began to spank him.

The laughter began slowly and gathered momentum. By the time Frank had finished, it had become a great wave of sound filling up the room.

Frank dumped Carson unceremoniously on the floor. Rising, he extended a crooked arm which Nellie slipped hers through. And like that, triumphant, they carved their way through a sea of thundering, clapping hands to the exit.

McIan jostled his way after them. Tears of laughter were still rolling down his cheeks when he joined them outside. 'That was the funniest thing I've seen in years,' he said slapping Frank heartily on the back. 'It'll be the talk of the Press Club for the next decade, if not longer.'

They walked round the corner to where the Riley was parked. Frank opened the door and helped Nellie inside. He was turning to walk round the car when McIan took hold of his arm. He stared up at the painter towering over him.

'You've made a really bad enemy though, Frank. Be careful. That one's the original viper.'

'I'll remember. Although it's not myself I'm worried about. It's Nellie. A man like him who goes in for muckraking could give her bad publicity.'

Nellie rolled down the window so she could be heard. 'I'm sure that was in his mind before he even spoke to me tonight. He wants to get back at me because of his brother.' She explained to them then about Geoff Carson.

'So we'll just have to wait and see what happens now,' Frank said grimly.

There were nearly halfway home when he suddenly let out a great roar. 'I'll never forget that till my dying day!' he spluttered.

Nellie joined in the laughter.

268

*

Two weeks later Frank and Nellie came down to breakfast, and found the papers laid out on the kitchen table by Myra, the *Daily Post* among them.

On page three Frank came across the leader, 'What Sort Of Woman Is This Glasgow Has Come To Idolize?' Underneath was Robin Carson's by-line. And underneath that a picture of Nellie.

The article was a long one, most of which consisted of an interview with Jim Biles out at the institution.

Frank read it through, then, wordlessly, handed it to Nellie. By the time she'd come to the end she was white-faced.

'Carson's made you out to be some heartless monster who's committed her adoring husband, while she's cavorting with a fancy man, namely me.'

Nellie glanced at the article again. 'The trouble is, there's nothing here I can prove is a lie. Most of it would be Jim's word against mine.' Then suddenly she burst out angrily, 'How can he say he worshipped the ground I walked on!'

'To read that, you'd think Biles was a saint and butter wouldn't melt in his mouth,' Frank said bitterly.

'At least there's nothing about Baz and me. That's something at least.'

'How will his wife take it if that comes out?'

'Not very well I shouldn't think.'

'And Carson knows about you two. That's for certain.'

Nellie bit her lip. She hated the idea of Baz and his family being hurt.

The telephone rang then and when Nellie answered it she found it was Baz.

'Have you read it?' Baz asked.

'A minute ago. Will it affect business?'

'I don't know. We'll just have to wait and see.'

'Baz. He knows about us. He said as much at the Press Club that night although your name was never mentioned.

269

He just kept asking me if it was true I'd slept my way to the top.'

There was a pause, the only sound the crackle on the line.

'Baz?'

'I'm still here, Nellie. Do you think he'll print about us?'

'After what happened at the Press Club I think he'll print anything that can harm me.'

'Damn!' Baz swore.

'What are you going to do?'

'Explain the situation to Rachel. I'd much rather she got it from me than him.'

'Baz, I am sorry.'

'You're not to blame. It's that dreadful man who is.'

'Does Rachel know about us, do you think?'

'I don't know. She's certainly never said, or even hinted.'

'Will you speak to her today?'

'I think that's best. I mean, he could print about us tomorrow.'

Softly she said, 'Come and see me before curtain up. I'll want to know how you got on.'

'I'll come just after the half. 'Bye for now, Nellie.'

'What a damn mess,' she said to a grim-faced Frank.

That night there was a full house at the Palace and Nellie was received as warmly as ever, taking nine curtain calls at the end, which was fairly average. According to Baz and the box office advance bookings hadn't slackened off any.

Frank was waiting for Nellie, as he always did, when the curtain came down, and after she'd changed and taken off her slap they made their way to the Riley which was parked close by the theatre in a side street.

He was just about to help Nellie in when a bottle came whizzing out of the night to smash against the windscreen, glass flying in all directions.

Frank went round the car at a run to grab hold of the figure who'd thrown the missile. The man yelled in terror as Frank lifted him off his feet and smashed him against a tenement wall. Frank drew back his fist to hit the man and in that instant a flashbulb popped.

Frank turned to see a second man rushing off down the street, a camera cradled protectively in the crook of his arm.

The first man squirmed, trying to break away, but didn't succeed.

'Who put you up to this? Frank demanded. 'As if I didn't know.'

The man shook his head.

'Let him go Frank,' said Nellie, coming to his side.

'I could punch his head in!'

'That would only make matters worse.'

He released the man and jerked his head in the direction the photographer had taken. 'Get!' he said.

Needing no second bidding, the bottle-thrower went clattering away.

'Are you all right?' Frank demanded.

She picked a few shards of glass out of her hair and coat. 'Shocked, that's all. That bottle gave me quite a turn.'

'A set-up,' Frank said between gritted teeth. 'A damn set-up. Well, they got the picture they wanted. I can imagine the article that's going to go with it.'

He surveyed the damage done to his car and shook his head in sorrow. 'I'll bet this isn't mentioned though,' he said.

With Nellie's help he picked up all the broken glass on the front seat and floor and threw it into the gutter.

The article appeared two days later and was headed, 'Nellie Wildchild's Boy Friend', and it was the picture of Frank hauling off to hit the bottle-thrower.

The article was short and basically a recap of the

previous one. Without actually saying so, it somehow gave the impression that Frank was a thug. Jim Biles was again very much the aggrieved party.

'The bastard,' Frank said, referring to Robin Carson.

Nellie looked grim. When she tried to pour the tea her hand was shaking with anger.

'Good-bye then. Take care of yourself,' said Babs through the car's open window.

'And you. See you soon,' Nellie replied.

Babs waved at her close mouth, then vanished inside.

Nellie always enjoyed being with Babs. Although she was now famous, and rich by Babs's standards, that hadn't come between them. When together they were still the two daft lassies who'd worked at Harrison's sweetie factory.

It was Sunday afternoon and Babs had been over for lunch. Her husband Phil had also been invited but had declined, saying he had a number of jobs round the house that desperately needed doing.

Nor had Frank been present. He'd been out since mid-morning on business, saying as he left that he wouldn't be back in till early evening.

Nellie slowly drove away from Babs's close, passing, a few streets further on, the place where she and Jim had lived.

Thinking of him made her remember she had some papers in the glove compartment which her solicitor had forwarded to her for perusal and signature. They were concerned with the divorce, which was now well under way, and they would also have to be signed by Jim. On a sudden impulse she decided she would go out to the institution and hand them to him personally rather than send them back to her solicitor as she'd intended.

It was a grim-looking place. Large, grey-stoned and Gothic, it had narrow slit windows in the walls and turrets on the roof. The overall impression was of a medieval fortress.

Inside it was gloomy with lots of tile and marble. There was a smell of polish in the air, mixed with something else. Hopelessness, she wondered?

She stopped a stern-faced, middle-aged nurse who told her where she could find Jim. She climbed three flights of well-worn stairs to his ward.

She was about to enter the ward when three men came out, one of them was her father, Davey. The other two were cronies from the Masons who'd often come round the house when she was at home. And, indeed, Turk Crombie, a tall hook-nosed man now staring at her intently, had called on Jim several times after the accident.

'Nellie,' Davey said.

She stared at him wordlessly. He was opening his mouth to say more when she swept past him. He swore and, for a moment, she thought he was going to come after her.

She took a deep breath to gather herself. The chance encounter had left her strangely shaken. Then she spied Jim at the far end of the ward.

Jim looked up in surprise as she sat down by his bedside. 'It's you,' he said, eyes flashing malevolence. 'You just missed your da.'

'Does he come often?'

'Fairly regularly.'

She gazed around. It was a long ward containing about thirty beds. Like the rest of the building, it was gloomy and almost lifeless.

'No grapes?' Jim asked mockingly.

She brought her attention back to him, aware that a number of people were glancing surreptitiously in her direction. She'd been recognized.

'I read what you had to say in the *Daily Post*,' she said.

'Oh, aye?'

'Not quite the way I remember it happening.'

'Well, it wouldn't be would it?'

There was a pause. Then Jim said, 'This Frank Connelly you're going out with, he's the same Frank Connelly you were once engaged to isn't he? The Fenian?'

'Yes.'

'Your da said he thought it was.'

'He came back to Glasgow and we met up again. We're going to be married after the divorce.'

Jim looked at her contemptuously. 'Are you turning?'

'No.'

'Is he?'

'As neither of us are practising Christians, the religious difference doesn't bother us. And speaking of the divorce . . .' she fished in her handbag to produce the papers she'd placed there from the car's glove compartment, 'I brought these for you. They require your signature. She placed them on his bedside table.

Jim glanced at the papers, then back to her. 'Why the personal service?'

Her eyes glinted. 'I was curious to see this place.'

'Nice, isn't it?'

'It could be worse.'

His lips thinned and twisted down into a cynical smile. 'I hope knowing it's a rat hole gives you some satisfaction.'

She smiled sweetly. 'It does.'

'You're really something,' he hissed.

She drew on her cigarette, the smile still playing round her mouth. 'When it comes to being mean and downright nasty, I had a good teacher. In fact, the very best.'

He glared at her, all his anger and frustration in his face. His one good hand opened and closed. He would have given anything to have been able to strike her.

'I'll give Myra your regards when I get back,' Nellie said.

His hand took hold of a corner of the blanket and viciously twisted it. He was imagining it was Nellie's throat. Like a pot boiling furiously with the lid on, he might explode at any second.

'Good bye,' she said softly. And without waiting for a reply she turned and walked down the length of the ward.

Whether as a result of her visit to the institution, or because it had already been planned, a few days later another article by Robin Carson appeared in the *Daily Post*, again an interview with Jim.

In the article Jim said that Nellie had climbed to stardom through the beds of various men, and named, as an example, Mister Basil Spira who owned and ran the Palace Theatre. He went on to say that she'd done this after he'd been paralysed and unable to do anything about it. And yes, he had kept on loving her after his accident. But that love had died the day she'd packed him off to an institution so she could live with her current lover, Mr Frank Connelly.

'You pig,' Nellie breathed when she'd reached the end of the article.

Frank had already left for his office, going in particularly early that day as he'd wanted to catch up on some paperwork.

Crystal tears were streaming down her face when she rang him and told him about the article. Frank said to hell with the paperwork, it could wait. He told her to put the kettle on, he'd be there as quickly as the Riley would bring him.

A few minutes past 11 a.m. on Sunday 3 September 1939 Nellie was glued to her wireless set listening to Chamberlain's historic words announcing that Great Britain was once more in open conflict with Germany.

She lit a cigarette with trembling fingers as the Prime Minister went on. War had been inevitable since Friday when Germany had invaded Poland, Britain having reaffirmed its pledge to Poland two months previously.

Still, she'd hoped, as had everyone, that somehow this

275

calamity would be averted. That a way would be found to stop the German insanity.

There was an unreal feeling in the air. Nellie was certain that unreality must be covering Britain like a blanket, as though time itself had stopped. As though the entire country were holding its breath.

Her brother Roddy was in the Army. She'd never been particularly close to him but he was her flesh and blood all the same. Now he would be in the forefront of whatever was about to follow.

Because she always found comfort and solace in singing, she started to do so now, a tune Betty had sung to her as a child.

But for once her singing didn't bring comfort and solace, instead a terrible ice-cold fear gripped her insides. A fear she was going to find would refuse to go away.

The following Wednesday morning Nellie and Frank were sitting round the breakfast table. Frank was reading the paper, the first few pages of which were crammed with war news.

On page four Robin Carson's by-line caught his attention. 'Jesus Christ!' he exclaimed after reading the first few paragraphs.

Nellie looked up. 'What is it?'

'Carson's at it again,' he replied tightly, reading on.

'What's he said about me this time?'

'It's not an attack on you, but an indirect one on me. He's insinuating that I'm a Fascist because I work for the Maestris.'

'A Fascist!' Nellie said, eyes opening wide. Leaving her chair she came round to stand beside Frank, leaning over his shoulder to read the paper now spread on the table before him.

She read, 'proof beyond question that the Maestri brothers of Covent Garden, London, have direct connections with the Fascist party of Italy. Weekly money is sent by the Maestris to the Italian Fascists for the furtherance of Italian Fascist aims and expansion.

'We would remind readers that it is only last May that Italy signed a pact with Germany. A country we are now at war with. And in April last, Italy seized Albania having by then conquered and cruelly subdued Abyssinia.'

'Oh!' Nellie whispered when she came to the bit which said, 'Mr Frank Connelly, Nellie Wildchild's close friend and associate, is the Maestri brothers' representative in Glasgow.'

Nellie read the article through to the end, then looked up at Frank. 'He doesn't actually say you're a Fascist.'

'No, but he bloody well implies that I am.'

'Do you think the Maestris are sending money to the Italian Fascist party?' Nellie asked.

'They must be, otherwise Carson would never dare state so emphatically that they are.'

Frank gathered the paper into his hands, screwed it into a tight ball, then threw it away from him. He barked out a loud laugh. 'You have to admire Carson. He just never gives up. I mean, just think of the time and effort that must have gone into digging up that sort of information. Even I, who work for them, didn't know the Maestris were Fascists, for God's sake!'

'You spanking him at the Press Club that night was funny at the time. But I regret it now. You lit a time bomb. A time bomb Carson is determined will blow my career to smithereens.'

'I'll put a letter of resignation in the post this morning. I can't go on working for the Maestris now,' Frank said.

But even as Nellie and Frank talked, the knot of fear in her stomach tightened yet further.

It was her last solo number before the interval and the cup of tea she was looking forward to. She threw out her arms when she reached for the high note. A note that came out pure and golden, sheer pleasure on the ear.

'Where's your Fascist china?' the voice yelled from somewhere at the back of the stalls.

She continued with the song, not sure she'd heard correctly, hoping it was a trick of her imagination.

'I said, where's your Fascist china the night?' the man repeated, this time in a roar, shaking his raised fist.

Immediately a murmur ran through the audience. Heads turned in the man's direction, but he didn't resume his seat. Instead he remained standing, glaring defiantly and aggressively at Nellie on stage.

Nellie faltered and then stopped singing. She was at a complete loss as to what to do. She could see Sandy staring at her from the corner. He was making a motion which indicated dropping the curtain. She shook her head. That was the last thing she wanted.

Slowly she walked downstage. 'Put the auditorium lights up,' she ordered. They came on as she reached the foots.

Her heart was thudding in her chest and suddenly her throat was dry as a desert.

The man who'd shouted was of middle height with dark hair and a sallow complexion. She could tell from his appearance that he was a working man, the sort of man to whom Fascism would be an anathema.

The audience was staring up expectantly at Nellie. Nor were all the faces she saw friendly. Quite a number were openly hostile.

'What makes you think my friend Frank Connelly is a Fascist?' she asked the man.

'It said so in the paper,' he shouted back.

'No it didn't. That article said the people he worked for were, it did not say he was.'

The man glanced around him. 'All tarred with the same brush if you ask me,' he said.

'Tell me something, who do you work for?' Nellie asked.

The man stared at her. 'Black Lion brewery,' he replied slowly. 'Why, what's that to you?'

'Isn't Black Lion owned by a Mister James Cameron?'

Everyone knew that, Cameron was a well-known figure in Glasgow. He nodded.

'A wealthy man, Mister Cameron I believe. How do you think he votes?'

'Och, Tory of course. What else would he be!'

'So you're a Tory then, I take it?'

The man stared at her in disbelief. 'Don't be bloody daft woman!' he spluttered.

'But you said to me that Frank Connelly must be a Fascist because he works for Fascists. By the same token you must be a Tory if you work for one.'

It was a fat woman halfway up the stalls who started laughing first. She was joined by her husband, then nearly everybody else.

The man stared around him in bewilderment. For a moment or two it was touch and go as to what his reaction would be, then he, too, much to Nellie's relief, started to laugh.

Nellie held up her hand for silence. 'I give you my word of honour, as one born and bred Glaswegian to another, that Frank Connelly is not, and never has been, a Fascist. That article in the *Daily Post* was a revelation as far as he was concerned. He'd never even suspected that his bosses were Fascists or that they were sending money to the Italian Fascist party.'

Nellie paused to let the man and the rest of the audience digest her words. She then said to the man, 'It's now up to you whether or not I go on.'

The man twisted his hands together. He cleared his throat and shuffled his feet.

'Well?' Nellie prompted.

'I believe you, woman. Let's hear you sing,' the man said suddenly.

The audience applauded, some people standing and shouting their approval, others whistling and waving their hands in the air.

Again Nellie appealed for silence. When she judged she

could be heard she said, 'Let's *all* sing the curtains in for the interval. A song I think most appropriate for this time.'

She began softly, the audience joining her almost right away.

> 'I belong to Glasgow, dear old Glasgow town,
> There's nothing the matter with Glasgow
> But it's going round and round.
> I'm only a common old working chap,
> As anyone here can see,
> But when I get a couple of drinks on a Saturday,
> Glasgow belongs to me!'

When Sandy brought the curtains slowly ringing in there was hardly a dry eye in the house.

Nellie was beside herself with excitement. It was the following afternoon and Baz had just been on the telephone to tell her the news that Robin Carson was leaving town.

According to Baz a journalist from one of the *Daily Post*'s rivals had been in the audience the previous evening. As a result of what had happened, he had written a piece in which he'd attacked Robin Carson for conducting a personal vendetta against her and Frank.

Nellie heard the front door click shut and instantly flew downstairs. Frank had been in town having had to do something or other. That was him back.

She rushed into his arms. 'You'll never guess what's happened!'

Frank stared down at her in astonishment. 'Not until you tell me,' he grinned.

It came out then in a tumble of words. 'Apparently this journalist described in detail not only what happened at the Press Club, but the way Carson plotted and lied against us. He's been given the sack and has left town. Isn't that absolutely marvellous?'

'You're certain about this?' Frank asked in a strangled voice.

'Oh, yes. No doubt about it. Carson's gone out of our lives forever.'

Like a man in a dream Frank walked away from Nellie and through to where he knew there was a bottle of whisky. He poured himself a large one, drank it right off, and poured himself another.

Nellie had anticipated a jubilation to match her own. Not this stunned, withdrawn silence.

'The thought of everyone knowing that he'd been publicly humiliated, along with everything else, was too much even for him,' Nellie said.

'Yes.'

'Men being what they are in Glasgow, he'd have been a complete laughing stock from one end of the city to the other.'

'Yes,' Frank repeated.

'I thought you'd be waving your wooden leg in the air on hearing it's all over.'

He turned to face her then. 'I've just come from joining the Army.'

Nellie grinned. 'You're having me on?'

'No, I'm going into the HLI.'

Her grin wavered and disappeared. The knot of fear that had been in her stomach ever since the war had started was suddenly so acute she thought she might be ill.

'Why?'

Frank ran a hand through his hair. His complexion had gone pale and muddy, his eyes were dull.

'I thought it would help,' he whispered.

'Help! How could it do that!' she screamed, a sudden fury erupting within her. Whatever had possessed him to do such a thing? Had he gone completely mad?

Shocked by this turn of events Frank groped for the words that would explain. 'It was an awful thing that happened to you last night at the theatre. When we went to bed I couldn't sleep. I lay awake thinking about it, and

281

Carson. It seemed to me he could possibly take this Fascist thing a lot further. Use it, along with Jim Biles, as a club to beat you with. You talked about time bombs; well, it seemed to me that by joining up I was very neatly defusing this particular one. How could he continue to imply I'm a Fascist when I've become a member of His Majesty's fighting forces?'

Nellie's fury died as swiftly as it had been born. Dear, beautiful, darling Frank – he'd done this for her. To protect her and her career. 'If only you'd waited a few hours more,' she whispered.

'If ifs and ans were pots and pans,' he said, shrugging.

'Oh Frank!' She was back in his arms, smothering him with kisses, loving him.

Sniffing, she pushed a stray lock of hair away from her face.

'I have to report to Maryhill Barracks first thing tomorrow morning.'

'So soon?'

He nodded, 'I'm afraid so.'

Nellie took a deep breath. Get hold of yourself girl, she told herself. What was done couldn't be undone. She'd have given her right arm if it could.

She stood at the window and watched him get into his car, raising her hand in farewell as the Riley's engines burst into life.

He rolled down the window and returned her salute. Their eyes met and, for a second, they were as one again. Then the moment was over and the Riley was moving on its way.

She watched the car till it was out of sight.

'Oh my darling,' she whispered, placing the palm of her hand against the bed, where his smell still lingered. Burying her face in the rumpled sheets, she wailed her grief.

8

It was fifteen minutes to curtain up when there was a tap on Nellie's door. She was already in her first-number costume and applying the final touches of her make-up.

'Come in!' she called.

The door opened and the stage doorkeeper popped his head round. 'There's a chap here says he's your brother and that he must see you.'

'My brother!' Nellie jumped up. 'Show him in.'

The door opened wider and a uniformed figure entered, his right arm heavily bandaged and in a sling.

'He *is* your brother isn't he?' the stage doorkeeper demanded. He'd known young men get up to all sorts of dodges to get into a female's dressing room.

'He is, indeed,' Nellie replied. Rising she took Roddy into her arms, careful of his wound, and kissed him on the cheek.

'You've changed so much, I swear I would have walked past you in the street,' she said.

'It's been a long, long time,' he replied.

She indicated the arm in the sling. 'Is it bad?'

He shook his head. 'Not really. I'm told it'll take a wee while to mend. They've shipped me home and now I'm on my way up north to a convalescent home. We weren't supposed to stop in Glasgow, but we had to change over from the Central Station to Queen Street and the train there's been delayed a couple of hours. I took the opportunity to sneak off and see you. If I'd had longer I'd have waited till after the show, but as things are I'm lucky to be here at all.'

'And how's Frank?' she asked eagerly. Frank had joined the same regiment as Roddy and had written to her early on to say the pair of them had become quite pally. He often mentioned Roddy when he wrote.

There was a pause, then averting her gaze, Roddy said softly, 'It's because of Frank that I'm here, Nellie.'

She turned away from her brother and sat. It surprised her to note that her hand was rock steady when she lit a cigarette. 'Wounded also?' she asked.

'There were four of us. Frank, myself and two other blokes. I can't say where it was I'm afraid, I'm not allowed to do that. Jerry caught us unawares with an artillery attack. The first shell landed right beside us. I was blown off my feet and collected this.' He tapped his arm.

'And Frank?'

'The other three are dead.'

Picking up the rabbit's foot Margo had given her she pretended to dust off excess powder.

'He wouldn't have felt a thing, Nellie. I give you my word on that.'

'Was his body badly – well, you know what I mean?' She looked at Roddy in the mirror and he glanced away. That was answer enough.

'They contacted his next of kin, which was his family in Drumoyne. But I knew you wouldn't know. I was going to write when I got to the convalescent home. But when this train thing happened I –'

'Thank you,' she said, interrupting him.

'I'm helluva sorry –'

'I appreciate you coming.'

'Frank was a good man, Nellie. Well liked.'

She rose and, crossing to the bottle of whisky she always kept in her dressing room, poured out a large dram. She handed it to Roddy.

'What about yourself?'

'Not just before a show.' She screwed the top back on to the bottle and slipped it into his pocket. 'For you and your mates on the journey north.'

He finished his drink and laid the glass down. 'I'd better be getting back.'

She took the hand of his undamaged arm and squeezed it. 'Stay lucky,' she murmured.

At the door he gave her a smile and bob of the head. 'Cheerio!' he said. Then he was gone.

'Five minutes!' the call was shouted along the corridor.

She scrutinized her make-up and hair one last time. In the opening number she wore her hair up, and as she walked to the stage, all she could think of, over and over again, was that Frank had always preferred it down.

Baz gave her a wave. She waved back, forcing a smile on to her face.

On arriving backstage she climbed down a flight of stairs to below stage. There, a stagehand was waiting to help her into a trap which would send her shooting into the air above the raked set now towering over her head.

When she was in position she thought of the letter she'd sent Frank only yesterday, telling him that the divorce had at last come through; that when they next saw one another they'd be able to get married.

And now that marriage would never be.

She heard the curtains swish open and the line go on stage. For a split second she thought she wouldn't be able to go through with the performance. Then she pulled herself together. It might be a cliché, but it was true none the less: the show had to go on. There was a full house out there waiting to see and hear *her*.

The stagehand nodded to her as her music cue was played. He pulled the lever that shot her up through the set. Clearing the trap she threw out her arms and legs in an aerial spreadeagle.

'Hello there!' she shouted.

'Hello there!!' the audience thundered back.

As she landed the line turned in on her and clapped their hands.

Seats banged as the audience rose to her. 'Nellie!' they cried. 'Nellie!'

She blew them kiss after kiss, the adulation washing over her, then launched into the opening bars of her first song.

She always sang well, but that night she was better than she'd ever been. That night she was singing for Frank. Somehow, somewhere, she was sure he could hear her.

Emma Blair

WHERE NO MAN CRIES

Glasgow between the wars. It was a town divided, taut with violence and steeped in hardship – a town with no time for dreams.

Angus McBain knew that better than anyone. Being poor in Glasgow had killed his father, aged his mother before her time, and crushed with fear and frustration everyone he knew. But Angus was different. He would never be content to stay where they had put him, doing the job the bosses allowed him, wanting only a woman of his own kind. Angus McBain wanted to be his own man, to make his own place – and to share all he had and was with the woman he so passionately loved...

Bestselling Fiction

☐ No Enemy But Time	Evelyn Anthony	£2.
☐ The Lilac Bus	Maeve Binchy	£2.9
☐ Prime Time	Joan Collins	£3.
☐ A World Apart	Marie Joseph	£3.5
☐ Erin's Child	Sheelagh Kelly	£3.
☐ Colours Aloft	Alexander Kent	£2.
☐ Gondar	Nicholas Luard	£4.5
☐ The Ladies of Missalonghi	Colleen McCullough	£2.5(
☐ Lily Golightly	Pamela Oldfield	£3.50
☐ Talking to Strange Men	Ruth Rendell	£2.99
☐ The Veiled One	Ruth Rendell	£3.50
☐ Sarum	Edward Rutherfurd	£4.99
☐ The Heart of the Country	Fay Weldon	£2.50

Prices and other details are liable to change

ARROW BOOKS, BOOKSERVICE BY POST, PO BOX 29, DOUGLAS, ISLE
OF MAN, BRITISH ISLES

NAME...

ADDRESS ....

....

....

Please enclose a cheque or postal order made out to Arrow Books Ltd. for the amount
due and allow the following for postage and packing.

U.K. CUSTOMERS: Please allow 22p per book to a maximum of £3.00.

B.F.P.O. & EIRE: Please allow 22p per book to a maximum of £3.00.

OVERSEAS CUSTOMERS: Please allow 22p per book.

Whilst every effort is made to keep prices low it is sometimes necessary to increase cover
prices at short notice. Arrow Books reserve the right to show new retail prices on covers
which may differ from those previously advertised in the text or elsewhere.